The Creoles Series

The Exiles

Gilbert Morris
&
Lynn Morris

THOMAS NELSON PUBLISHERS®
Nashville
A Division of Thomas Nelson, Inc.

Published in Nashville, Tennessee, by Thomas Nelson, Inc.

Scripture quotations are from the King James Version (KJV).

Publisher's Note: This novel is a work of fiction. All characters, plot, and events are the product of the author's imagination. All characters are fictional, and any resemblance to persons living or dead is strictly coincidental.

ISBN 0-7394-3380-6
Printed in the United States of America

To Kate Larimore—

Thank you, my dear Kate, for being who you are!

There are some dark things in this old world, but you have cheered my journey with your lovely light!

The Creole Heritage

In the early nineteenth century, the culture of New Orleans was as rich and wildly varied as the citizens' complexions. Pure Spanish families, descended from the haughty dons, still dwelt in the city, and some pure French families resided there, but many were already mingled with both Spanish and Africans. Acadians—or "Cajuns" as they came to be called—lived outside of the city. This small pocket of Frenchmen had wandered far from their homes, but like many groups in the city, they stubbornly kept much of their eighteenth-century heritage intact and ingrained.

Of course there were many slaves, but there were also the *gen de coulur libres,* or free men and women of color. Some of these were pure Africans, but most of them were the mulattoes, griffes, quadroons, and octoroons who were the result of French and Spanish blending with slaves. There were Americans, too, though they were strictly confined to the "American district." And there were Creoles, people of French and Spanish blood who were born outside of their native countries. Creoles born in New Orleans were Louisianians, but they were not considered to be Americans.

All well-born Creole families sent their children to receive a classical education at the Ursuline Convent or the Jesuit schools, and both institutions accepted charity children.

This series of novels traces the history of four young women who were fellow students at the Ursuline Convent School:

- *The Exiles:* Chantel
- *The Immortelles:* Damita
- *The Alchemy:* Simone
- *The Tapestry:* Leonie

PART ONE

· 1810-1813 ·

Aimee

HAVANA, CUBA, JULY 3, 1810

Aimee Fontaine looked out of the open carriage and immediately shut her eyes. She turned and threw her arms around her husband and cried, "Cretien, we'll all be killed!"

He held her tightly and said, "We won't be killed, darling. It's not far to the docks, and once we get on board the ship we'll be safe."

Opening her eyes, Aimee moved her head back far enough to get a good view of Cretien's face, and the very sight of it encouraged her. Faults her husband might have, but if Cretien Fontaine was a coward, no one had ever found out about it. His chestnut hair escaped the tall black top hat, and his brown eyes glowed as they always did when he was excited. He showed no fear whatsoever.

"They've gone crazy," she whispered, holding on to Cretien's arm.

"Revolutionaries are always crazy," Cretien said. He turned to the driver, saying, "Get in the back with Elise, Robert. I'll drive."

"But, sir—"

"Mind what I say!" Cretien's eyes flashed, and Robert got up awkwardly and fell into the back, where Elise Debon was crouched down, her large eyes frightened. Cretien took the lines and slapped them on the backs of the pair of bays, holding the horses firmly. "They're crazy fools! They don't even know what they're fighting for."

Others besides Cretien had made that remark concerning the uproar that had shaken Cuba to its very foundation. The countryside was alive with flames where men, apparently driven mad by the revolutionary fervor, had set fire to the homes of innocent people. The government had tottered and collapsed, and now Havana was packed with a mindless mass of humanity.

Darkness had fallen, but men carrying torches held them high, and the flickering red flames cast shadows over cruel faces loose with drink. The air was filled with drunken cries and screams of women who were being attacked regardless of their politics. Gunfire rattled, sounding a deadly punctuation.

"We'll never be able to get through this crowd, Cretien," Aimee whispered.

Indeed, it did look impossible, for the street that led to the docks was filled with milling people. Many of them were armed men, but some were the helpless victims of the revolutionaries.

Cretien pulled his hat down firmly, reached low, and pulled the whip from the socket. "Hold on, everybody!" he cried. He slashed the rumps of the horses furiously, and the bays lunged forward against their collars. "Get out of the way! Clear the way!" Cretien yelled. He stood to his feet and whipped at men who reached out to pull him from the carriage.

Once Aimee saw the whip strike a man right across the cheek and leave a bleeding cut. The man fell back with a scream and was seen no more.

Aimee hid her eyes, for the horses ran over anyone in their way, and the wheels bumped over the bodies that had fallen. The carriage careened wildly, and the shouts grew louder. A gunshot sounded clearly close to the carriage. Aimee's heart seemed to stop, but the marksman had missed.

"We'll be all right," Cretien said. He sat back down but kept the horses at a fast clip. "There's the ship, down there." A few moments later he pulled the horses up short, and they stood trembling and snorting under the light of the lanterns that hung from posts on the dock. *The Empress,* one of the new breed of steamships, loomed large and black against the ebony sky. "Robert, you see to the luggage. I'll take care of the women."

"Yes, sir!"

Aimee stood, and Cretien lifted her into his arms and set her down firmly on the dock. She clung to him for a moment, but he gave her a quick hug and said, "We're all right now. Don't worry. I'll get you and Elise on board, and then I'll come back to help Robert with the luggage."

Aimee gratefully leaned against her husband, but they had not gone three steps toward the gangplank when their way was blocked by a roughly dressed group of men. All had a wolfish look, and their eyes were wild with drink.

"Hold it there!" one of them said. "We'll take your money."

"That's right. He's an aristocrat." The speaker, who wore a crimson rag around his forehead, pulled a knife from his belt and laughed drunkenly. "His kind's gone forever. Give us what you've got, and maybe we'll let you go."

In one smooth motion, Cretien pulled a pistol from under his coat and aimed at the man bearing the knife. The shot struck the ruffian in the upper arm. The wounded man shouted, "That's the only shot he's got! Get him!"

The men moved forward, eyes glittering. Suddenly another shot rang out, and a short, stocky man staggered and grabbed his thigh.

"He got me!" he cried.

Robert, Cretien's manservant, stepped out and said, "The rest of you had better leave."

But the three were so drunk they could not think. They all drew knives and, screaming, surged ahead. Cretien reached into the carriage and produced a cane. He pulled a sword from the hollow container, and when one of the men came close he swung the blade in a circular motion. The tip of the sword cut a gash in the chest of the man.

"I'd advise you to leave before you are all dead," Cretien said tightly.

"Come on, let's get out of here!" the leader cried. Since three of the four had been wounded, his words were convincing. They all turned and made their way, cursing and holding their wounds.

"Come along, Aimee," Cretien said at once. His face was pale, and the violence had shaken him, for he was not a man of action. "And you, Elise, I'll get you on board. Robert, start loading the luggage. I'll be back to help you."

Ten minutes later Cretien was greeted by a barrel-shaped man with a clipped white beard and mustache. "I'm Captain Smith. You had trouble on the dock. It's a good thing you made it. The roughs are out in force."

"So I noticed." Cretien glanced at the milling crowd, then turned to face the captain. "Is there any chance they will attack the ship?"

"Not likely! They tried that once, but my men are all armed and fine shots. They won't try that again!"

"Good! We need to get my wife and her maid to our cabin. It's been quite an experience."

"Certainly. I'll take you myself." Captain Smith led Cretien and the two women to a steep stairway, and when they reached the lower deck, he led them down a narrow corridor to a door. "This will be yours and your wife's room, sir. And your servants—we have separate accommodations for them."

"Thank you, Captain. When will we be in New Orleans?"

"Two days at the most, barring engine trouble. When you get the ladies settled, we'll have something for you to eat."

"That would be kind of you, Captain Smith."

Aimee stepped through the door and took a look around the cabin, lit by a single lantern. It was a small room with two beds, a chest, a portable toilet, and a vanity with a washstand.

"Take care of your mistress, Elise. I'll go help Robert with the luggage."

"Come back quickly, will you, Cretien?" Aimee whispered.

"Of course. You rest yourself. I won't be long."

As soon as Cretien left, Elise fluttered over Aimee, helping her take off her coat and bonnet. "We'd all have been murdered if it hadn't been for the master."

"Yes, Elise, I think we would." She hesitated, then sat down on the bunk. "He's a strong man, and I thank God that he is here to take care of us."

Cretien leaned back in his chair, studied his hand, then pushed some chips forward. "I'll meet your bet and raise you ten." He felt good, for he had slept well the previous night, after a good supper provided by Captain Smith. His wife had slept little enough, but there was nothing he could do for that.

Cretien smiled at the uncertainty in his opponent, a slender man with a razor-thin mustache and hooded green eyes. "Well, Monsieur Sedan, what do you say? Would you like a chance to win some of your money back?"

Sedan threw his cards down. "I never play a man when he's riding on his luck." He pulled a cheroot from his inner pocket, bit the end off, and lit it. When the tip was glowing he said, "Perhaps tomorrow."

"We'll be in New Orleans tomorrow. This may be your last chance."

But Sedan was not interested. He was obviously a professional gambler, and he got up now and left the table. As Cretien collected his chips, a voice at his side caught his attention.

"You're a lucky man with cards."

He turned around to see an attractive woman in a low-cut, pale blue dress. Her hair was yellow and her eyes a deep blue. She had the assurance of a woman who knew the world at least as well as he did, and he stood up at once and nodded. "Lucky in cards, at least. My name is Cretien Fontaine."

"I'm happy to know you, sir. I'm Nan Strickland." She looked expectantly at him, and when he showed no recognition she laughed at herself. "I'm an actress, you see, and I always expect to be recognized."

"May I buy you a drink, Miss Strickland?"

"Certainly." She sat down and studied him boldly.

The waiter brought them drinks, and Cretien began telling her about his last few days.

"You were caught in the revolution?" she asked, sipping her drink.

"Yes. Things have gone badly in Cuba."

"You probably lost all your property. I hear that's what happened to many."

Cretien smiled. He knew he made a handsome picture as he sat there, with his perfect teeth, thin and aristocratic face, and patrician features. He was graceful and cultured in a French manner, and totally confident in a way that told Nan Strickland he was at ease with women. "Not at all. As a matter of fact, I made a profit. I saw this coming months ago." He lifted his drink and smiled at her. "Never stay in the middle of a revolution."

"You are fortunate."

"Yes, I am."

"Where will you go?"

"I've bought a sugar plantation outside of New Orleans. I'll be in town a great deal, of course."

Nan gave him a brilliant smile. She reached into her reticule and brought forth a small card. "My company will be at the Majestic for some time, depending on how well we are received. Give this to the doorman. He'll give you a good seat."

She rose and held out her hand, and Cretien stood as well. He bent over to kiss her hand and smelled her perfume. Then he rose to his full height and looked down at her. "I'll look forward to that."

Nan Strickland smiled. "Give your wife my best wishes."

"I'll certainly do that."

He watched as the actress walked away. She disappeared through the portal, and he sighed, cashed in his chips, and took his money. Leaving the saloon, he went right to the stateroom. It was later than he had thought, and he would have to make excuses.

When he stepped in, he found Aimee already in the lower bunk and said, "Elise, that'll be all tonight."

"Good night, sir. Good night, madame."

"Good night, Elise. I hope you don't get seasick again."

When the door closed, Cretien spoke at once. "I'm sorry to be late." He began to remove his clothes and noted that she was watching him cautiously. "I didn't drink too much, my dear. Don't worry about that."

For a moment Aimee looked sober, and then she smiled. "Come here and kiss me good night," she said. She held up her arms, and when he came to her and kissed her, she held him fiercely. "I'll be glad when we're off this boat and in our own place."

Cretien held her tightly. In other circumstances he would have made love to her, but she had been drained by the events of the past two days. And to his shame, the image of Nan Strickland came to his mind. He ignored it and said, "We'll be in New Orleans tomorrow. We'll find a good hotel and look the city over. It's going to be a good life there, my dear."

For a moment she held him, and then she whispered, "I wish we had a child. I know you're disappointed that I haven't been able to give you a son."

Cretien held her. He knew that this was something that was never far from her heart, and he said quickly, "No, it will be all right. I have you and that's enough."

His words brought balm to her spirit, and she whispered, "Good night."

He settled himself in his own bed and very quickly his breathing became regular. Aimee lay awake for some time, still shaken over the violence of the revolution, but thinking of New Orleans. *O God,* she prayed, *give us a good life there.* She finally went to sleep, and her last thought was, *It's not too late. I'm still young enough to have a child if the good God pleases.*

Chapter two

The Empress eased up to the dock, meeting it with such a slight bump that Cretien hardly felt it. He turned to Aimee, who was standing beside him, put his arm around her, and said, "Well, my dear, we are here. Our new home."

Aimee stared out at the busy port and exclaimed, "There are so many ships! I never saw such a busy place!"

The port of New Orleans was indeed busy—one might almost say frantic. Ships and boats and crafts of every kind plied the river, some skimming over the water under full sail, others easing in slowly. The sound of steamboats with their shrill whistles rent the air. The river made a large S-curve, and it seemed that the lengths of the banks were made of nothing but docks.

The masts of the ships, their sails furled, lined the docks. "It looks like a forest of bare trees," Cretien remarked. Then his eye caught a sight that pleased him. "Look, they're loading sugar onto that ship, Aimee! Soon it will be *our* sugar. We're going to do well here. I feel it in my bones."

Aimee leaned against him, and when his arm tightened about her, she felt a surge of desire for a life of peace and contentment. Life in Cuba had been difficult, for the scent of revolution had been strong for the past few years. Both she and Cretien had known they would have to leave sooner or later, and she was grateful that they had sold their land and gotten away without losing everything.

The burly first mate was shouting orders to the crew, and as the gangplank was lowered, Cretien said, "Let's find Robert and Elise and go ashore. I'll be glad to get off of this boat and get my feet on firm land again."

Together they turned to go below. Just before they reached the stairs, they encountered an attractive woman with blond hair and blue eyes. She gave Cretien a bold smile of recognition, and he bowed slightly. Aimee said nothing. She was accustomed to women being attracted to her husband; what would be the point of creating a scene?

In their cabin they found that Robert and Elise had collected their things, and in a short time they were leaving the ship.

As they walked down the gangplank into the hubbub of the port, all seemed to be confusion. Passengers were lined up to board the ship. Peddlers were everywhere, calling in a polyglot of languages. Aimee heard English and French, of course, plus Spanish and others that she could not distinguish.

Cretien took charge and engaged a carriage driven by a muscular young man with inky black hair and white teeth stark against his golden tan. He spoke a mixture of French and English that the newcomers found difficult to understand.

"Ah, monsieur, my name is Jacques. Me, I weel take you anywhere to which you go."

"We want to go to a very good hotel, Jacques," Cretien said as he offered a hand to aid Aimee into the carriage.

"That would be the St. Charles. I theenk you weel like it there, but it is ver' expensive."

"I think I can afford it, Jacques," Cretien said with a slight smile.

Jacques helped Robert load the trunks, then stepped back up into the carriage. He spoke to the horses, a fine matched set of grays, and at once began talking to the group. He was a curious fellow, wanting to know everything about the new arrivals. "There are many come from Cuba because of the revolution. I hear," he said, "over three t'ousand. More than two t'ousand of them black people have come already the last two months. Was it bad over there?"

"Yes, very bad."

"Well, you weel like it here in New Orleans. While you are here I hope you weel avail yourselves of my services."

"We won't be here long. I have a sugar plantation to the west."

That sent Jacques into a lengthy dissertation on the advantages of raising sugar over cotton, but as they moved into the downtown section, the visitors expressed interest in the city. When Cretien mentioned that they had never been there before, Jacques said, "Oh, it is a great city. Plenty to do. Your people, the Creoles, have brought good things to the city. Every one of you people love to go to the theater, no?"

"Yes, that is true. You have a good theater here?"

"Many of them. The best."

"What street is this?" Aimee asked.

"St. Charles Avenue. You see, this is the *Vieux Carré*—the good part of town. The other part is where the Kaintocks stay. Very bad."

"Kaintocks? Who are they?" Cretien asked.

"The men who bring the flat boats with their goods down the river. They are rough men, these Americans. Stay away from them, sir, I would advise you."

St. Charles Avenue was paved with cobblestones. Most of the other streets had *banquettes,* or sidewalks, which were simply planks or sometimes a single log pegged into the ground. Wooden drains served as gutters, and in some instances there were open ditches containing garbage and refuse of every description.

"It smells bad," Robert whispered to Elise.

"Yes, it is terrible. I hope our plantation will not smell this awful."

Robert, a tall, saturnine man of forty, patted Elise on the shoulder. "The town was made by men. The country was made by God."

Elise laughed. "You say such funny things."

Aimee spoke to Jacques. "The streets must be very bad when it rains, those that are not paved."

"Oh, you would not believe! It is so bad you cannot get anywhere, no!"

They passed a large party, over two hundred people, some carrying lanterns and many disguised with masks. They were a noisy group, banging old kettles and shovels and tongs with clanging metal.

"What is that, Jacques?" Cretien asked.

"Oh, that is a *charivari*. A wedding. That is a big one."

Then a cart passed by, bearing a rather strange sight. Aimee asked, "What is that, Jacques?"

"Oh, that is a widow, and that is an effigy of her husband in the coffin and her present husband is there by her side."

"Is that common?" Cretien asked, staring at the cart. "It seems rather—crude."

"Me, I don't know why they do it," Jacques shrugged. "Maybe the bride wants her new husband to see he can be replaced if he doesn't behave himself. You'll see t'ings stranger than that in this place."

Finally Jacques drew up the carriage and waved his whip. "The St. Charles. The rates are high, two dollars and a half a day, but there is a table for gentlemen that provides dinner from three to five."

"What about the ladies?"

"Oh, the ladies, too, of course."

The St. Charles was an enormous building, seeming to stretch for a full block. The lobby had a high ceiling, glowing chandeliers, and paintings on every wall, adding color to the scene.

Cretien moved to the desk, where a small man with a pair of sharp gray eyes said, "Yes, sir. May I serve you?" He spoke in French, and Cretien responded, "I need a room for myself and my wife, and two for my servants."

"Yes, sir. Will you be staying long?"

"I think not. Just a few days."

"You will like our hotel, sir. First time in New Orleans?"

"First time in the United States."

"Ah, I trust you will have a good stay. Are you traveling far?"

"I bought a sugar plantation a few miles west of New Orleans."

"Then you would be interested in our auction."

"What sort of auction?"

"Slaves, of course. You will find them under the rotunda. I think it is going on now."

Curious, Cretien resolved to look into the matter, but he knew that Aimee was tired. "Thank you," he replied. "I must get my wife settled first."

Cretien and Aimee followed a hulking servant upstairs, and after he put their luggage inside the room and left, Aimee looked around with pleasure. She was tired but she loved the room.

"It's so beautiful, Cretien! I've never seen such gorgeous wallpaper—and look at the woodwork!"

"I'm glad you like it. Well, suppose we go out and buy ourselves a fine meal to celebrate our first night in Louisiana."

"That sounds wonderful. I am hungry."

The two went downstairs and learned that the Bienville, one of the best restaurants in New Orleans, was right down the street. They soon found themselves seated in an ornate dining room, swarmed by a waiter who rapidly gave them a verbal menu of the offerings.

They dined well that night on lobster and a delicious salad. After they had eaten, they returned to the hotel, and just before they went to sleep Aimee put her arms around her husband and drew him close. "We are going to be very happy here, dear."

Cretien returned her caress. "Yes, we are. We will make a new life for ourselves in this place!"

Cretien arrived at the offices of Oliver Harcourt, where he was greeted by the lawyer whom he had never met in person. The two had done business through the mail, and it was Harcourt who had recommended buying a sugar plantation instead of cotton and had negotiated the purchase.

Harcourt was a tall, dignified man with an aristocratic air. He had silver hair and wore a dark brown suit with a spotless white shirt and a black string tie.

"I think you will find that I got a good buy for you in your plantation, Monsieur Fontaine."

"I was somewhat hesitant. There are many sugar plantations in Cuba, but I have never engaged in that sort of trade."

"With the right workers you should have no trouble. You must have a good overseer, and I checked carefully into the man who is there now. His name is Simon Bientot. He knows all about the work and is an amiable sort. I interviewed him myself. And his wife, Marie, would be a good housekeeper, but of course that is up to your wife."

"I'm very grateful to you for your help, Mr. Harcourt."

"We're anxious to see good people coming to our part of the world." He frowned slightly and shook his head. "Of course, the revolution brought a great deal of the other sort." Then he smiled and nodded. "But I can see that you are a man of the world who knows good living."

"I'm glad you think so."

"There is one matter that I should mention. I assure you I looked at a dozen plantations, and this one was the best. However, it has no house that would be suitable for you and Mrs. Fontaine."

"What sort of house is there?"

"It is no more than a cottage. I think, sir, you will have to think about building your own house."

"I would like that very much. I have looked forward to building my own home for some time, and my wife has a box full of ideas about it."

"Well, when it's time to begin I can recommend builders. And of course many of the slaves are expert craftsmen. It might pay you to invest in a few of those. Plenty of them are available at fair prices."

At that moment a knock sounded at the door. Harcourt looked up and said, "Come in."

A woman entered, carrying a small child. Harcourt looked irritated. "Yes, Mrs. Wells, what is it?"

"I don't think Neville is well, sir. Shall I take him to the doctor?"

"Yes—yes, take him, Mrs. Wells! You don't need to ask me everything."

The woman flushed, then turned and left.

"Your son?"

"Yes, his mother died at his birth. His name is Neville."

"He looks like a fine boy."

For a moment Harcourt hesitated, and then he said, "He's like his mother." Somehow he made the words sound like an accusation.

Uncomfortable, Cretien quickly said, "I must go now. My wife will be wondering about me. We'll be leaving to see the plantation early in the morning."

Cretien left the office and walked the streets for a while. New Orleans was a colorful city with no tall buildings, for the sands of Louisiana would not permit such things. His mind leaped ahead, and, as always, he was excited at the thought of a new project.

He took a turn through the old town where the Americans, the Kaintocks, stayed. He was surprised to see the large number of brothels, saloons, and gambling houses. The streets were crowded with rough looking men, and he thought, *I wouldn't like to be here at night without a pistol.* He turned and went back to the hotel, looking forward to seeing the plantation in the morning.

Jacques had made himself available to take the Fontaine party to the plantation. He was ready and waiting early, and after a good breakfast Cretien and Aimee found themselves passing through the wilds of Louisiana. After leaving the city of New Orleans, "wilds" was the proper way to describe the countryside. The land was flat, of course, much as it was in New Orleans, but the pale earth seemed to grow darker and wetter as they rode farther away from the city. The large trees that they did not know were called sugarberries by Jacques, and the Louisiana birds flocked to them for their sweet, reddish fruit. Live oaks were the most spectacular trees. They towered some seventy or eighty feet, and some of the lower limbs spread out to enormous distances, adorned with Spanish moss, which looked like huge birds' nests. The streams they passed were the color of milk chocolate, almost as if the earth had melted; and once, as they passed by a wide stream, an alligator raised his snout.

Aimee shivered. "What a horrible beast!"

"The Cajuns, they like to hunt the alligator. They use their hides and even eat their meat," Jacques offered.

"I wouldn't eat one of those things if I were starving!" Aimee exclaimed.

"Well, I don't know about that. We've eaten snails," Cretien teased her.

"A snail is better than that thing!"

They stopped once to water the horses at a small stream, and Aimee was pleased by the white birds she saw.

"They are called egrets," Jacques said. "And look. There is a blue heron. He is a serious-looking fellow, no?"

They watched the heron as he moved slowly, his long legs seeming inadequate for such a large body. Once his head flashed down as quickly as a thought, and he came up with a small fish. He tossed it into the air, caught it expertly, and swallowed it whole. The party watched the bulge as it went downward, and Cretien laughed. "He doesn't bother chewing, does he?"

The air grew hotter as they made their way, and the humidity was much worse than in Cuba. Aimee fanned herself and pulled her dress away from her neck to let the air circulate. "Is it always this humid?"

"No, the winter here is nice—not as humid. You will like it then." Jacques turned, his white teeth flashing at her. "Sometimes you don't know whether you're in the ocean or on dry land, it is so wet. But you will get used to it."

As they drew nearer, Jacques pulled up at a shack to ask directions, and an old woman came out. She spoke French, and when Cretien asked her if she knew the way to the plantation, she grinned toothlessly and pointed. Then she came closer and said, "You will live there, sir?"

"Yes, it will be our home."

"Ah, if you want a juju or a love potion, you come to me. If you have an enemy, I can put a curse on him that he will die screaming."

"I don't think we will require that," Cretien laughed.

"Then perhaps a love potion. You come and see me. I can make any spell you want. You come and see Ma Tante."

"I don't need a love potion. I've got all the love I need right here." Cretien smiled and put his arm around Aimee.

Thirty minutes later they pulled off the main road and went down a much narrower lane until Jacques said, "That must be it."

They had been passing through cane fields, but now they had

come out into an open space. A cottage occupied the center of a small ridge overlooking the fields, and several smaller shacks, obviously slave quarters, were off behind it.

"Don't be disappointed, darling," Cretien said quickly. "We will build a fine house. Even today we'll find a location, and I'll get started at once."

As the carriage pulled up to the house, a woman came out. She was in her forties, a solid woman with a pleasant face and black hair covered by a kerchief. She smiled and curtsied. "May I help you? My name is Marie Bientot."

Cretien introduced himself and said, "Is your husband here?"

"No, he is out at the far field, but I will send someone for him." She turned around and called, "Brutus!"

A huge black man, who was carrying wood from a pile, dropped it and came over. He was an enormous man, muscular, with a rather sullen look.

"Brutus, go fetch my husband at once. Tell him the master's here."

Without a word the black man turned and plodded away.

"What a massive fellow. He looks rather villainous," Cretien murmured.

"He's not the best of the slaves, but he is strong. Will you come inside the house, sir, and you, madame?"

They got out of the carriage and went inside. "My husband and I live over there." She waved her hand toward the window. "But I wanted to fix the house up."

"It's very nice, Marie," Aimee said.

"You look around, and I will fix you a lunch. We will have a fine dinner tonight."

Cretien and Aimee wandered around the house. It was a very modest place, but it was clean and large enough and seemed to be well kept. Then they stepped outside.

"It's not much, is it?" Cretien frowned. "I thought it would be better than this."

Aimee turned to him, reached up, and touched his cheek. "It will be very nice when we fix it up. And we'll be here every day while the house is going up."

Cretien smiled at her. "You're a patient woman. Most women would rather stay in town at a fine hotel."

"No, this will be our home until we build the big house. We will call it Fontaine Maison, for your name will be on it."

Cretien reached out and took her in his arms. He kissed her and said, "*Our* name will be on it. We will have a good life here, *mon chère!*"

Chapter three

A sense of pride came to Aimee Fontaine as she walked out of the house to greet her visitors. She thought of the almost two years that had passed as Fontaine Maison was rising, and she was filled with a strong sense of possession. The house had become her life, for although Cretien was drawn often to the city, where he enjoyed the theater and dining and excitement of cosmopolitan life, Aimee loved the plantation.

She paused for a moment as the carriage pulled up and turned to look at the exterior of the house. The French influence on the structure was strong. She had wanted to make it a miniature Versailles, but not quite that formal.

Fontaine Maison was a raised structure with large columns in the lower story and colonnettes in the upper. It had a typical French roof slanting upward to a peak, and she had designed it with many, many windows so that every room would be bathed in light. The house was surrounded by a white fence that also protected a large garden. In years to come it would be more attractive, but at least the seeds were sown.

Aimee felt a strong love for the place, and at the same time a guilt of sorts. She had prayed that she would not make the house an idol, but it had become a haven for her, and she loved it with all of her heart.

A tall man stepped out of the carriage and turned to help a woman. Aimee at once advanced, saying, "Monsieur Despain, Madame Despain, I welcome you to Fontaine Maison."

Charles Despain was the mayor of New Orleans, and his wife, Margaret, was one of the social leaders in the city. The Fontaines had visited many times with the Despains in their home.

Despain removed his hat and bent over Aimee's hand to kiss it. "We are an imposition, I fear."

"Not at all. Come inside. My husband is not here, and I'm afraid he won't be back until tomorrow."

She turned to Margaret, who kissed her. Margaret Despain, an attractive woman in her late forties, had a real affection for Aimee. Hers was one of the true friendships that Aimee had formed since her arrival in Louisiana.

Now Aimee said, "Are you hungry? There is food ready."

"No, first you must show us the grounds," Margaret insisted.

When they had seen the outside, Aimee urged them to come in. "It is a little cold for March. Come inside to the fire."

They entered the house, where they were served *cafe au lait* and pastries. "Our cook is a Cajun," said Aimee, "and fixes the most fiery dishes you can imagine. She makes the best gumbo in the world."

"'In the world' means New Orleans. I don't think gumbo is enjoyed anywhere but Louisiana," Despain said.

Aimee took them on a tour of the house, and the pair exclaimed many times over the exquisite furnishings.

"It feels so much like a home!" Margaret exclaimed. "Many grand houses seem more like museums, but this house has a comfortable feel about it."

"I must confess I love it, Margaret. Too much, perhaps. It's easy to learn to love things instead of God."

Margaret laughed and put her hand on her husband's arm. "I think you should preach a little of that doctrine to my husband. He's stocking up with houses and land and money as if he were going to live forever."

Despain laughed shortly. He was, indeed, a man who loved things, but he did not like to be reminded of it. "Well, I know I won't be on this earth forever, but I intend to enjoy the time I have here. Now, show us some more of the house."

The three ended their tour in the drawing room. It was a large room with deep burgundy rugs on the polished hardwood floors and velvet curtains of the same color pulled to one side at each of the floor-to-ceiling windows. The walls were papered with a flocked gold-and-burgundy paper and were decorated with numerous paintings of landscapes, all with gilded frames.

A large stone fireplace took up almost the whole wall at the far end; the grate and accessories were made of ornate wrought iron, and a large mantel above held tiny porcelain boxes and vases of all shapes and sizes. There were four high-backed chairs of red-and-ivory damask flanking the fireplace, and a large couch of ivory damask took its place among these. More of the same chairs were placed along the walls of the room, with highly polished mahogany tables and glass lanterns at the sides of some. A beautiful piano stood open with an array of music on its stand.

Despain said, "It's a bit of a shame, isn't it? I suppose you'll be spending less time here when you go to your new town house."

A silence came over the room, and the Despains saw distress in Aimee Fontaine's eyes.

"A house in New Orleans?" Aimee said, a thickness coming to her throat. Suddenly the room was uncomfortable.

"My dear, you should not have said that!" Mrs. Despain said.

Mr. Despain flushed and stammered an apology. They had lunch and then quickly made their departure. No one spoke again of the house in town. As soon as they were in their carriage, however, and pulling away from Fontaine Maison, Margaret turned to her husband.

"You are a fool, Charles! Why did you have to mention the house?"

"I'm afraid you're right, but I didn't know it was a secret."

"Well, it obviously was! Sometimes I wonder how you ever managed to get elected to any office. You're the most tactless man who ever lived!"

Despain slumped down in his seat and pulled his hat down over his eyes while his wife continued to rebuke him. Finally he threw his hands up in a gesture of despair. "Well, how am I to know what to say and what not to say? I supposed that Cretien had told her about the house."

"Well, he obviously hadn't. He was planning a surprise." Margaret shook her head. "I'm glad you didn't mention seeing Cretien having dinner with that actress. What's her name?"

"Nan Strickland."

"She's nothing but a harlot. If I ever hear of you running around with harlots, I'll see to it that you're sorry!"

"I've got no intention of running around with harlots, and you know it!" Charles protested. "And besides, you don't know that Fontaine is guilty of anything—except indiscretion. He should know better than to be seen in public with a woman like that."

"Oh, you mean it's all right in private?"

"I give up. Have your own way."

"I'm worried about the Fontaines, Charles. Cretien is gambling a lot, and sometimes he doesn't go home for days."

"It never pays to meddle in other people's marriages. They have to take care of themselves. Let's talk about something else."

Cretien came back excited, full of plans for buying the property next door to their plantation. Aimee, on the other hand, was quiet. She ate practically nothing of the excellent dinner, and when they moved into the drawing room, where Robert served them coffee and small cakes, she sat before the fire without saying a word.

Cretien finally sat down and gave her an odd look. "What's wrong, dear? You've hardly said a word."

"The Despains came by today."

"Yes, so you told me. I'm sorry I missed them."

Aimee turned to face him. "Charles told me that you bought a house in New Orleans." She saw something like guilt sweep across her husband's face, but he quickly recovered.

"Blast the man! It was meant to be a surprise. A Christmas present for you."

"A Christmas present? You're buying me a *house* for Christmas?"

"Well, yes, and I've been dickering for months on the place."

"But why do we want a house in New Orleans when we have Fontaine Maison?"

Cretien put his arms around his wife and drew her close. "For variety, sweet. I love this place as you do, but there's so little to do here, especially in the winter. When we go to town we have to live in hotels, but now we can have the best of all worlds. It's a small house, but so beautiful! Not like this place, of course, but comfortable. We can have guests there. We can go to the theater and then come home. You'll love it."

Aimee listened as Cretien spoke. While his plan pleased him, it only made her anxious. She knew that her husband was not suited to the life of the city. He had weaknesses that he would have been shocked to know that she had discerned.

But since the deed was done and impossible to avoid, Aimee made herself smile. "I'm sure I'll love it, dear."

Cretien was pleased. He kissed her and waltzed her around the room. "We'll go tomorrow, Aimee. I can't wait to show it to you! We'll be able to move next month."

Cretien's eyes danced with excitement. Aimee knew he loved her, but she also knew that he was a selfish man. In her private moments, she had wondered many times if he had married her for her money.

Aimee again forced a smile and said, "I can't wait to see it, Cretien. I'm sure it will be very beautiful."

Chapter four

Aimee twisted so much in her chair that Elise exclaimed, "Madame, you are so jumpy! I cannot fix your hair."

Aimee looked into the mirror and gave a smile of pure joy. "I'm sorry, Elise. I just can't seem to keep still today."

"You are very happy, madame. I am glad to see it."

Indeed, Elise was glad to see her mistress in such good spirits. Thinking back over the past few months, when they had first taken up residence in the town house on Chartres Street in the French Quarter, the maid had noticed that Aimee was not happy. This had been a puzzle to Elise, for to her the city was exciting—not nearly so boring as the Fontaine Plantation had been. She had found many suitors here, but she was aware that her mistress longed for the life in the country. Now she continued to brush Aimee's hair and said, "Why are you so happy, madame?"

"I just am," Aimee said. She turned suddenly and said, "Oh, you may pick up my new dress at Monsieur Benet's shop today, Elise. I don't have the money for it. Just tell him to put it on our account."

"Shall I go now?"

"Yes, but it's cold and wet. Take the carriage."

"I will not be long."

As soon as Elise left her bedroom, Aimee rose and walked around the room. She seemed to be overflowing with energy, which was unusual enough, but there was a joy within her this day that she could not contain. Despite the dreary weather, she wanted to sing or run.

She opened a drawer and pulled out her journal from beneath some clothing. She had begun the journal when they had first come to the town house the previous August. Now she looked at the first entry:

August 18, 1812

The house is very nice. It has a fine courtyard and is close to the theater. Right down the street is the Ursuline Convent, and we are very close to Place d'Armes. We can go to the cathedral with no problem each Sunday. I wish I liked it more. Cretien is so excited, but I am already lonesome for the plantation.

She turned the page and saw the entry she had made a week later:

August 25, 1812

I wish I were back at Fontaine Maison!

Their lives had become a series of fashionable balls and masquerades. Almost every night there was a visit to some theatrical performance, where Aimee would join Cretien in one of the boxes with the Creole belles and their chaperones. Below the boxes were rows of seats for ladies. Many evenings they went to the dances, where the young men wore bright colors and boots with fancy stitching. Each carried a *colichemarde,* a sword cane wide near the hilt and tapering suddenly to a rapierlike blade.

The colichemarde was a popular weapon, and many duels were fought over little or nothing. One of Cretien's young friends had prepared for a duel at St. Anthony's Square, just behind the cathedral. There he fought with another young man and fortunately escaped with only a minor wound.

With true Gallic passion, New Orleans incited the pleasure-loving Creoles to entertainment, food, wine, luxury, and display. Page after page of the journal recorded Aimee's visits to the Theatre d'Orleans with Cretien, and she smiled when she read her opinions.

October 2, 1812

The play was stupid and not well acted, but no one seemed to notice but me. I think the acting here is terrible, perhaps because the municipal council controls almost everything in the theatre. No one can put on a play without submitting a script of it to the mayor, and if he likes it, he fixes the day and the hour for the performance. If he doesn't, it will not be put on. There's even a fine for any actor or actress who fails to appear upon the stage at the exact time called for in his or her part. And they passed another act just recently that time between acts must not exceed fifteen minutes. It's really a foolish sort of life. I enjoy the opera, but it is not something one wants to attend every night. Cretien, however, could go every night and never tire of it.

She turned another page, and this sentence caught her eye:

October 14, 1812

This life is not good for Cretien. It tempts him, and he cannot overcome his weakness.

Aimee stared at the entry, remembering how she had seen Cretien on the street in the company of an attractive woman. He had not seen her, and she had never rebuked him for it. But she had begged him to go back with her to the plantation, and he did—but only for a few days. He then left her there alone and went back to the city for two weeks. When he did come back, grieved and repentant, she had forgiven him. She always did.

Reading the record of the past months dimmed the glow in Aimee's eyes. But suddenly she laughed with pure joy and began to write:

November 12, 1812

God has given us a miracle. I am with child! I am certain now that God has given us a miracle. We will have a child in May. I will tell Cretien this evening, and God willing, he will be as happy as I.

"You seem upset tonight, darling," Cretien said later that very day. He was dressing to go out and turned to her when she did not speak at once. When he saw tears in her eyes, he rushed to her side. "What is it? Is something wrong? Have the servants displeased you?"

"No, I am only crying because I'm so happy."

Cretien was puzzled. "Well, that's wonderful. I know you'd rather be at the plantation, but I think you would be very lonely there now."

"I don't think I am ever going to be lonely again." Aimee smiled suddenly and reached out. She pulled his head down and kissed him. "We are going to have a child, Cretien."

Cretien Fontaine stared at his wife. During the first years of their marriage he had been anxious. But as the years had gone by and no child had come, he had concluded that Aimee was barren. Now he tried to assemble his thoughts. "Why, I can't believe it! Are you certain?"

"Yes, I waited until I was sure before I told you. Now our lives will be so different. We will have a little one to think of."

Cretien laughed. "That is true. Our lives will be better. We will have a son."

"Perhaps it may be a girl."

"No, it will be a boy. I feel it." He put his arms around Aimee and held her gently, as if holding something very precious. "I am a selfish man," he whispered, "but I will be a good father. You will see."

Cretien paced the floor. He had kept a tight reign on himself during Aimee's pregnancy, spending more time with her than ever before. The idea of having a son had grown more and more pleasing to him. He planned the boy's childhood, the games he would play with him, his education. They would go to Europe together. They would be friends. He fixed the date in his mind—May 20, 1813—the day his firstborn son came into the world!

Six hours ago the doctor had come, and for most of that time Cretien had paced the floor. Now he heard the door open, and Doctor Franklin stepped out. "Well, your waiting is over. You may come in and see your wife and child."

Cretien brushed by the doctor. When he saw Aimee lying with her face worn and haggard, he swallowed hard and then rushed to her side. Falling on his knees, he took her free hand and said, "My dear, are you all right?"

"Yes, I am fine." Her voice was weak, but there was pride in her eyes.

"Here, let me hold my son," Cretien said.

Doctor Franklin had come in behind him. "Oh, but you have a beautiful *daughter,* sir."

Aimee was dazed with the pain of the ordeal, but at the doctor's words she saw something change in Cretien's expression. His eyes had been filled with joy, but he suddenly dropped his head as if to cover his emotion. Recovering quickly, he looked up and said, "Here, then. Let me hold my daughter."

"I know you wanted a son, Cretien, but now God may give us one. He has given us this child."

"What will you name her?" he said, holding the bundled child rather awkwardly.

"I have been singing in my heart ever since I knew she was coming. We will call her Chantel. She will be our song. Chantel Renee Fontaine."

"It is a beautiful name, and she is a beautiful child." Cretien handed the baby back, and now his disappointment was plain on his face. He had never been a man, Aimee knew, who could hide his emotions. She promised herself, *We will have a son if God wills it.* She held the child closely to her breast and, reaching out, took Cretien's hand. "She will bring joy into our life."

"I'm sure she will," Cretien said. He got to his feet and released her hand. "You will soon feel better. I will take you back to Fontaine Maison."

"Yes, Cretien. Please take me home."

PART TWO

· 1822-1827 ·

Chantel

Chapter five

In November 1822, fall had come to the coast of Louisiana. The trees had shed their leaves and now held their naked arms to the sky, but at the end of the year, it seemed that heaven had decided to bless the land with a mild, springlike warmth. The creek that wound around the western edge of Fontaine Plantation was as rich and brown as the chocolate that nine-year-old Chantel loved to have in the evenings.

As she sat beside the creek attaching a piece of meat to the end of a thin string, a warming breeze came from the east and blew her carroty red hair back from her forehead. Once she looked up and grew very still, as a mother raccoon with five masked cubs came out of the woods and dabbled in the water no more than fifty feet away. She watched as the cubs played like puppies, splashing in the stream while their mother felt carefully for mussels or crawdads. When she captured one she would share it with the cubs, who fell over themselves to reach the delicacy.

For Chantel this was the best that life had to offer. She loved the out-of-doors, the animals, the birds, even the snakes and bugs that abounded in her homeland. Time spent in the house studying dull books was a torment to her, but once outside, the bayou, the streams, and the woods of pine that teemed with life of all sorts became her world.

Eventually the coons moved upstream around a bend, and Chantel lost sight of them. With a sigh she tossed the baited string out into the water. It sank slowly, and she wound the free end of the string around her forefinger, waiting for a bite.

As she sat there her mind was busily engaged and her eyes moved constantly, taking in the snowy white egrets that had lit in the field beyond the stream following the slow-moving cows. One of them suddenly flew up and perched on the neck of one of the larger cows. *What is he doing up there?* Chantel wondered. *He must be picking bugs or something off of her back.* She watched carefully and filed the scene in her memory, determined to ask Brutus why the egrets and the cattle got along so well.

Overhead the skies were a dark gray, and a rolling mass of dirty off-white clouds made their way along the western horizon. They looked like huge cotton bolls, and she entertained herself by deciding what they looked like. One, she decided, was a horse, another was like an elephant, and yet another, she decided, like the dragon in one of the picture books she had treasured since she was a small child.

The smells that came to her were no less interesting than the sights. The thick smell of the stream and the fresh scent of pines loaded with turpentine came on the breeze. There was also an odor of burning wood that made her look, but she saw no sign of smoke. The brown stream purled at her feet, making a soft, sibilant sound where it broke over the banks, and she sat there, content.

Suddenly the string in her hand moved slightly, and Chantel reached out with her free hand and gave it a tug. Finding some resistance, she pulled the string in slowly and carefully. Finally, when she saw a large crawdad at the end, she said, "Got you!" She caught the crawdad with two fingers. He wiggled as she pulled him free, but she held him high, laughing.

"You can kick all you want to, Mr. Crawdad, but you're going to be supper for me! Now, you get in there with your brothers and sisters." She dropped it into a bucket and glanced in at her catch. The bucket was almost a quarter full, and she could hear the scrapings of tiny feet and faint clickings of claws as they frantically tried to escape. "Sorry, but that's what God made you for, to be our supper."

Chantel stood up and stretched. She was wearing a faded dark-blue dress that came to her knees, and an old coat that she had a fondness for. It was two years old, and she had grown so rapidly that the cuffs struck her six inches above her wrists. She wore black stockings, and her black leather shoes were worn and muddy. Beside her on the bank lay a straw hat with a frayed brim.

As she stretched higher, her body seemed no thicker than one of the reeds that grew along the banks of the river. Her feet and hands were very thin and delicate. No one had ever called Chantel Fontaine beautiful, for her mouth was very wide and her prominent cheekbones seemed to give her face a fullness that did not match her body. She had good teeth, but her best feature was her perfect complexion: smooth and very fair.

Baiting her string again, Chantel tossed it out into the water, then tied the free end around the bail of the bucket. She moved up and down the banks looking for signs of turtles and was delighted when a large fish came up, struck at something, and then disappeared about ten feet out from the bank. "I'll catch you, Mrs. Fish! You wait and see if I don't. Brutus and I will come back and catch you on a trotline."

She began to sing a song as she moved up and down the bank. Chantel sang a great deal, giving her name credence, and her voice, though thin, was clear and true.

Chantel saw a long, thin stick on the ground and picked it up. She held it for a moment, then grasped the thicker end and held it out as if it were a sword. She began moving back and forth as if parrying the blows of an opponent, muttering under her breath, "Take that, you villain! Oh, you would, would you? Don't think you're going to get away!"

She darted back and forth, turning and wheeling and crying out to her imaginary villainous opponent. Then she suddenly dropped the sword and fell down in a heap. She looked up piteously and held her hand out. "Oh, kind sir, spare me! I am a poor, helpless girl and have no friends!"

Then Chantel was on her feet and became the man, speaking in as deep a voice as possible. She bowed and said, "Do not fear, mademoiselle, I am Captain Fontaine, and I will save you from the villain that would harm you. Here, let me carry you to safety." She bent over and pretended to pick up a form and moved away.

Her game went on for some time as she played many roles in the drama that was birthed in her head. Chantel spent so much time alone that making up games had become her chief entertainment. There were other children in the area, to be sure, but most of those who lived close enough to her home to visit were either older or younger. So she had become a solitary child, creating imaginary worlds.

Forgotten were the crawdads and the string, which began to pull from one side to another as Chantel moved, speaking lines, peopling the open space beside the stream with unseen companions. She had just finished a speech when a voice from behind startled her.

"What are you doing here, girl?"

Chantel whirled, and her face reddened, for her father stood there watching her. As always, he was finely dressed; today he wore a pair of gray trousers strapped under his feet and a gray cloth coat with a black fur collar. A fur cap on his head covered his chestnut hair. There was censure in his eyes, and he shook his head. "Your mama has been worried about you. Why do you run away without telling us where you've gone?"

"I'm—I'm sorry, Papa." Chantel dropped her head, unable to meet his eyes. She drew a figure in the dirt with the toe of her shoe, then managed to look up. She hated to displease her father, but she saw that his lips were turned down and his brow knit with a frown. "I will not do it again."

"If you would study your schoolbooks as hard as you play, it would be well."

Chantel had no answer for that, and he had warned her before about her laziness in the classroom. Desperately she tried to find something to say, but this was not unusual when she tried to speak to her father. At times he was happy and showered her with affection, but this would be followed by long periods when he seemed to forget that he had a daughter. Chantel lived for those times when he would come and pick her up and throw her in the air, and then give her a hug and a kiss, or when he would play games with her in the parlor or read to her the stories from a book.

"Come along. It's late. You'll have to tell your mother you're sorry."

"Yes, Papa."

Chantel scrambled to get her crawdads, not forgetting to pull in the one that was on the end of her line. As she tossed it into the bucket, Cretien shook his head, his face cloudy. "You are absolutely filthy, girl! And you're dressed like the daughter of a slave."

"I didn't want to get good clothes dirty when I came for the crawdads, Papa."

"Fishing for crawdads indeed! You should be learning to draw or do embroidery like a lady."

Chantel picked up the bucket, her face red. Silently she trudged beside her father, who said not another word to her all the way to the house. Finally he spoke. "Get rid of those things and get cleaned up."

"Yes, Papa."

Running around the house with the crawdads thumping in the bucket, Chantel flew into the kitchen and slammed the door behind her. She ran up at once to Clarice Debeau, the cook. "I've caught lots of crawdads, Clarice."

"Look at you!" Clarice said. She was a thickset woman of thirty-five, short and strong, and had a real affection for the daughter of the house. "You're so dirty!"

"I'm going to wash right now. Could we have *étouffée* tonight?"

"It's too late for that. Maybe tomorrow."

"All right, Clarice." Chantel spun about and left the kitchen. She ran upstairs to her own room, breaking in like a whirlwind. Chantel loved her room, and for one moment she stood still and let her eyes run over the mahogany canopy bed, with its pink and white lace coverings, the brilliant white curtains held back with pink lace ties, the delicately carved rocking chair holding porcelain dolls in frilly dresses, and the dark burgundy rug in the center of the room. On the other side of the room she took in the small desk with bookcases on both sides filled with colorful leather-bound books that she had not yet read, the shelves with delicate figurines of dancers in all poses, and the pictures of beautiful faraway places on the walls.

She took off her jacket and the worn dress, and going to the washstand she poured water from a flowered pitcher into an enamel basin. She splashed her face quickly and washed her hands, then dried off on a thick towel.

Wheeling, she ran to the large walnut armoire, pulled it open, and yanked out a dress. Quickly she pulled it over her head and then went to the mirror and began trying to do something with her hair. Because it was red, she endured much teasing from other children. Adults always remarked on it, too, and seemed compelled to pat her on the head. More than once she'd had to restrain an impulse to keep from doing something shocking—like spitting on them or slapping their hands away. Determinedly she picked up a brush and comb and tried to get some of the tangles out of it. Her eyes watered as she yanked at it, pulling at her scalp.

The door opened, and Elise came flying in. "You're late!" she exclaimed. "Here, let me do your hair."

Willingly Chantel surrendered the brush and comb to the maid and sat there while her hair was put into some sort of shape. "I caught enough crawdads to make *étouffée,* Elise. You can have some tomorrow."

"And your father had to go looking for you. He was upset." Elise took a few more swipes at the hair, tied it up efficiently with a ribbon from the table, and said, "Now, go quickly."

"Yes, Elise."

Chantel left her room at a run and dashed down the stairs. Then she slowed to a stop and managed to walk in with some appearance of grace.

The dining room she entered was beautiful indeed. It was a very large room with embossed wallpaper in gold. Each wall, it seemed, had innumerable pictures and mirrors with carved, gilded frames. The ceiling was very high, with heavily carved cornices, and was painted a brilliant white, and there was a beautiful marble fireplace with its mantle holding porcelain figurines of all sorts. A brass and crystal chandelier with etched glass globes hung over the highly polished table, set now with the best of china, crystal, and silver. The delicately carved chairs had seats upholstered in a white fabric with bold red- and pink-colored roses. The floor was covered with a deep crimson carpet, red silk draperies fell over lace curtains at the floor-length windows, and the oversized sideboard displayed crystal and china of different sizes and shapes.

Aimee smiled and said, "Come in and sit down. Clarice has made us a very good dinner."

"Yes, Mama." Chantel took her seat and waited until Robert and Clarice came in with the food. It was one of her favorite dishes: chicken creole, with its spicy red gravy, rice, corn bread, and stewed okra with tomatoes.

Aimee said, "My, you're getting sunburned."

"Yes, and that's not good," Cretien said. He paused with his fork halfway to his mouth and shook his head with disfavor. "A lady should have a nice white complexion. You're going to be as black as Brutus if you don't stay out of that sun, child."

"Oh, I don't think it's going to ruin her complexion," Aimee said quickly.

Cretien argued the point and then, as he saw Chantel eating rapidly, he said sharply, "Don't gobble your food down! You're eating like a pig."

Again Aimee interposed. "She has such a good appetite. Being outside gives it to her, I suppose, and that's a good thing."

"Well, she eats enough. I don't see why she can't gain weight. She looks like a stick."

Chantel's face turned pale at her father's thoughtless words. Her mirror told her that she was not beautiful, and children called her "bird legs" and other cruel names.

"What did you do all afternoon, dear?" Aimee asked.

"I just went out in the woods. I caught some crawdads. Clarice said we could have *étouffée* tomorrow."

"That's nice. It's one of my favorite dishes."

The conversation moved in a more pleasant direction, and eventually Cretien's mood softened. With a smile he said, "I think our daughter is going to be an actress when she grows up."

Aimee was surprised. "Why do you say that, dear?"

"Because when I found her, she was acting out a play. Quite well, too. She was doing all the parts. Had a sword fight and a love scene and a dying scene. It was like being at the theater in New Orleans." He laughed and shook his head. "It was a very good performance, Chantel. I enjoyed it."

As always, Chantel flushed at her father's praise. She beamed at him and said, "It was from the play you took us to last month."

"I'll have to be careful what kind of plays I take you to see," Cretien said with a smile. "Some of them are not wholesome. But it was a good sword fight. Maybe I'll teach you how to use the foils when you get a little older."

"I'm old enough now, Papa!"

"Well, maybe you are. We'll see."

Aimee smiled then and said, "Why don't you tell her our surprise, dear?"

Cretien gave his wife a swift glance and nodded. He studied Chantel for a moment, then said, "We're going to have company, Chantel."

"Who is it?"

"Let me give you a hint. Our visitor will be very small. No bigger than this." He held up his hands, holding them about eighteen inches apart.

"I know. It's the puppy I've wanted!"

"No, it's even better than a puppy. Come here."

At once Chantel was out of her seat and around the heavy table. When Cretien picked her up in his arms, she felt a security and a delight in being noticed. Her father put his lips close to her ear and whispered, "We're going to have a baby."

"Oh, Papa, how nice!" She reached up and put her arms around her father's neck and hugged him. He laughed and unwound her arms, saying, "Go embrace your mother. She's the one that will be bringing the baby to us."

Chantel slipped from his lap and ran over to receive her mother's hug. "When will it come, Mama?"

"Very close to your birthday. Maybe on the same day. Wouldn't that be something, if we had two birthdays on the same day!"

"We could save money." Cretien smiled, his eyes sparkling. "I'm hoping you'll have a little brother. Then we can all three raise him to be a good, strong man." Echoing his wife's thought, he added, "It will be close to your birthday when the baby is born. What do you want for your birthday?"

"A horse."

"Well, you don't mind asking for the moon!"

"Can I have one, Papa? Please!"

"Yes, you may have a horse."

"Dear, do you think she's old enough?"

"Of course she is. She needs to learn to be a horsewoman. Then she can go riding with her father."

"Papa, will you really get me a horse?"

"Yes. I'll bring it to your party."

"Does anyone else know about the baby?"

"No one."

"Can I go tell Clarice and Elise?"

"Yes, you may."

As Chantel shot out of the dining room, Aimee said, "That child adores you, Cretien. She just glows when you pay attention to her. Don't you see it?"

Cretien was well aware of his failings as a father. He looked down at the table and fumbled with his napkin, then looked up and caught her eye. "I know. I'll try to be more affectionate with her."

Aimee knew that part of the reason for Cretien's lack of affection for their daughter was that Chantel was not a beautiful girl. "She's not pretty now, but she will be someday."

"Oh, that doesn't matter," Cretien protested.

But Aimee bit her tongue, for she had almost said, *Yes, it does to you. You like beautiful things.* Instead she said, "When will you get the pony?"

"There's no hurry. I'll look around for a good one."

"She'll love it, Cretien. She treasures anything you give her." A smile turned the corners of Aimee's lips upward. "Do you remember the doll you bought for her when she was four? She's almost worn that thing out. It's all Marie and I can do to keep it sewn together. She sleeps with it every night."

Cretien smiled. He was mellow with the thought of having a son to raise and said, "Chantel is a good child. Just not what I expected. She's so—so boyish."

"She will outgrow that. Don't worry."

"I hope so. I'd hate to see a woman of eighteen running around in a ragged dress catching crawdads."

Chapter six

The day was dying, and now the sun sent the last few pale rays through the window of Chantel's room. It illuminated the carpet and touched the mirror on her vanity briefly with its pale light. She looked up from the book before her and caught a glimpse of her own face. As always, her features displeased her, and she looked down quickly and began writing again.

She had begun her journal at her mother's suggestion, on the same day that her parents had told her of the baby to come.

Her father agreed, saying, "It might help her penmanship a little."

"Oh, no," Aimee had protested. "No one sees a young lady's journal except the young lady herself."

Strangely enough, as much as she had once disliked some studies, Chantel had found a pleasure in keeping her journal. Perhaps it was because no one ever checked it for spelling or punctuation. She wrote rapidly as her thoughts flowed through her, and never paused to correct anything.

May 2, 1823

Today *is the day the baby will be born! I hope it's a boy because Papa wants one so much. I don't care whether it's a boy or a girl.*

I'd love to have either *a baby brother or a baby sister. Whichever it is, I'll be happy with it!!!*

The doctor came early this morning, and Mama is having a bad time. I don't like to hear it—the cries that come from her room. The doctor is worried, too, although he tries not to show it. I tried to talk to Papa, but he's too worried to listen to me, so I just stay quiet as a mouse and pray that Mama and the baby will be all right.

It's been a wonderful *time for me, waiting for the baby—until today. Papa has been* so *happy, and he's taken me to the theater several times! I* love *to go with him, but I know he's ashamed of me because I'm not pretty like other girls. Mama says I will be prettier when I get older, but I don't think so.*

I was hoping the baby would be born on my birthday, but it's all right that it's a few days early. My birthday is only eighteen days away, and think what I will have! *I will have a* new *brother or sister, and I'll have* my new horse, *which Papa promised me. If it's a mare, I'll call her Lady. If it's a gelding, I'll call him Pegasus. I'll* never *be lonesome again with my new baby brother or sister and my new horse!*

Hearing footsteps coming down the hall, Chantel quickly closed the book and ran to the chest against the wall. Opening the drawer, she shoved the journal beneath her clothes, rose, and turned just as her father came in. He stood looking at her, and for one terrible moment Chantel was afraid that her mother had died. She knew that women did die sometimes from having babies, and it had been a fear on her heart almost constantly. "Is— Is Mama all right?"

"Yes, she's fine—and you have a new baby sister." Her father's voice changed when he said "baby sister," and instantly Chantel knew that he was very disappointed. She wanted to tell him how sorry she was that it wasn't a boy, but that didn't seem very fair to the girl who had just been born. She said breathlessly, "Can I see Mama?"

"Yes. Come along."

Chantel accompanied her father down the hall, and when she stepped into the large master bedroom, she saw her mother in bed with a bundle in her arms. Doctor South was putting something in a black bag, and Marie was cleaning up.

"Come here, dear."

Chantel went over to stand beside the bed. Her mother's face was pale and drawn, and her lips looked very thin and white. "Here's your new baby sister."

Chantel leaned forward and looked at the little face that peered out of the blanket. She had never seen a newborn baby, and for a moment she felt disappointed. "She's so red, Mama!"

"All babies are red. You were too. She's going to be beautiful."

"I hope so," Chantel said. She reached out and touched the fine blonde hair on the baby's head. "What color are her eyes?"

"All babies have blue eyes."

"Really!"

"Yes, indeed. I'm hoping she'll have brown eyes like your father."

"What's her name, Mama?"

"Veronique."

Cretien had come to stand on the other side of the bed. He said nothing while Chantel asked questions. Finally Aimee turned to him, and he made himself smile. "She's a fine child," he said quietly.

Aimee felt a pang of disappointment. She had prayed so hard for a boy! Now her heart was heavy, because Doctor South had told her that it would be dangerous for her to have other children. She knew that he had informed Cretien of this, and she saw a heaviness and a sadness in his face, despite his attempts to hide it.

"Can I hold her, Mama?" asked Chantel.

"Yes, but be very careful."

Chantel was very careful indeed as she took the baby, holding her as if she were a very fragile piece of fine glass. She looked down into the face. "We're going to be the best of friends always and always," she whispered.

After several minutes Doctor South said, "I think you'd better give your sister back to your mother now, and you scoot on along."

Chantel carefully placed the baby in her mother's arms, then leaned over and kissed them both. "I'll be back when Doctor South says I can."

As soon as she left the room, Doctor South gave the parents a few instructions, then added, "That's one of the healthiest babies I've ever seen. She's a fine girl. Congratulations, monsieur."

"Thank you, doctor, for everything."

As soon as Doctor South left, Aimee held her hand out, and Cretien took it. "I'm so sorry it's not a boy."

Cretien tried to smile, but she saw that he was unhappy. She squeezed his hand and said, "We must adopt a boy."

His face grew tense. "No," he said firmly. "Blood is everything! I wouldn't want a child that wasn't mine by blood."

Bending over, he kissed his wife, then reached over and, almost with reluctance, touched the child's head. "She's a fine child," he repeated quietly, then turned and left the room.

In the silence of the room, holding the baby close to her heart, Aimee Fontaine felt one of the most intense moments of sadness she had ever known. She should have been crying out for joy with a new baby healthy in every way, but she knew how Cretien had longed for a son. And now she had failed him. Tears ran down her face, and she made no attempt to wipe them away.

The days seemed to fly by after the birth of Veronique—at least for Chantel. She spent every moment possible with the baby, helping with her all she could. She watched with amazement as her sister nursed and asked her mother a thousand questions concerning babies.

Aimee laughed and waved her hand in the air. "You want to know everything about babies."

"But they're so wonderful, Mama!"

"Yes, they are wonderful, indeed, and I'm glad that you love her so much."

"We're going to be best friends."

When she was not holding the baby or watching her being cared for, Chantel was singing to her. She had learned many nursery songs already and could rock the baby and sing for hours without growing tired. This pleased Aimee and astonished Cretien.

"I never thought she would be such a good little mother," he whispered, watching Chantel as she rocked Veronique. "She's much older than her years in this way at least."

Yet time also seemed to move slowly because Chantel was counting the hours until her birthday. Papa had promised her a horse! The delight of her life was when her father would put her on the saddle in front of him and take her for a ride on his big stallion, Caesar. Chantel was constantly at the barn, and whenever a foal was born she could hardly be dragged into the house for the joy of watching the spindly legged but beautiful creatures as they learned to walk.

Finally, as it always must, time went around, and the morning of May 20 arrived. Cretien had left two days earlier on a business trip to New Orleans. Chantel was giving Veronique her bath, at which she had become very good indeed. Carefully she washed the silkened skin, marveling at the tiny wrinkles in the hands and the small fingernails. She sang a song as Aimee sat watching.

Chantel said, "Papa will be back for my birthday, won't he?"

"I'm sure he will, dear. He wouldn't forget your birthday." Aimee smiled and said, "How does it feel to be ten years old?"

Chantel thought for a moment and said, "Just like it did to be nine years old. I thought I would feel older."

She soaked the baby's hair, rinsed it carefully, and then tickled her. The baby chortled, which pleased her. Looking up, she said, "When will I be grown, Mama?"

"Not for a long time."

"I want to be grown up."

"Don't wish your life away, my dear."

"Didn't you want to be grown up when you were nine years old?"

"My goodness! I can't remember that far back. Here, let me help you get this child dressed." The two of them dressed the baby and then Chantel said, "I'm going down to help Clarice make the cake. She said I could."

"All right. Don't be a bother, though. Remember, the guests will be coming at one o'clock, and you want to be all dressed and ready."

"I will, Mama. I'll do my hair just right, and maybe Elise will help me."

"Just a moment," Aimee said. A smile touched the corners of her lips as she brought a small package out of her pocket. "I want to give you your present now—a special present just from me."

Chantel took the small package and unwrapped it quickly. Opening the box within, she pulled out a locket on a gold chain. "Mama, it's beautiful."

"It belonged to my mother." Aimee smiled. "Look inside."

Chantel opened the locket and stared at the miniature painting. "It's a picture of you!"

"Yes, and someday you'll put a picture of yourself in it and give it to your daughter. Do you want to wear it?"

"Oh, yes, Mama!" Chantel could barely stand still, and when the locket was fastened, she threw her arms around her mother. "Thank you so much, Mama! I'll always love it. May I go show it to Clarice?"

"Yes, run along."

Running downstairs, Chantel went at once to the kitchen and found the cook in the midst of making the birthday pastry. "Clarice, look at my new locket!"

The locket was duly admired, and Chantel said, "I came to help you make the cake. Hello, Miss Marie." She talked like a magpie, informing them of the progress of Veronique and her excitement about the horse. "I hope it's a gray horse. I've always liked gray horses," she said.

Clarice and Marie were amused. "What makes you think you're going to get a horse to ride?" Marie asked.

"Oh, Marie, you know Papa promised! That's why he went to New Orleans. I just know."

"You will break your neck," Clarice warned. "I do not think it is a good thing."

"I will not!"

"That's what horses are good for. To fall off of and break your neck."

"Oh, Clarice, why do you talk so foolish!"

When Chantel left to get ready for her party, the two women stared after her. Marie said, "She loves her Papa so much."

"And he cares so little for her!" Clarice snorted.

"Hush! It is not for us to talk about the family."

"I've heard you say it, so I suppose I can too."

"The master is a strange man. He wanted a boy so much. Perhaps he will have a son next time."

"And then he will pay all the attention to the son," Clarice replied, "and our little Chantel will get none. Poor child! She just soaks up his love when he gives any—which isn't often."

Marie Bientot was an astute woman. She knew as well as Chantel and everyone else who was intimate with the family that Chantel was a lonely child who loved her father with every fiber of her being. She also knew how self-consumed Cretien Fontaine could be. He was good enough to his wife and not abusive to anyone, but his first consideration was his own comfort.

Marie sighed and shook her head. "I'm glad the baby was a girl and not a boy. Chantel would no longer get any notice at all!"

Chantel found Brutus shoeing a horse and stood watching with fascination. "Doesn't it hurt the horses when you put those nails in their feet?"

"These ain't feet, missy. These is hooves. And no, they ain't got no feelin' unless you go too deep and hit a nerve—which I ain't never done."

Chantel and the large slave were good friends. Brutus was amused by her interest in the workings of the farm, and it was not unusual to see the small girl sitting astride his massive shoulders as they walked through the fields of sugar cane. He taught her how to catch crawdads, took her fishing, and taught her the names of the animals and birds and trees in the countryside.

He listened as she told him about the horse she was to get, and promised to shoe it for her whenever it was time. When she left singing, as usual, Brutus shook his head. "That child is a sight in this world! She purely is," he muttered. "She sho do love hosses. I hope her papa gets her a good 'un."

There was no other way to put it: the party was a failure.

Eight children from the surrounding plantations came, but only one, Claude Dumair, was anywhere close to Chantel's age. The others were either several years younger or several years older. Aimee and Marie had planned the games, and the food was delicious. Chantel opened her presents, forcing herself to smile and politely thank each child who gave her a gift.

Aimee saw that Chantel could not stop looking toward the road, at every moment expecting her father to come riding up on his stallion, leading the horse he had promised her.

As time went on and Cretien did not come, Chantel's heart began to grow cold. She was glad when the last child left. She turned to her mother. "Papa didn't come to my party."

"I'm sure something held him up, dear."

"He promised to come, and he promised to give me a horse." The words were spoken in a whisper, and Aimee saw the eyes of her daughter fill up.

"He didn't come," she said, turning and running out of the house.

"Chantel!" Aimee called out. "Chantel! Come back!" But the child kept on running.

Aimee Fontaine was a calm and generous and loving woman, but now someone had hurt her child. An anger began to grow in her, and soon it was white hot. She stood there trembling, so angry that she wanted to strike out and beat her fists against something. Instead she took a deep breath, walked stiffly to the rosewood secretary, and sat down. Getting a sheet of paper, she dipped her pen in ink and wrote in large letters without any heading:

Come home at once and bring a horse for your daughter—the one you promised her!

She formed an exclamation point, then blotted the letter, folded it, put it into an envelope, and sealed it with wax. She strode into the kitchen, where she found Robert polishing the silver. "Robert," she said, holding out the envelope, "take this at once to your master."

"Why, yes, madame. Shall I wait for an answer?"

"I expect he will be coming back with you." Polar ice was never colder than Aimee's tone, and as she turned and left the room, Robert stared after her.

"Never seen her like that before! I can imagine what's in here," he said to Elise.

"I hope she told him what a sorry excuse for a father he is," Elise said. Tears came to her eyes. "I hope she did."

"Well, I'll find him. I know all of his spots," Robert said grimly. He put the envelope into his pocket, put on his coat, and left the house. A few moments later Elise heard the sound of hoofbeats and looked out the window to see Robert driving a large bay gelding at full speed down the road.

Cretien was winning and, as always, this made him feel good. The stakes had gotten high, and as he pulled in the pot, he shook his head. "You gentlemen are not lucky tonight."

"No, I believe you have all the luck, Cretien." The speaker was a tall, swarthy man with a sharp-pointed mustache. He looked up suddenly and said, "Isn't that your man Robert?"

Cretien turned and saw Robert striding across the room. "Why, so it is!" he said.

"Madame Fontaine asked me to give you this, sir," Robert said to him.

Cretien took the envelope, but his eyes were on Robert's face. Robert had been with him for a long time, and the two got along well. Now, however, there was a fixed hardness on the face of his manservant.

"Is someone sick?" he asked quickly. "One of the children?"

"No, sir."

The answer gave no information, and Cretien opened the envelope. He pulled out the single sheet of paper and read the stark message. Licking his lips, he put the letter back into the envelope and carefully put it into his pocket. "I'm cashing in," he said. "I have to go."

"Is there some sort of problem, Cretien?"

"I'm afraid so. I'll give you a chance to get even next time I'm in town."

Robert stood, silently waiting until his employer had collected his winnings, then followed him outside the gambling room.

As soon as they were outside, Cretien turned and said, "Go to the house and pack my things, then meet me in front of the hotel. We'll be leaving in an hour."

Robert nodded and left, saying not a word. Cretien watched him go, then turned and broke into a half run. He did not stop until he got to a stable and called out, "I need some help."

Chantel cried herself to sleep, then slept fitfully. She awoke to the sound of a voice calling her name, and at first she thought it was just another dream. The voice called her name again.

"Chantel, wake up. It's Papa."

She came out of sleep and found her father kneeling beside her bed, holding a candle with his right hand.

"Papa, what is it?" she said, groggily struggling to sit up.

"Are you awake?"

"Yes, I'm awake." Chantel saw her father's tense face, and fear came to her. "Is something wrong with Mama?"

"No, not at all."

"Is Veronique all right?"

"She's fine. Come with me. I have something to show you."

Chantel stood up barefooted, but suddenly her father blew the candle out and set it down. He picked her up in his arms and went out the door. Chantel blinked against the lights that were burning and saw her mother standing at the foot of the stairs. Again she felt a wash of fear, but her father's arms held her tight. She reached up and put her arms around his neck and her face against his chest. When they went outside it was dark, but a lantern threw some light on the scene. She saw Robert standing there holding the lantern high.

"Happy birthday, daughter."

The events of the day rushed back to Chantel, but when Cretien turned around she saw a small horse standing next to Robert.

"Happy birthday," her father whispered. "She's all yours. A fine mare."

In all her life Chantel had never felt as she did at that moment.

Gone were the tears and the heartache that had crushed her. She stared at the horse and whispered, "For me, Papa?"

"All yours, little one. Why don't you go get acquainted with her?"

Chantel felt herself being lowered, and she ran barefooted toward Robert, who was holding the mare with his other hand. She stopped, reached up, and the mare whickered at her and lowered her head carefully. Chantel felt the velvet nose, and tears came into her eyes. She began to cry and could not stop.

"I love you, Lady," she whispered, and then she turned and ran back up the steps to her father. "I knew you wouldn't forget, Papa. I knew you wouldn't!"

Cretien Fontaine felt shame such as he had rarely known. Turning slightly, he saw Aimee standing in the open door. Their eyes met, and as Chantel said again, "I knew you wouldn't forget!" he looked down. He held the child close, then he kissed her cheek and said hoarsely, "I'll never be late for your birthday party again, daughter. I swear it!"

Grasping the reins of her mare firmly, Chantel sat straight in the saddle, filled with joy. She glanced at her father, who was riding Caesar, and thought, *He is the handsomest man in the world.*

Cretien turned and smiled at her. "A good morning for a ride, eh?" He saw that her eyes were dancing bright, but now there was the air of a little girl's eagerness about her that he had learned to recognize. "I wish everyone in the world could get out and ride like this with a fine rider like you."

Chantel's face revealed the pleasure that welled up inside. She turned away so that he could not see how happy he had made her. Ahead she saw a tree across the path and said, "Let's jump it, Papa."

"Do you think you can do it?"

"You just watch. Come on, Lady." Chantel leaned forward and spoke encouragingly to the mare, who broke into a swift gallop. When she came to the log, Chantel cried out, and the mare jumped it easily.

Chantel looked back, crying, "I did it, Papa!" She watched as her father took the jump and pulled up beside her.

"That was fine! You've become a good rider." He studied her for a moment and then shook his head. "But you're going to have to learn to ride sidesaddle sometime."

"Oh, Papa, that's no fun! Riding with your leg crooked around an old saddle horn!"

"That may be, but it's the way ladies ride."

"I think it's silly!" Chantel turned to face her father, her brow kneaded. "I want to ride just like you do."

"Well, we'll worry about that when you get all grown up. In the meanwhile you've gotten to be a fine rider."

Chantel flashed a smile. "You know, Papa, the last six months have been the best time of my whole life."

"Is that right? Well, I'm glad to hear it. I hope the rest of your life will be just as good."

"Papa, do you think I'll ever be pretty like Mama?"

Cretien hesitated. In truth he was disappointed that his daughter had not inherited Aimee's beauty. She was entirely different, and he sought words carefully so that he would not hurt her feelings.

"Let me tell you something about beauty, daughter. You have one thing that I admire very much." He saw her eyes brighten and he smiled. "You have a fine carriage. You're a tall young lady, and you're going to be even taller when you grow up. A fine carriage and good bone structure, which you have—nothing can take the place of those." He turned to look at a small bird pouring out a symphony of song.

He gazed at the bird for a moment and then turned back and said, "I knew a lady once in France. She had the same sort of bone structure that you have, Chantel. And when you studied her face alone she didn't seem exceptionally attractive. But she carried herself well, and somehow other people began to think she *was* attractive."

He thought for a moment about the days that he had spent in Paris, and there was a queer twist in him—a stray current of something out of his far past, half regret and half a pale sentimentality. Shaking himself, he said, "Now, you're going to be just like that woman. You're going to think yourself beautiful."

"But how can I do that?"

"That's what you must find out for yourself. We, all of us, have to find out things about ourselves, Chantel."

Chantel thought about his words and then said, "You know, I want to do so many things. Last night when I saw Veronique looking out the window she saw the moon, and she reached out for it. But she didn't know she could never get it."

"Reach for the moon, Chantel," Cretien said strongly. "You may not get it, but you must never give up trying. Some poet or other, I forget who it was, said, 'Always reach for the stars. Some day you might get one.' Something like that."

The two talked as their horses walked side by side, until Cretien said, "I think we'd better get back now. It's getting a little bit late."

"Just a little ways further, Papa."

"No, I have things to do."

Reluctantly Chantel reined Lady around, and when they started back, she said, "When will you have to leave, Papa?"

"Next week, I think." He turned and smiled. "I'll bring you back something from the city. What would you like?"

Instantly Chantel said, "I would like a pistol."

Her answer brought a burst of laughter from Cretien. He was fascinated by the mind of this daughter of his. "A pistol! What in the world would you do with a pistol?"

"I would protect myself. And if a burglar came in the house, I would shoot him."

"I think eleven is a little young to be shooting burglars. Wherever do you get such ideas?"

"Oh, I don't know. I just think of them."

"I believe you've been reading too many romances."

"But I love the stories, Papa. Don't you?"

"They're all right. But you have to remember, Chantel, they're just stories. Not real life." He did not speak for a time, and then he said, "I'll bring you back something from town, but it will be much nicer than a pistol. Maybe a new dress or some shoes."

"I'll like whatever you bring, Papa—but someday when I grow up I'll get myself a pistol and carry it in my reticule. Then I won't have to be afraid of anyone."

Cretien turned to study his daughter. He did not understand her in the least, but he shrugged and thought, *Maybe a man never understands a child. Especially a female one.*

∽

A cold breeze from the north bit at Chantel's face, but she ignored it. She was wrapped up in heavy clothes and wore gloves that were really intended for more sedate pastimes than trot lining in the river. She sat in the back of the flat-bottom boat, watching as Brutus propelled them along by tugging at a heavy line. Every ten feet or so he would stop and examine a shorter line that was tied to the long one that stretched along the banks. One end was tied at the bank and another to a cypress tree that pushed its way upward out of the murky waters of the river.

"Let me put some bait on, Brutus."

"No, missy, you'd better let me do dat," he replied. He turned to smile at her, and the late afternoon sun caught his ebony features. His weight pushed the front of the johnboat down into the water. He reached into the bucket at his feet, pulled out a crawdad, and skillfully hooked the wiggling creature just beneath the top of its shell. He examined it critically, then lowered it into the water, still holding onto the main line.

"You cotch us a good catfish, Mr. Crawdad," he said.

He was humming a tune, and as he moved along to the next set line, Chantel said, "What's that song, Brutus?"

"Just a song I know."

Chantel asked him to sing it again, and the second time she sang it with him.

"You sho is got a good singin' voice, missy," Brutus said. He started to speak, then suddenly he halted and turned quickly. "We got somethin' on the line up ahead there! Feels like a big 'un!"

"Can I help pull it in?"

"No, indeed! These catfish can be mean critters. They got horns on 'em with pizen in 'em. But you kin watch. And then later on you kin have some good, fresh, fried catfish. Hold still now!"

Chantel watched with excitement as Brutus propelled the boat. She saw the line dipping and straining, and, as always, wished she could help.

Brutus kept a tight hold, and once he turned and said, "He shore is a big 'un. Must be big as Jonah's whale." He turned back and soon he said, "Gonna have to pull hard to get dis 'un in. You watch now. Don't let him git close to you when he get in de boat."

After what seemed like a long struggle, Brutus gave a tug, and a huge catfish came dripping and flopping into the bottom of the boat. He was the biggest catfish Chantel had ever seen, and she saw him swing his head around.

"Watch out for dem horns now! Lemme get 'em off." Brutus approached the fish carefully, for the dorsal fin and the two side fins both had spikes that could hurt fiercely. He waited his chance, ran his huge hand in the fish's lip, and gripped down. Chantel saw the mighty mouth close, but Brutus was not paying attention. With a pair of pliers he reached down and snapped off the dorsal fin, the horn, and then the two side fins. "There, dat'll hold you, I reckon."

"He's so big!"

"Biggest one I ever cotched," he said. "Now, I reckon as how we might as well go home. We got enough fish for one night, and mo' than I expect. Everybody will have fish at Fontaine Maison tonight." The fish flopped and thrashed around the bottom of the boat as Brutus dropped the line down. It sank immediately because of the weights he had tied to it. Picking up a paddle, he sent the small craft over the water with powerful strokes.

As always, Chantel chattered like a magpie, speaking about the things she was going to do when she grew up. "You know," she said, "I think I might be a doctor."

Brutus broke his strokes for a moment and stared at her. "But dey ain't no lady doctors dat I knows of."

"Well, there will be when I get to be one."

"Don't see why fo' you want to be a doctor. It's a pretty messy job, and you allus havin' to be around folks in trouble. Why don't you just be a lady like yo' mama."

"I can be that, too."

Brutus laughed deep in his chest. "You sho got a mess of things you gonna do when you grow up. Looks like it'd take two or three lifetimes to get 'em all in."

They were almost to the landing when suddenly two large black birds dropped out of the sky and lit on the limb of a cypress.

Brutus stared at them. "Dat's bad luck right there."

"What is?"

"Why, dem black birds! Every time dey come you can figure on somethin' mighty bad happenin'. Maybe I'll break a leg or somethin' like that."

"Oh, don't be silly, Brutus! They're just old blackbirds."

"You think what you want, missy, but last time I seed two birds like dat come down and light, the next day I lost my good knife."

"Well, it didn't have anything to do with the blackbirds," Chantel said defiantly. "Now, I want to watch you clean the fish."

"Shucks, dat's a messy job. I don't know why you want to see dat." He smiled suddenly at her, his teeth white against his ebony skin. "You more interested in things than any girl I ever seed—or any man either, for that matter."

He paddled the boat so that the prow drove in on a bank, then stepped out and held it, saying, "You watch out for dat fish. He might bite yo' foot clean off."

Chantel laughed, but all the same she carefully avoided the huge catfish. She watched as Brutus tied the boat, then reached out and got the fish by the lip.

"Dis here fish must weigh thirty pounds! We're gonna have good eatin' tonight. Come on. I'll let you watch me clean 'im." They had started for the house when Brutus paused to look upward. "Dat sky looks mighty bad."

"It does look like rain," Chantel agreed.

"It done been rainin' so much. That river ain't gonna take much more." He shrugged and said, "Well, come on. Let's get dis here fish cleaned." He cast his eyes up at the rolling black clouds and shook his head sadly.

The rain came down in solid sheets, slanting as though driven by a powerful east wind. Simon Bientot was soaked to the skin. The water dripped off his hat in a miniature waterfall as he trudged along, the ground squishy with each step. As he came up on the front porch and stood under the overhang, he looked back in the direction of the river, lines of worry creasing his forehead. He took off his hat, wiped his face as best he could with a sodden handkerchief, and knocked on the door. It opened almost at once, and Aimee Fontaine stood there. She stepped outside and said, "What is it, Simon?"

"Miz Fontaine, I'm worried about that river. It's plum out of its banks already."

"But it's never flooded here."

"Yes, ma'am, it did, a long time ago. The old-timers told me that. This whole area was under water. That was before the house was built, of course, just a few shacks here. But it took 'em all away."

Aimee looked out at what seemed like a world submerged. Already the low places had become small lakes, and the water fell from the sky like a deluge. She was silent for a moment, then said, "I think it will be all right."

"I reckon we'd better leave, Miz Fontaine."

"No, we're not going to do that. It may get up to the house, but we're on a rise here. It won't get to us."

Simon argued. "What about folks in the lower lands? They are almost sure to get water in their houses."

"You can bring them all here. We'll take care of them until it stops raining and the water goes down."

Simon was not satisfied, but he realized that Aimee's mind was made up. "All right, ma'am, but I'm worried. And I think you should be, too."

Aimee turned and went back into the house, where she found Chantel rocking Veronique in the nursery.

"I never saw it rain so hard, Mama," Chantel said.

"I don't believe I ever have either. And I expect New Orleans will be flooded. It's so low there."

"But the water won't come in here, will it, Mama?"

With all the confidence she could muster Aimee replied, "Of course not. It'll stop raining, and the water will go down. It goes down very quickly. Now, let's give Veronique her bath."

After the bathing was done, Chantel went out and stood on the porch. The sound of water cascading off the house and striking the ground was louder than she had ever heard it. Thunder rolled almost constantly, and the sky was lit up with blinding white flashes. She was frightened by the power of the elements and quickly turned around and went back inside. She closed the door, muting the sound, but still the storm was like a beast prowling around. Chantel went to the nursery to sit beside her mama, who was rocking Veronique.

Simon nodded with relief. "You made the right decision, Miz Fontaine. We've got to get out of this place. The water's almost up to the level of the house."

"It's going to ruin our beautiful home."

"We can work on it after the water goes down, but now let's get out of here. Everybody else is all ready."

Aimee had finally acknowledged the inevitable. Ever since Simon's first warning, the rains had fallen steadily, though for a time they seemed to have stopped. Now the rain was slowing, but all around the big house a sheet of water continued to rise. The slave quarters were already flooded, and there was no other choice.

"Come along, Chantel."

"Where are we going, Mama?"

"We're going over to the Bascom Plantation. Mrs. Bascom sent word that we could stay there until the waters go down. Hurry now."

Chantel gathered her treasures together, including her journal and the doll that her father had given her, and placed them in a canvas sack. She went outside to the barn. Brutus had already saddled Lady, and Chantel stepped into the saddle and tied her sack around the saddle horn.

Brutus held the lines and said, "I tole you bad luck was comin' when dem two birds came down." He handed the reins to Chantel and said, "You be keerful now." Then he turned and hurried back to three wagons that had been loaded with the slaves and their possessions.

Simon Bientot came to greet Aimee as she came out of the house holding Veronique. "You ride with Tallboy. He's a good, steady driver, ma'am."

"Is everybody ready?"

"Yes, ma'am. Come along." Bientot walked with her to the wagon where a tall, thin young man pulled his hat off and nodded. "How do, Miz Fontaine."

"Hello, Tallboy." Aimee got into the wagon and settled back with Veronique in her arms, as Tallboy put on his hat and looked to the overseer.

Bientot nodded and climbed into the wagon, saying, "All right, let's find some dry ground."

The wagons moved through the floodwaters in a small procession. Chantel touched Lady with her heels, and the mare obediently moved forward. She guided the mare until she was even with her mother and said, "Do you want me to ride with you and help with Veronique?"

"No, I can take care of her. You be careful though."

"I'm afraid, Mama!"

"It's all right," Aimee said and smiled. She extended her hand, and Chantel reached down and took it. "We'll be fine. You'll see."

At that moment something touched Chantel. She held on to her mother's hand until the wagon dropped into a pothole, and they were separated. Chantel steadied Lady and moved on ahead to ride along with Bientot.

"It'll be all right, Miss Chantel. You sure you don't want to ride in the wagon with me?"

"No, I want to ride Lady. The rain has stopped, so I'll be fine."

"All right. You stick close to the wagon though."

The journey was slow, for Bientot was cautious. They followed the line of the road until finally they came clear of the water. Mud was everywhere. "The river's right up there," he said to Chantel. "Do you hear it?"

Chantel had already heard the distant rumbling that sounded like far-off thunder.

"It's out of its banks. I hope the bridge is still in place. If it ain't, I don't know what we'll do."

Chantel rose in her stirrups from time to time and finally, when they made a turn around a group of cypress trees, she saw the bridge. "It's still there, Simon!"

"Well, that's good!" Simon said with relief. He guided the horses until they came to the roaring river. The original banks were completely underwater, and the crest of the flood was striking the top of the bridge itself so that water flowed over it.

"We can't cross that bridge, Simon, can we?" Chantel stared at the raging torrent with fear.

"We've got to," Bientot said grimly. "Come on. I'll go across first." He stood up in the wagon and said, "All right. Come along, everyone. It'll be fine. You come with me, Chantel."

"All right." Chantel guided Lady across the bridge. The water seemed to grab at the mare's feet as it flowed over the bridge. The muddy torrent was beyond anything she had ever seen, and when she reached the other side she gave a sigh of relief. Simon drove the wagon thirty yards away, then halted and got out. The others were coming, and he said, "It looks like your mama and Tallboy's waiting till everyone else is across."

Chantel stood there and could not control the trembling in her limbs. She had climbed down from the mare and was holding the lines, but everything in her strained toward the figure of her mother and sister. "I wish they'd hurry!" she whispered.

The last of the wagons rolled across, and then Chantel saw Tallboy slap the lines on the horses. They started up skittishly and got to the edge of the bridge. They did not want to go, and she heard Tallboy calling to them, "Get on there! You get on there, you hear me, hosses! Cross that bridge!"

Her eyes were fixed on her mother and sister, and she waved at their wagon. "Come on, Mama!" she cried.

Her voice could not reach across, but she saw her mother, who was sitting on the front seat, smile and wave her free hand while holding Veronique with the other. Finally Tallboy forced the horses onto the bridge, but the team fought him all the way.

"Those fool horses! I wish they'd come on," she heard Bientot say under his breath.

She wished the same thing and watched as Tallboy finally got out of the wagon and went to the head of the team. "He's going to lead them across, Simon."

"I wish I'd gone with your mother," Bientot muttered. "Come on, Tallboy, get those horses moving!"

The bays behaved somewhat better, but not much. Tallboy pulled at them, and finally they started forward. They had reached the center of the bridge when suddenly there was a loud cracking sound, and she saw Tallboy suddenly go to his knees.

"The bridge! It's breaking!" Bientot shouted. He started for the bridge, but halted abruptly at the edge.

Chantel stared, horrified, as the bridge, with a creaking, groaning noise, suddenly parted in the middle. The force of the water caught it and pushed the center of it out.

"Mama!" Dropping Lady's reins, she ran forward. Even as she ran, she saw Tallboy swept away by the water—and then she saw the wagon caught by the force of the stream. Her eyes were on her mother, who was holding Veronique tightly. The bridge was swinging parallel with the stream, and suddenly the horses, screaming almost like women, dashed forward. As the wagon hit the water, the current caught it and turned it around. It floated, but was swung from side to side.

The animals tried to swim, but the current rolled them over. There were loud cries from the servants and slaves, and Chantel heard the sound of her own voice screaming. Just a fragment of the bridge was left standing, and as she rushed toward the river, the wagon suddenly rolled over and disappeared.

Chantel would have gone right into the raging water, but she felt arms around her and heard a voice saying, "Nothing we can do, missy. Come on back."

Chantel fought against Brutus's strong arms, but Simon Bientot's voice repeated, "Nothing you can do, Miss Chantel."

And then Marie was there, and she fell against the woman's breast crying and calling out her mother's and sister's names.

Chantel clung to her father's hand as they stood in the cemetery. To her it was a natural enough thing that the bodies of the dead would be interred above ground. In this low country, water was sometimes only as much as two feet below the surface; when a grave was dug it would fill up with water faster than the diggers could work.

They stood beside a structure of white marble to which was attached a bronze plate, bright and shiny, with the names of her mother and sister and the date: November 19, 1824.

The priest's voice came to her in a barely audible hum, but she could make no sense of the words. Ever since the tragedy, she had eaten so little that she had become much too thin. She had bad dreams every night, and even as she stood there she relived the horror, seeing the wagon go down in the muddy waters and take her sister and mother out of her life.

The priest's voice droned on. Chantel remembered how her father had come home the day after the deaths shouting and striking at the slaves for not saving them. He had cursed Bientot and acted like a wild man. He had refused to believe that they were dead and had organized search parties on both sides of the river. After two days her mother's body was found—but the body of Veronique was never recovered.

It seemed wrong, somehow, that Veronique's name was on the mausoleum when her little body was not there. Chantel's grief rose to a pitch, and she felt suddenly unable to stand. Her father caught her as she slipped, and she buried her face against his chest, her arms around his neck, until the funeral was over.

When they reached the house, she stepped inside. Everything in it spoke of her mother and of her baby sister, too. Chantel turned to her father, whose face was pale and had lines drawn in it she had not seen before. "What will we do without them, Papa?"

"We have to do the best we can, dear."

"I don't believe Veronique is dead."

"You must accept it. We must both accept it and move on."

The weeks that followed were terrible for both father and daughter. The floodwaters receded, and the river shrank back into its original banks. The cold weather came with December, but when Christmas came there was no attempt by either of them to make any ceremony.

The house was full of memories, and Chantel had nightmares that came tearing at her, bringing her awake, sobbing and almost screaming.

She stayed away from the house a great deal, riding her horse or just walking through the woods.

One day Simon Bientot said to Cretien, "The child is not doing well, is she?"

"No, she's not. Neither am I, Simon. I didn't know how much I loved them until I lost them."

One cold day in January Chantel could not be found. It was not unusual for her to take long walks or rides, but when she and Lady were not back by late afternoon, Cretien grew worried.

Marie said, "Sir, we must start looking for her. Something could have happened."

Cretien thought a moment. "I believe I know where she is." He mounted his stallion and rode to the cemetery. As he approached, he saw Lady tied to a tree at the edge. He tied his own horse, then walked to the mausoleum where he found Chantel lying on the cold ground, shivering. Her head was pressed against the cold marble. Cretien's heart went out to her, and he knelt down by her side. "Come, dear. We must go home."

Chantel turned, and her face looked even thinner than usual. Her eyes seemed abnormally large, and her face was pale. She reached up and put her arms around his neck.

"We must go on, Chantel, no matter how hard it is."

Cretien felt her arms tighten, and her face was muffled against his chest. But he heard her whisper, "You're all I have, Papa."

Cretien Fontaine could not speak, for his throat was tight. He picked the child up, took her to the horses, and held her on his saddle, leading her pony by the lines back toward the house. As she clung to him, he said, "You'll always have me, Chantel."

Chapter eight

Chantel compressed her lips as she wrote steadily in her journal. The hot sun flooded in through the window of her room, revealing millions of tiny motes dancing in the pale light. From far off came the sound of the field hands singing as they did their work, but the sound made no impact on her.

July 14, 1826

Papa finally came home late last night. I heard him and got up, and he looked very tired. I'm glad he's home. He stays away so much now that I get lonesome.

Leaning back in her chair, Chantel considered the next entry. She had confided secrets to her journal that she would not want anyone to see. It had become a substitute, in a way, for her mother, with whom she always had been able to share.

After Mama and Veronique left us, Papa stayed at home most of the time. But after six months he began going to New Orleans. He didn't stay long at first, but as time went on he spent more and more time there instead of here at the plantation. I wish he would take me with him! I get so *lonesome!*

I've just finished a geography lesson with Mrs. Pettis. She is so boring! *That woman even makes geography dull. We were studying Hawaii, and she told me all about the annual rainfall but not a word about the beautiful dancers and the sea and the natives in their canoes. Why does she always want to talk about the boring things and never about the exciting and beautiful things? Why, I learn more from* Brutus *than I do from her!*

The sound of a barking dog interrupted her, and she got up and went to the window. She had grown, and at the age of thirteen was the tallest of all the girls in her rather small society. Her frame was as slender as ever. She had grown up like a weed, and while other girls of her age were developing womanly features, she thought herself to be as skinny as a rake handle. The thought troubled her, and she went to the mirror and stared. Her face was no more beautiful than it had been when she was ten. Her eyes looked enormous, but they were such an odd color. True, her hair had darkened somewhat and was no longer carroty red, but it was still so thick that she could hardly drag a comb through it. Most of the time it was full of tangles, except when Elise insisted on combing it out.

Going back to the table, Chantel sat down and continued to write. The words came slowly, and for a moment she did not want to put them down. But she had vowed she would tell all in her journal:

I dream about Veronique so often. I dream about Mama, too, and they're such awful dreams! People don't like it when I go to their grave so often, so I have to sneak off when no one knows where I've gone. It's strange how I feel about Veronique. I just can't believe that she's dead. I *know she's alive—I don't care* what *they say!*

It did help to say things in her journal, to write down the things that she would not say to anyone else.

Suddenly she heard her father's voice calling her, and she quickly concealed the diary in the armoire.

"Aren't you dressed yet?"

"I was just getting ready to dress, Papa."

She stood there feeling very much alone, for since her father had started going to New Orleans she had felt the sense of distance between them grow. Even when he was home, he did not spend as much time with her as she would like. It had been over two months since he had gone out riding with her.

Cretien broke the silence. "I've got something to tell you."

"Is it bad?"

"No, it's good. At least I think it is. We're going to live for a time in New Orleans in the town house."

"You mean I must leave Fontaine Maison?"

"You've always enjoyed going to the town house and seeing the city," Cretien said. "You like to see new things."

"But I always knew I was coming back here. I love this place, Papa."

"Well, you'll love that place, too. We'll come back here on visits. I promise."

Chantel thought quickly, *If I'm there, I'll get to see more of Papa, and that will be so good.* "All right, Papa," she said, brightening. "When will we go?"

"Probably tomorrow. We'll have to pack a lot of your things. Do you need me to help you?"

"No, I can do it myself. I'm thirteen years old now."

Cretien smiled. "All right, then. We'll try to get away by Wednesday. That will give you plenty of time to get packed. Now get dressed. Breakfast is on the table."

The move to town was a great change for Chantel. She had said good-bye almost tearfully to Brutus and Marie and Clarice. Elise would be coming with them to be her own maid, and she was glad of that.

The first week was exciting, for Papa took her out every night but one, usually to the theater. The Creole life included a great love of drama, and it was possible to go to a different production every night of the week.

Only at night, when she was alone in her room and trying to sleep, did she feel her loss. She not only ached for her mama and Veronique, but she missed her horse and the servants and the out-of-doors as well.

She continued to have bad dreams of the death of her mother, but they were not as vivid as they had been.

One day she was in the courtyard playing with the neighbor's cat when her father stuck his head out the window. "Come and get ready, Chantel. I want you to do an errand with me."

"All right, Papa."

Running inside, she climbed the stairs and quickly put on a fresh dress, a coat, and a bonnet. "Where are we going, Papa?" she said.

"I've got to see my lawyer. His name is Mr. Harcourt."

"Can we go to Place d'Armes?"

"Yes, we can. As a matter of fact, his office is just off the square."

"Do I look all right?"

Cretien gave her a quick glance and nodded. "You look fine. Come along."

They walked to Place d'Armes, which was close to their house and not worth getting the carriage out for. The streets were crowded and, as always, the plaza was full of activity. Artists had set up their easels and were painting pictures of the cathedral. Others were selling their wares and calling out as the two passed. A juggler was juggling six balls, and Chantel was fascinated. "Give him some money, Papa."

Cretien laughed, reached into his pocket for a coin, and put it in the box on the ground.

"Could I learn to do that?" Chantel asked.

"I expect you could if you wanted to, but who would want to? There are better things for young ladies to learn." He looked down at her and studied her for a moment. She was growing every day, it seemed. *She's taller than Aimee right now, but skinny as a rail! I would think at her age she would begin filling out a little bit. Other girls do.*

Cretien said none of this aloud but listened as she chattered on about the activities on the square. He turned in at a door and led her up a pair of stairs. To the left were two doors, both of them marked with the sign *Harcourt and Son, Attorneys-at-Law.*

Opening the door, Cretien waited until Chantel was inside and then closed it behind him. A clerk was sitting behind a desk, and he rose at once. "Well, good afternoon, Mr. Fontaine. I suppose you need to see Mr. Harcourt."

"Yes. Is he in?"

"He's not busy at the moment." The clerk moved over and knocked on the door. When a voice answered, he opened the door and said, "Mr. Fontaine to see you, sir."

Chantel heard a voice say a rather gruff "Come in," and she entered with her father. A tall, heavyset man was sitting behind a desk. He rose at once and came over to shake her father's hand. "Good to see you, sir. And who is this young lady?"

"My daughter, Chantel."

"I'm very happy to know you, Miss Chantel." The big man turned to a young man who was working at a high desk over by a window. "This is my son, Neville."

Chantel looked at the young man as he came over and shook hands with her father. When he reached out and took her own hand, she saw that he had a nice smile. He was not nearly as tall as his father nor as handsome as hers; still, she liked it when he bent over in a bow and said, "I'm delighted to meet you, Miss Chantel."

"I have met you before, Neville," Cretien said.

"I'm afraid I don't recall, sir."

"You were only two years old. It was the first time I was ever here." Cretien turned and said, "So, you've taken your boy into the business."

"Yes, and I must say he's going to be a fine attorney." Oliver Harcourt glanced quickly at Chantel and shook his head. "This is going to be a rather dreary business for a young lady." He turned to his son, saying, "Neville, take Miss Chantel somewhere for something to drink. Perhaps even a bite to eat."

"That will be my pleasure," Neville said. He turned and pulled a coat from a rack, put it on, then put on a top hat. "If you'll come with me, Miss Chantel," he said, "we'll see what we can find."

Chantel was intrigued when he put his arm out just as if she were a grown lady, and she took it at once. They left the offices and were soon on the street. Neville chatted, asking questions and listening carefully as she spoke. Chantel liked this, for many grown people would ask a question and then wouldn't listen when she answered. She wished he were taller and more handsome, but he couldn't help what he looked like.

"Would you like some ice cream?"

"It's a little cold, but I always like ice cream."

"Well, perhaps something warmer. How about some gumbo?"

"Oh, yes . . . but it won't be as good as our cook makes at home."

"Probably not, but I know one place that has very good gumbo. It will be a close second."

Neville led the young girl to a small cafe where he was greeted by name by a large woman wearing a white apron. She had silver hair and merry brown eyes and remarked, "Ah, you have a lady with you."

"Yes, this is my very special friend, Miss Chantel Fontaine. Miss Fontaine, may I introduce Madame Charmain."

"I am happy to know you," the woman said, beaming. "Come now and sit down." She winked at Chantel, saying, "You must be careful. This handsome young fellow will get away from you. All the ladies are after him."

Chantel giggled at that, for Neville Harcourt was not at all handsome. She liked it, though, when he seated her and sat down and let her order for herself. The gumbo was accompanied by a basket of rolls that smelled so good that she bit into one at once.

As they ate, Neville asked her about herself, and she found herself talking far more than she usually did to strangers. She liked this young man very much.

"Are you married, Mr. Neville?"

"No, I'm not."

"How old are you?"

Neville laughed. "I'm eighteen. And let's see, I would guess that you're about sixteen. Is that right?"

Pleased at being taken for older than she was, Chantel said, "No, I'm just thirteen, but I'm going on fourteen."

"Well, that's a surprise. Tell me, do you like New Orleans?"

"I like it all right, but I miss my horse."

"Oh, you have a horse!"

"Papa's having her brought to New Orleans, and he's going to keep her in a stable. Then I can go riding. Do you have a horse?"

"As a matter of fact, I do. Perhaps we could go riding together sometime."

"Oh, that would be nice!"

The two ate the spicy gumbo and the rolls and then drank hot chocolate. They sat for a while talking, sipping the tasty drinks, and finally Chantel grew silent.

"What are you thinking about, Miss Chantel?"

"I was just wondering about my mother and my sister." The memory came sweeping back through Chantel, and she forgot for the moment where she was. She could almost hear her mother's laughter and see her face. Without thinking she said impulsively, "Where do you think people go when they die, Mr. Neville?"

"You mean good people?"

"Oh, yes, good people like my mother."

"I think people who love God go straight to heaven."

The words warmed Chantel. "I asked our priest, and he said that they go to purgatory, and they have to suffer there for a long time until they can get out. But I don't believe that."

"Well, I'm afraid I don't believe it, either. As a matter of fact I was reading in the Bible last night about a man who died and went to heaven that same day."

Chantel looked up. She had a line of chocolate across her lips and dabbed at it with her handkerchief. "Really! That's in the Bible?"

"Yes, it is."

"I'd like to read it, but we don't have a Bible."

"Don't have a Bible? Well, come along."

Neville paid for the food and waited for her. Once again he put his arm out, and she took it, feeling very grown up as she walked along the streets of Place d'Armes.

Neville led her to a bookstore and went inside. He was evidently a frequent guest, for he was greeted by name by the proprietor, a short, swarthy man with bushy black hair and a ferocious beard to match.

"We're looking for a Bible."

"Well, you know where they are, Mr. Harcourt," the proprietor said. "Let me know if I can help you."

Harcourt led Chantel to a shelf and studied the books for a moment. "This looks like it might be very nice." He pulled out a book and opened it. "Can you read this print all right?"

Chantel took it and studied it. The cover was black and rather thick, but when she opened it, she saw that the print was large and plain. "Yes, it's very easy to read."

"Very well then. This will do."

He took the book to the proprietor, paid for it, and the two left. "Let's sit down on that bench over there. We can watch the people, and I'll let you read the story that I mentioned."

They sat down on the bench, and Neville said, "Let me see. Yes, here it is. It happened at the time Jesus died. You know about that, don't you?"

"Oh, yes, He died on a cross. I have a silver cross that I wear sometimes, but I'm not wearing it today."

"I'm sure it's very pretty. Now, read right here." He handed her the book, put his finger on a line, and nodded.

Chantel read aloud about Jesus being crucified.

> *And when they were come to the place, which is called Calvary, there they crucified him, and the malefactors, one on the right hand, and the other on the left.*
>
> *Then said Jesus, Father, forgive them; for they know not what they do.*

Then when she got to verse thirty-nine Neville interrupted her. "This is what you really need to pay attention to," he said.

She read:

> *And one of the malefactors which were hanged railed on him, saying, If thou be Christ, save thyself and us.*
>
> *But the other answering rebuked him, saying, Dost not thou fear God, seeing thou art in the same condemnation?*
>
> *And we indeed justly; for we receive the due reward of our deeds: but this man hath done nothing amiss.*

And he said unto Jesus, Lord, remember me when thou comest into thy kingdom.

And Jesus said unto him, Verily I say unto thee, To day shalt thou be with me in paradise.

Chantel could not take her eyes off the page for a time. She turned and said, "And the thief went to heaven that day?"

"That's what Jesus said. He went to paradise, and that is heaven, isn't it?"

Suddenly Chantel saw that the young man's eyes were misty. "Why are you crying?" she said.

Neville pulled a handkerchief out and wiped his eyes. "Oh, sometimes I get moved when I think about Jesus dying for me."

Chantel stared at him. She had never seen a grown man cry. Women cried, but not men, and it troubled her. "I'm sorry it made you feel bad," she said.

"It didn't make me feel bad, Chantel. It made me feel good. Come along. We'll go back to the store. I'll get a pen, and I'll put your name and the date in the front of this Bible. It'll be something to remember the first time we met."

When they returned to the office, Chantel found her father ready to go. He smiled and said, "Was she a great deal of trouble, Mr. Harcourt?"

"No trouble at all. We had a fine time, didn't we, Miss Chantel?"

"Yes, we did. Mr. Neville has a horse, and when we get Lady here he's going to ride with me."

"That is most kind of you, sir," Fontaine said.

As Chantel and her father left the office, she almost told him of the gift, but something stopped her. Unsure of how her father would react, she decided to keep it a secret.

Two weeks after her meeting with Neville, Chantel was riding Lady in the park. Robert had brought the mare from the plantation, and Chantel enjoyed a ride several days a week. Now she put Lady into a gallop, pulling her up to where Robert was waiting.

"Did you have a good ride?" he asked.

"Oh, yes."

She turned the mare over to a groom, patted her, and said, "I'll be back soon, Lady."

On the way home in the carriage Chantel saw three beautiful young ladies in the back of an open carriage.

"They're so pretty. Who are they?"

Robert had been watching the women also. His tone was neutral. "They're quadroons."

"What are quadroons?"

Robert cleared his throat and said, "I don't think I can discuss it with you, Miss Chantel."

Later, when she was alone with Elise, Chantel asked her maid about the quadroons.

"Oh, you don't know about them! Well, they're young women with some Negro blood in them."

"Really? But they were white as I am!"

"Well, some of them are, and they're very beautiful. They have a quadroon ball here, where the young men go to look them over. If they like them, they sometimes take them into their houses as mistresses."

Chantel listened breathlessly. She could not believe that such beautiful young women would become mistresses, but Elise insisted it was true.

That night her father was out, and Chantel stayed awake reading. She had planned to read a new novel, but instead she took out the Bible that Neville Harcourt had given her. She was fascinated by the Gospels—mostly by the figure of Jesus. Before this time Chantel had thought of Him only as a statue with a painted face that she saw in church, but the words of the Scripture leaped out at her. She had not dreamed that anything true could be so exciting. It was better than one of her romances.

As she finally closed the Bible and hid it along with her journal, she wondered why she felt guilty about it. She had asked her father once if he had ever read the Bible, and he said, "No, that's for the priest. Ordinary folks can't understand it."

She thought about this one night a couple of weeks later as she drifted off to sleep. Her father's statement puzzled her, for while it was true that much of the Bible seemed difficult, she could understand the stories about Jesus. She had found also that reading the Bible just before she went to sleep seemed to give her a more restful night. She could not understand this, but as she lay there thinking about Jesus healing the lepers, healing the blind, or talking to a woman at a well, He seemed very real to her.

Chapter nine

Chantel found that living in the French Quarter had its advantages. It was true enough that she missed many things about her home at Fontaine Maison, but she only dwelt on these thoughts in bed at night, unable to sleep. She was still troubled from time to time with nightmares of her mother's death, and more than once her father, awakened by her cries, came in to soothe her.

Living here, she saw much more of her father, and Elise had become a close companion. There were few young people for her to associate with, but on the whole she had adjusted very well.

As she looked out the window to the street below on a fine August morning, Chantel felt happy. She waved at Robert, who was working in the flower bed, and called to him, "Good morning, Robert!"

"Good morning, Miss Chantel. A fine day."

Chantel drew back and started across the room to her desk. Her room was beautifully done, but she sometimes felt uncomfortable in it. Everything was so new and fragile. On the light blue walls hung pictures in delicately carved wood frames. The dark blue carpet on the floor repeated a pattern of lighter blue and white flowers, and the mantel of a small marble fireplace held white china figurines of ballet dancers in various poses. There were roses and vines carved into the bed's headboard, and the armoire, desk, bureau, and washstand all matched. A thick comforter and fluffy pillows of white with light blue trim covered the bed, and light, airy curtains of the same material covered the windows.

Chantel stood before the full-length oval mirror and studied herself critically. She was still growing like a stalk of sugarcane! She had grown even since coming to New Orleans, and more than once Elise had rebuked her for stooping over. "You're going to be a fine, tall woman. Be proud of it. Why would you want to be a short, dumpy thing? No, you will stand tall and be proud!"

But looking in the mirror, Chantel was unhappy. She was wearing only a pair of drawers and a vest and could not see any signs of the womanly curves that other girls her age had begun to manifest. Her hair continued to grow darker, which pleased her, but she wished for the thousandth time that she had inherited her mother's good looks.

Now she held up her hand with her fingers outspread and frowned. "I've got fingers like a gorilla." Then suddenly she laughed. "You've never even seen a gorilla, you foolish thing!" She turned from the mirror and began dressing. She put on a light green dress that matched her eyes and a pair of white stockings, then slipped her feet into new black shoes that still pinched a little bit. She gave her hair a few quick swipes, tied it with a ribbon, and left her bedroom.

As she entered the dining room, she found her father sitting there sipping his coffee. He looked up and said, "Good morning, sleepyhead."

"Good morning, Papa."

"I trust you slept well?"

In truth Chantel had not, for she had been troubled with dreams, but she knew her father did not like to hear this. "Very well, Papa. And you?" She sat down and began to eat.

"It's almost time for you to begin school," her father remarked casually.

"Papa, do I have to go to that convent?"

Cretien had told her earlier that she would be attending the Ursuline Convent a few blocks from their house. Chantel had begged to simply have a tutor, but her father had been firm. "You must learn the things that a lady has to know," he had said in a tone that brooked no argument.

"I'm sure you'll like it there. There will be girls your own age, and you need to be with young people."

"Yes, Papa."

A moment later Cretien said, "Would you like to go to the theater tonight?"

"Oh, yes!"

"I thought you might. We will go to The Majestic. They're doing a musical that has a great deal of good singing and playing."

"Oh, that will be wonderful!"

For a moment Cretien hesitated, then he said, "We will not be alone. I have asked a lady to accompany us."

"A lady, Papa?"

"Yes. Her name is Emmeline Collette Culver. I think you will like her very much."

Something stirred within Chantel, but she said only, "Is she an old lady, Papa?"

"Oh, no. She's not at all old. She's very pretty. You will like her."

All day long Chantel was in a state of excitement, and she almost drove Elise crazy deciding what to wear. When she was alone Chantel cared little for dress, but when she was going out with her father she let Elise dress her in the very finest fashion and fix her hair carefully.

For this event Elise selected a high-waisted dress of white silk with delicate garlands of flowers in light pink, yellow, and blue. The gown had long, narrow sleeves that ended in white lace at the cuffs. The high neckline and the long skirt were edged with white lace, and she had a spencer jacket of dark blue velvet to wear over the dress.

Chantel stood in her underwear waiting for Elise to put on the dress. She turned to her with a worried expression. "Elise, why aren't I filling out like other girls do?"

"That's the way it is sometimes," Elise said, looking critically at the dress. "Yes, this one will do. You look very nice in it."

"Am I going to look like a stick all my life?"

Elise heard the troubled tone and at once put her arm around the girl. "Of course not, *mon chère*. You are going to be a beautiful woman—tall and well-shaped, and very pretty indeed."

"No, I'm not. I'm going to be an old stick with an ugly face!"

"Do not be ridiculous. When I was your age I was the same way." She smiled, remembering. "I did not start becoming a woman until I was nearly fourteen, and I cried myself to sleep every night." Seeing that Chantel wasn't convinced, she said, "You just wait. A year from now it will be all different."

The words comforted Chantel. Elise had become her confidante and told her of the changes that would come in her body as she passed into womanhood. Her mother had hinted about such things, but it all seemed to be very mysterious. She returned Elise's hug and said, "Thank you for being so nice."

"There, there. Of course I'm nice. I get paid for that."

"No, you don't. You get paid for doing my hair and helping me with my dress. You're nice just because you're nice."

Elise laughed, and a light danced in her eyes. "I am glad you think so. Now, let us ready you for your engagement with your father."

"A lady is going with us tonight. Her name is Miss Culver."

"Ah, yes, I know."

"You do?" Chantel demanded.

"Why—yes, I have met her. She is a very nice lady."

"How did you meet her?"

"Oh, I don't remember. I think at a dinner your father gave while you were still at the plantation."

Chantel sensed the evasiveness in Elise's reply—unusual in this straightforward woman who had few unspoken thoughts. It troubled her, but she asked no more. "When I come back," she said, "I will tell you all about the play."

Downstairs Chantel found her father ready to go. She wanted him to praise her appearance, but he merely said, "Come, we're late." Then he added as an afterthought, "You look very nice. Elise does a fine job."

"Thank you, Papa."

Robert drove them in the larger closed carriage to a section of the city that Chantel had not seen. Her father left her in the carriage, where she waited impatiently. Then he came out with a lady.

He helped her in, then got in and sat down beside her. "Chantel,

I would like for you to meet Miss Emmeline Collette Culver. Miss Culver, this is my daughter, Chantel."

"I'm so happy to meet you, Chantel."

Chantel had not known what to expect, but she was surprised by the beauty of the woman who smiled at her. Miss Culver was a small woman, but she was exquisitely formed, and her face was attractive indeed. She had dark hair and dark eyes and seemed genuinely glad to meet her.

"I was so glad I could go with you and your father. Do you like the theater?"

"Oh, yes, Miss Culver!"

The conversation went well, and she could tell that her father was pleased at her behavior toward the woman.

The rest of the evening was fun for Chantel. She loved the play and laughed and actually sang along with some of the choruses under her breath. Miss Culver, who was sitting across from her father, said, "She is named right, Cretien. She is a real songbird."

"Oh, yes, she sings constantly. I believe she's going to grow up and be an opera star."

"That would be wonderful," Miss Culver said with a smile.

After the performance Chantel talked excitedly. She had been rather shy at first, but Miss Culver drew her out. When the carriage stopped, she leaned forward and said, "We must do this many times, Chantel."

"Yes, please. I enjoyed meeting you, Miss Culver."

Chantel sat there until her father returned, and when he got into the carriage and settled back, he asked, "How did you like our guest?"

"She's very pretty."

"Yes, she is."

"Have you known her a long time, Papa?"

Cretien hesitated briefly, then said, "Why, yes, for quite some time." He changed the subject. "Well, you begin school next Monday. I will be expecting fine reports."

"I will do the very best I can, Papa."

"I'm sure you will, my dear."

When they got inside their house, Cretien bent over and kissed her cheek. "Go to bed now. It's late for you."

"Good night, Papa. I had such a good time, but I always have a good time with you."

Chantel went quickly to her room and at once withdrew her journal. She sat down and wrote of the evening at great length.

> *Miss Culver is very pretty, and I like her. Papa has known her a long time, and I hope she liked me.*

For a time she stared at the entry and then was aware of a strange sensation. She had liked Miss Culver well enough, but deep inside she also resented her being there. She added:

> *She's very nice, but I would rather have Papa all to myself.*

Closing the journal, she put it into its hiding place and then went to bed. She did not dream of her mother that night, but of being an opera singer on a stage.

"So this is your daughter, Monsieur Fontaine."

"Yes, Sister Martha, and I hope she will prove to be a fine student."

Sister Martha was a tall, angular woman with a pair of sharp gray eyes. She wore the black habit of a nun and examined Chantel closely. "I'm sure you'll do your best to please your father and me and your other instructors, won't you, Chantel?"

"Oh, yes, Sister Martha."

"Fine! You will be living in with us for a time. I suppose your father has told you."

The words struck Chantel hard, and she twisted her head quickly to look at her father.

"Sister Martha and I decided it would be better for you to stay at the convent for a time. Later on you may come back home."

"But, Papa—"

"I meant to tell you about this, but it slipped my mind."

Chantel instantly knew that this was not true. Her father often put off things that were unpleasant. She had come to the convent hopeful and excited. Now a heaviness settled upon her, and she dropped her head.

Sister Martha saw the girl's reaction and said quickly, "I'm sure you will enjoy it here. You will have plenty of companions, and though the studies are hard, we will find entertainment for you. And you will see your father very often. Is it not so, monsieur?"

"Why, certainly!" Cretien reached over and put his arm around Chantel. "I will come and get you, and we will go riding in the park. And I will take you out often to the theater."

Chantel blinked back her tears and tried to smile, for she knew her father did not like to see her sad. "All right, Papa," she said. "Please come often."

"Now then. Say good-bye to your father, and I will introduce you to your instructors. Then you will meet some of your fellow students."

Sister Agnes was a short woman with a round, reddish face and brown eyes. Chantel knew at once that she would be a hard woman to please.

"All right, girls. This is our new scholar, Chantel Renee Fontaine. I will let you introduce yourselves to her. Then we will begin our class."

Sister Martha had brought Chantel to a classroom where Sister Agnes was teaching a group of fifteen girls. Chantel saw at a glance that some of them were very young, no more than nine or ten. Others seemed older, as much as fifteen, perhaps sixteen.

Sister Agnes examined Chantel with a steely glance, assigned her a seat, and said, "We will now proceed with the lesson. Chantel, you will have to study hard to catch up, for you are beginning late."

"Yes, Sister Agnes."

"I permit no laziness in here. You will work hard and do extra work until you are up with the rest of the class. You understand?"

"Yes, I will do my very best."

"I expect it." Sister Agnes turned to the board and wrote out an algebraic formula. She turned and began to call out names. "Angelique, you will solve this problem."

A tall girl of about fifteen, rather pretty but with a sullen expression, went to the board. Her lower lip was stuck out in a pout, and for a time she struggled with the problem. Finally Sister Agnes said, "You are a sluggard, Angelique. Come here."

Angelique looked frightened, but she came over to stand before the stubby nun. "Put out your hand." Sister Agnes took out a footlong ruler, and when Angelique held out a trembling hand she struck it sharply twice. Angelique winced and went to her seat with a sharp reprimand.

Several other girls tried the formula, and none of them could solve it. Each received the same punishment. Finally Sister Agnes said, "All right, Laurel, you are our star student in algebra. Come and work the problem."

A short girl with a round face and rather heavy figure came forward. She did better than the rest, but when she turned, Sister Agnes snorted, "I am disappointed in you, Laurel! Take your seat. You will do twenty extra problems for tomorrow."

"Yes, Sister Agnes."

Sister Agnes glared at the group, and finally her eyes lit on Chantel. "Well, have you had any training in algebra?"

"Yes, a little."

"Come and work this problem then."

A snicker went around the room as Chantel got up, and she heard the girl named Angelique whisper, "What a beanpole! She's skinny as a snake."

Chantel's face reddened, but she went to the board. Her instructor in mathematics had been one of the priest's assistants. He was an amiable young man and had quickly discovered that whatever brain cells make a person adept at algebra, Chantel had. He had been delighted with her progress and had gone through advanced problems with her.

Chantel took the chalk and worked the problem rapidly. When she put down the answer, she said, "I think this is right, Sister Agnes."

Sister Agnes's eyes grew round. "Well," she said with surprise, "it is correct! Very good! Very good indeed, Chantel!" Then she turned to the class and for five minutes shamed them for letting a new student show them all up. She said, "Some of you need help. I will expect you, Chantel, to help the slower students—which seems to be everyone."

"I'll be glad to do anything I can to help, Sister Agnes."

Chantel took her seat, and the lessons went on. After the algebra class several of the younger students came up and introduced themselves. A slender, doe-eyed girl named Helen begged for help. "I just can't get this into my head, Chantel."

"It's easy. I'll help you," Chantel assured her.

And then they were interrupted by a voice that said, "Well, Stick Legs, are you happy that you've embarrassed the rest of us?"

Chantel turned to find Angelique and Laurel standing there. The other girls had drawn back, and Sister Agnes had left the room. Laurel suddenly reached out and struck Chantel in the chest with her fist. "You think you're so smart! Well, you'd better not be too smart, or you'll be sorry!"

Angelique reached out and pulled Chantel's hair. "Don't be thinking too well of yourself. We're the oldest students here, and you'll do exactly as we say. You'll polish my shoes tonight. You understand me?"

"I will if Sister Agnes tells me to."

"You'll do it if I tell you to!" Angelique snapped, her eyes gleaming.

"Why don't you shut up, Angelique!" Chantel turned to see a girl with hair as black as a raven and eyes to match. Those black eyes were glinting now with anger, and she stepped in front of Angelique and pushed her backward. "You're not the pope, so stop acting like you're somebody important!"

Angelique's face turned red and she shouted, "Get out of my face, Damita!" When Angelique tried to shove the dark-haired girl aside, she instantly received a resounding slap on the cheek. Grabbing her face, she screamed, "I'll tell Sister Agnes on you!"

"Go on and tell, you little squealer." Damita turned to Chantel and laughed, her eyes dancing. "You don't have to do anything Elephant Nose tells you. If she tries to make you polish her shoes, just shove them down her throat. I'll help you if you like."

"You stop calling me names!" Angelique shouted.

Damita laughed and suddenly reached out and pulled Angelique's nose. "I'll just pull it a little longer!" Angelique let out a scream and struck out at Damita, who dodged the blow easily and struck Angelique in the face. Laurel at once threw herself at Damita, and the smaller girl was knocked backward. Chantel leaped at Laurel and, grabbing a double handful of hair, began to drag her away.

Four more girls joined the battle while the others stood watching, most of them shouting as the fight raged.

Suddenly the door opened and Sister Agnes dashed into the room, shouting, "Stop this! What's going on?" Her face was flushed and she pulled Chantel away from Laurel, demanding, "We don't do such things here."

"She started it, Sister!" Angelique cried. "She just starting hitting us!"

"You are a liar, Angelique!" Damita's black eyes glowed, and she turned to face the nun, saying, "Angelique and Laurel were the ones who started it."

"I can't believe that!"

Damita faced the nun fearlessly. "You never believe the truth about them. They cause all the trouble here, and you're so afraid of their parents because they're rich and give lots of money to the school, that you let them get by with it!"

Sister Agnes' face turned red, then pale. She started to shout at Damita, but then changed her mind. "You are insolent, Damita Madariaga! Your parents will hear of this!"

Damita laughed suddenly. "They will hear of it, because I will tell them. And we both know that my father gives more to this convent than anyone else!"

"That's enough!" Sister Agnes said, but Damita's words had a strong effect, for she said with an effort, "Take your seats, all of you." She stared at Chantel and said, "There was no trouble here until you came. You will be punished—and I will tell the Mother Superior of your doings!"

Chantel waited all day to be called before the Mother Superior, but to her relief, nothing came of it. She went to her classes, and that night before dinner, Damita came to her. She was smiling as she said, "I'll bet you were scared you'd be called for punishment, weren't you?"

"Yes, I was."

"I knew you wouldn't be," Damita grinned. "That old Agnes knew she'd get in trouble if I told my father about her."

"It was nice of you to stand up to Angelique and the others for me."

"It was fun!" Damita turned and motioned to two girls who were standing off to her right. When they came close, she said, "This is Simone d'Or."

Simone was a tall, strongly built girl with long blond hair and dark blue eyes. She had a squarish face and a determined chin, an easygoing girl, but with a trace of rebelliousness.

"It was nice of you to come to my defense in class."

"I've been waiting to punch those girls!" Simone said. "Don't you knuckle under to them!"

"None of us are going to do that," Damita said. Turning to the fourth girl, she said, "This is Leonie Dousett." She put her arm around the small girl and laughed. "You're so meek I was surprised to see you tackle that girl. You've got a tiger in you, Leonie!"

Leonie smiled shyly. "I was surprised at myself. It's the first fight I ever had." Like Chantel, she had auburn hair. She was small, almost frail, with a timid air about her. She had the sweetest spirit of any of the four. "I never hit anyone in my whole life."

Damita's dark eyes were glowing, and she had a way of speaking that underscored her fiery spirit. "Listen, we're going to cut down Angelique and those crows who hang out with her!"

"Good!" Simone nodded. "I'm sick of them all."

"Everyone is, but everyone's scared of them," Damita said. "Now, I've been thinking ever since the fight. We four are going to put a stop to their bullying, and here's the way we'll do it—if one of them picks on any girl in this school, the four of us will make her sorry!"

"How will we do that?" Leonie asked.

"I can think of lots of ways," Damita nodded. "We'll gang up on her after lights out!"

"But she'll tell on us!" Leonie protested.

"Good! Then we'll catch her alone and get her twice as much and cut all her hair off!"

Simone giggled, "I like it! We'll be sort of a secret club."

Chantel said, "We'll be the Four Musketeers—just like in the book! One for all, and all for one!"

The girls began to giggle, and suddenly Chantel was happy. She had felt so alone, but now she had three friends. She put her arm around Damita, saying, "I don't feel so bad now, Damita."

"All for one—and one for all, Chantel!" said Assumpta Damita de Salvedo y Madariaga. She did a dance as they moved toward the dining hall. "I hope Angelique tries something pretty soon! I can't wait for the Four Musketeers to show their might!"

Angelique Fortier had been a tyrant too long to give up her power. She had been humiliated by Damita, but it was the new girl that aroused her hatred. She waited no longer than Chantel's first night to seek her revenge. She made a plan with Laurel Dutretre, and late that night, she struck.

The two girls crept into the room that Chantel shared with five other girls and fell on Chantel while she was asleep.

Chantel cried as hands dragged her out of her bed.

"Now you're going to get it!" Laurel declared.

Angelique had a belt and struck Chantel across the legs with it.

Chantel was of a rather placid temperament, but the blow enraged her. She threw herself onto Angelique and grabbed two handfuls of hair. Angelique screamed at the top of her lungs while Laurel began to pummel Chantel.

Suddenly the room filled, and Chantel was freed from the grasp of the two girls. She came to her feet to see Damita, Simone, and Leonie—all in their nightgowns. Damita was carrying a belt, and she said, "I thought you'd try something like this! Hold them down, Musketeers!" The Musketeers surrounded Laurel and Angelique and held them down.

The cries quickly brought Sister Martha into the room, and she snatched the belt from Damita's grasp. "What in the world are you doing?" she demanded.

Angelique was crying in great blubbery sobs. "They got us in here with lies, Sister!" She clung to the nun, inventing lies at a rapid rate.

"She's a liar!" Damita said. "She and Laurel came in here to whip Chantel, and we gave them a taste of the their own medicine!"

Sister Martha held up her hand. "I'm going to get to the bottom of this." She turned to a shorter, younger girl whose face already showed fear. "Who started this, Mary Ann?"

The young girl took one frightened glance at Angelique, who gave her a vicious stare and held up a fist behind Sister Martha's back.

"It—it was her. The new girl."

At that moment Chantel knew that her fate was set. She listened as several girls—all frightened of what would happen to them if they implicated Angelique and Laurel—lied boldly to Sister Martha.

The nun turned to Chantel. "I'm disappointed in you, Chantel. Your first night and already in trouble. I'm going to have to punish you severely. You will report to me tomorrow morning before classes. Now, all of you go to bed. If I hear one more word out of any of you, you will all be very sorry."

Sister Martha left, and the girls all went to bed, but not before Laurel hissed one more comment. "You're not going to like it here, Stick Legs! We'll make you wish you had never been born!"

Chantel tried valiantly, but it was useless. Sister Martha believed the testimony of the other girls and said, "You must learn to control your temper, Chantel. I'm restricting you for the next week from all recreational activities. You will have extra work in class. I will not use the rod on you this time since you are new, but the next time you will receive a beating. Do you understand?"

Chantel lifted her head high. "They lied about me. I don't tell lies, Sister Martha."

Sister Martha hesitated. There was such fearlessness in the girl that she could not feel easy about her decision. She well knew that some of the older girls bullied the others, but they were sly, and she had been unable to catch them in it. While she could not relent, for discipline must be upheld, inwardly she resolved to keep a closer eye on what was happening inside the dormitory.

Chantel was punished for what took place in her room, but she didn't care. Damita, Simone, and Leonie encouraged her—and Damita threatened Angelique so fiercely that she and all her clique were intimidated.

After this rather rough introduction to her new life, Chantel found the school bearable. She had been hungry for friends, and now she had three of them! Everyone in the school, including the nuns, recognized that these four were knitted together in some sort of mystic bond.

Sister Martha remarked to Sister Agnes, "I think those four are going to be all right. I've been worried for some time about Angelique. She's a cruel girl—but those four seem to have found a way to deal with her."

"Yes, they have," Sister Agnes agreed. "With a belt! I was shocked at first, but the 'Four Musketeers'—as they call themselves—have actually brought a good thing to the other girls."

"They're very strong willed, aren't they? Except for Leonie, of course."

"Yes, they are. But it took something like this to stop Angelique and her crowd from persecuting the others."

Chantel's life fell into a pattern. She did well in her studies, for she was by far the most advanced student of all the girls. She did especially well in mathematics and in languages, but she did not do as well in the other areas, such as sewing and the domestic sciences.

Many weeks later, Chantel went home for a visit with her father. He had received a recent report from the school about Chantel. "Sister Martha sent me a report of misbehavior. What were you thinking?"

Chantel looked at her father and told the whole story about Damita and Laurel—and about the Four Musketeers. "I'm telling the truth, Papa. All the others are afraid of Angelique and Laurel. They're horrible girls. They steal from the younger ones and anyone who is weak." She held her head high. "It is the truth. I swear it."

Cretien stared at his daughter. He knew that she was an exceedingly truthful girl. Only once that he knew of had she told him a lie, when she was no more than seven or eight. She had come to him the next day in tears confessing her fault, for she had been unable to live with it. Since that time he had never found her to be untruthful in any way.

Now he said, "I am sorry it is that way."

"May I come home and live with you, Papa?"

Cretien nodded. "Yes, I think that might be best. You will still attend classes, but you will not be subject to those awful girls."

"Oh, Papa, I'm so happy!"

Cretien held Chantel. He saw the joy in his daughter's eyes and felt shame. "It will be all right, *mon chère.* Don't trouble yourself any more."

Life became bearable for Chantel once she came home. She knew Sister Martha had been surprised by her father's decision, but there was nothing the nun could do about it. Every day Chantel had breakfast with her father. Robert or Elise walked with her to the convent, where she stayed until four o'clock. The weekends, of course, were free, and she often rode Lady in the park.

The riding pathways were not crowded one fine day in August when she and Lady were out enjoying the bright weather. When Chantel saw a man riding a bay horse ahead, she determined to pass him. She kicked Lady's flanks and spoke to her, and the mare broke into a run. As they passed the man, Chantel heard the bay pick up his pace and a voice call her name. Soon the rider pulled up even with her, and she saw with surprise the smiling face of Neville Harcourt.

"Mr. Neville!" she cried and pulled Lady down to a walk. "I've looked for you many times, but I've never seen you here."

"I've been a little busy lately. It's so good to see you. You look fine, Chantel. How are things going with your schooling?"

Chantel hesitated, then she remembered with warmth how Neville had taken her out of his father's office and treated her like an adult. Words tumbled from her lips as she began to tell him all about her experiences at the convent. Finally she stopped and blinked. "I'm talking too much."

"Not at all. I'm very interested. And I'm very glad you're living at home again. Tell me all your other problems."

Chantel giggled. "You don't want to hear them all."

"Yes, I do. I've thought about you a lot."

"I hated to disappoint my father. That was the worst thing about all that trouble at school. He really wanted a son, Mr. Neville."

"I think you can leave the *Mister* off, Chantel. We're good friends, aren't we?"

Chantel smiled warmly and nodded. "Yes, I suppose we are. Anyway, my father always wanted a son, but he only got girls."

"Well, I can understand his disappointment. But he did get a fine young lady out of it. He ought to be proud of you."

"I don't think he is, really."

"Of course he is." Neville assured her, and tried to bolster her confidence. "But you're not the only one who has problems."

"You have problems? I didn't think adults had problems like young people."

Neville laughed. "This is the happiest time of your life. Everything's downhill from now on, Chantel." He saw her expression, reached over, and tweaked her hair. "I'm just teasing you. You'll have a beautiful life."

"What are your problems, Neville?"

Neville Harcourt was silent for a moment. He studied Chantel's eager face. "Well, my father is unhappy with me."

Chantel was amazed. "But why?"

"I'm not really interested in the law. I do the best I can, but I don't think I'll ever please him. And he doesn't like my appearance."

Immediately Chantel turned her face on him. "Why, you look fine!" she said. She ducked her head and said, "My father's disappointed in my appearance, too. I'm not beautiful like my mother."

"But you're not grown yet. In another year or two you'll have men following you around the streets of New Orleans begging you to marry them."

Chantel laughed. "That's silly!"

"It is not! It's true."

"That's what Elise says. I don't believe either one of you. They call me 'Stick Legs' at school."

"Don't pay any attention to them."

"What's wrong with the way you look?" Chantel asked. "I think you look very nice." Actually she had not thought he was handsome at all when she first met him, but she had since changed her mind.

"Well, I'm not a large man, as you can see. As a matter of fact, I expect when you're grown, you and I will be about the same height. My father wants men to be big like he is."

"Don't you pay any attention to him! You look very nice," she said again.

Indeed, Neville had a pleasant face. He was always neatly dressed, and although he was not as large as her own father or as Mr. Oliver Harcourt, he was well-knit and cut a handsome figure in his riding clothes.

"Well, I suppose we've told each other all of our problems."

As they rode on, Chantel found herself able to talk to Neville quite freely. "I've been reading the Bible you gave me a lot."

"Do you like it?"

"Yes, I do. It's so exciting. I've read all of Matthew, Mark, Luke, and John."

"What did you think, Chantel?"

Chantel was silent. The Catholic church taught that only priests were qualified to read and interpret the Bible. She did not want to be disloyal to her own beliefs, but, indeed, the New Testament had become one of her favorite pieces of reading. "I love Jesus," she said softly. "He was so kind, and He helped everybody."

"I'm glad you see that. I feel the same way."

"And they were so mean to kill Him. Why did they have to do that, Neville?"

"Well, it's a little bit complicated."

"I'm very intelligent. You can explain it to me," Chantel said firmly.

"You're not overly modest though. Well, it's like this, Chantel. All you have to do is look around to see that something's wrong with the world. There's evil everywhere, injustice, and people getting hurt.

That's because of sin. When sin came into the world, it didn't stop with Adam. All of us, his descendants, are affected by it."

"I know. I confess my sins every week to one of the priests."

"We all need to confess our sins. Do you remember John the Baptist?"

"Oh, yes, I liked him. Herod killed him. He was a mean king."

"He certainly was. Do you remember the first thing John the Baptist said when he saw Jesus?"

Chantel thought hard. "He said, 'Behold the Lamb of God that taketh away the sin of the world.'"

"Exactly right! You have a fine memory. Well, what did he mean by that?"

"I don't know. I didn't understand it."

"As you read the Old Testament you'll find out that the Jews always sacrificed a lamb, the most perfect lamb they could find. They confessed their sins to the priest, and the priest killed the lamb, and symbolically the sins of the people were on that lamb. The lamb couldn't really take away sin, although God could, of course. But when Jesus came John said, 'Here is the *real* Lamb of God!' So, when Jesus died, Chantel, all the sins of the world were on Him."

"I get scared when I read about Him dying."

"So do I. Perhaps because God had forsaken Him."

"How could that be?"

"Because the sins of the world were on Him—my sins and yours. All people sin. But now all sinners can be forgiven because Jesus died for our sins."

Chantel was silent. She was an introspective child with an ability to reason far beyond her years. Finally she said, "Catholics have to do penance. You're not a Catholic, are you, Neville?"

"No, I'm what you would call a Protestant."

"Do you have to do penance?"

"Not as you would think of it."

"When I tell the priest I did something wrong, he makes me say twenty Hail Marys or do without something good that I like."

"It probably does you good to fast, and prayer is always a good thing. But actually when I sin, I do things quite differently."

Chantel was fascinated. "What do you do? You don't go to a priest?"

"As a matter of fact, I do—but not to one that you can see."

Chantel's eyes were huge. "You can't see him? Is he invisible?"

"In a way. The Bible says that Jesus is our High Priest, and that we can go directly to Him and confess our sins. When you go home, look in First John. Not the gospel of John, but the first letter in the back written by the same man who wrote the gospel. Look at the first chapter, verse nine. It says this: 'If we confess our sins, He is faithful and just to forgive us our sins, and to cleanse us from all unrighteousness.'"

Chantel listened carefully and then said, "So, you just pray and ask God, and He forgives you?"

"That's right. When I was sixteen, I asked Jesus to come into my heart, and He did. And He's been there ever since. I hope you'll ask Him into your heart, Chantel."

All this was strange to her. She looked at him and said, "I don't understand it, Neville. It's too complicated."

"You have a good heart, Chantel. God won't let you go wrong. I pray for you every day. Did you know that?"

Chantel was shocked. "Do you really?"

"I really do."

Chantel felt warm. "Thank you, Neville," she said. "That makes me feel very good."

The two finished their ride, and Chantel went home. She wanted to tell someone what had happened, but somehow she knew that what she had heard would not sit well with her father, who was a staunch Catholic—in doctrine at least. She did not even tell Elise, who was also a Catholic. Everyone she knew was a Catholic, but Chantel knew she would think long and hard about what Neville had said.

Chantel usually said formal prayers before she got into bed, but this night was different. "God," she said, "Neville prays for me every night, and I'm praying for him. Make his father like him better." She hesitated, then said, "And I need to be forgiven. I was so angry with Angelique and Laurel. I really hated them. That was wrong. Jesus never hated anybody, so I ask you to forgive me." She waited for a moment, expecting perhaps to hear a voice. But hearing none she said, "Amen," and got into bed.

"I have something to tell you that may be a little difficult for you to understand, Chantel."

Chantel was sitting at the breakfast table with her father. She had mentioned her ride with Neville but did not reveal the details of their conversation. She looked at her father curiously. "I'm going to have to go back and live at the school?"

"No, indeed, you're not. This, I think, is very good news if you'll have it so."

Chantel could not understand his meaning. "What is it, Papa?"

"Well, you're going to have a new mother."

Instantly Chantel seemed to grow cold. She stared at her father, speechless, and finally she said, "Is it Miss Culver?"

"Yes, I have learned to care very much for the lady, and I want to marry her. She could never take the place of your mama, of course, but I hope you will accept her."

Chantel could not speak, and Cretien saw that she was deeply shocked. He tried to calm her fears, but his words did not seem to register. Finally he said, "I hope you will come to accept Collette. We will never forget your mama or your sister, but life goes on." He leaned over and kissed her, but when she did not respond, he shrugged and left the room.

For a time Chantel sat there, then she got up and went out in the courtyard. She grasped the black iron bars that fenced the house off from the street. People passed by, but she did not see them. Finally she grew angry.

"Why does Papa have to get married? We don't need her!" She could not think of anything else to say. She could not even think clearly. She stared up at the sky and said, "God, You're not fair! I don't need a mother! Nobody can take my mama's place. Why would You let this happen?"

She knew she was being foolish, but she couldn't help it. She stood there gripping the cold iron bars, tears running down her face, and she feared for what would happen in the days to come.

Chapter ten

Chantel squinted at the book before her, holding it so tightly that her fingertips grew white. Her mouth twisted to one side in an angry grimace—and suddenly she lifted the book in one hand and flung it as hard as she could. "I hate poetry!" she shouted.

The book sailed across the room, pages fluttering, and struck a delicate porcelain vase of fresh flowers. The blow sent the vase off the table, and it smashed on the floor, scattering broken glass and white blossoms everywhere.

Chantel stared at the wreckage. Before she could move, the door opened and Elise hurried in, her eyes wide. "Are you all right?" She looked over at the fragments of the vase and the scattered petals. "How in the world?"

For one moment Chantel tried desperately to think of some excuse. Then she sighed. "I threw my book." She went over and began to pick up pieces of glass. "I didn't mean to break the vase. I just threw the book before I thought."

"Here, you'll cut yourself. Let me clean this up," Elise said quickly.

The two cleaned up the mess together, carefully looking to be sure there were no shards of glass scattered on the carpet that could cut Chantel's bare feet.

Then Elise said, "Here, sit down and let me fix your hair."

Chantel marched over to the chair in front of the dresser and sat glumly staring at her features while Elise began to brush her hair.

Elise spoke lightly enough, but it was obvious that her young mistress was not in a good mood. "What's the matter? You're out of sorts this morning."

"Did Papa come back yet?"

"No, as a matter of fact, I was coming up to give you this. Robert came back this morning and brought it."

Quickly Chantel took the small envelope, extracted the note, and read her father's message:

Dear, your mama and I are going to stay with her family in Baton Rouge until Monday. I know you will be a good girl. Be sure and go to Mass Sunday morning with Elise.

Chantel stared at the words, then crumpled the note into a small ball and threw it across the room.

"That's no way to treat your papa's note!"

"I don't care! He's never home."

Elise ran the brush through the thick, lustrous hair and tried to speak soothingly. "You must remember he has only been married three months. It's only to be expected that he and his bride would want to spend a great deal of time together."

Chantel suddenly rose and said, "I don't want my hair brushed any more!"

"Well, what do you want? I can never please you these days."

"I want to go somewhere and get out of this house."

"All right. Get dressed, and we'll go shopping over at the square. After all, it's almost Christmastime. Do you have any money?"

"Yes! I've been saving it, and I'm going to spend it all."

Despite her bad mood, Chantel enjoyed her walk around the plaza. It was a fine morning, warmer than usual for December. She was wearing a fine wool coat that her father had bought her. She remembered how the two of them had shopped all over New Orleans for it and had finally found what she wanted at Holmes Department Store. That had been a good day! But the feel of the coat only reminded her that her father was not with her now.

They passed a store with a sign in the window that Chantel found intriguing: *Indian Doctor*. She turned to Elise. "Does that mean he's an Indian—or that his patients are Indians?"

"Oh, who knows? There are so many charlatans in this city I can't keep them straight."

Chantel read the advertisement. "Doctor W. K. Lowe, by long intercourse with many different tribes of savages, and much practice, is able to give relief in desperate cases. Can cure scurvy, bilious complaints, fits, fevers, agues, diabetes, ulcers, cancers, and bedsores."

"I'll just bet he can," Elise scoffed. "Come on, Chantel. Don't ever let yourself fall into the hands of someone like that."

The plaza was crowded for such an early hour, swarming with colorfully dressed blacks. Many of the women wore *tignons,* a madras head kerchief. Indians were a common sight, many of them having emigrated from Santo Domingo, and several negro nursemaids pushed perambulators along the streets. An enormous African woman bellowed out at the top of her powerful lungs, "Blackberries—berries very fine!" Another was selling pralines out of a basket, some brown, some pink, some white coconut.

They passed by the Place d'Armes hotel with its low-pitched high roof and arcaded side. All around them snatches of English, French, German, and Spanish made a perfect babble on the air. The market was so crowded with sellers and buyers that it was almost impossible to move about.

"This is a bad time to come," said Elise.

"I like it," Chantel said. She led the way down the street, threading her way between the people. Once she passed by a bald-headed gentleman sitting in a rocking chair at the door of the *Pharmacie*, reading the *Abeille de la Nouvelle Orleans.* Beside him his grave spouse was sitting reading the *Propagateur Catholique.* Peering into the dim recesses of the store, Chantel could see rows of shelves laden with bottles of drugs. A strong scent emanated from the shop.

Suddenly Chantel paused in front of a shop and said, "Let's go in here." Before Elise could protest, she had stepped inside a shop that advertised guns and knives.

There were several customers inside, all male. One of them was staring down the long barrel of a rifle, and he took his eye off to gawk at the two who entered. He grinned and said to his friend, who was twirling a heavy pistol, "Watch out, Jake, the females are comin' in."

A short, balding man with alert gray eyes came over. He was wearing a black suit and a rather colorful neckerchief. "May I help you ladies?"

"I want to look at your pistols."

The shopkeeper hid a smile, or tried to, and said, "Certainly, miss. What sort did you have in mind?"

"A small one. One that I can hold."

The shopkeeper motioned to a counter with a glass top. "Here is our collection of smaller guns." He opened the lid and took out a sample. "How does this one feel?"

Chantel took the small gun, which was like none she had ever seen. "It's so little," she said. "It just fits."

"This one fires only two shots, you see. One over and one under."

"Who you plannin' on shootin', missy?" the man named Jake inquired.

Chantel turned to look at him and said frostily, "I haven't decided yet." She turned back to the shopkeeper. "How much is it?"

"That one is fifteen dollars."

Chantel shook her head. "I don't have quite that much. I'll have to get some more from my papa."

"Your papa will never let you have a gun, Chantel! Now come out of here!"

Chantel ignored Elise, saying, "I'll be back when I get the rest of the money. I only need six more dollars. You save it for me, you hear?"

"Oui, mademoiselle! I will certainly save it. And what might your name be?"

"I am Chantel Renee Fontaine."

The shopkeeper glanced toward the men, who were taking all this in, and said, "I will write it down and await your return."

Chantel waited until they were outside and walking again in the milling crowd. "He was making fun of me, but I'm going to buy that gun."

"What do you want a gun for?" Elise demanded.

"When I get older I'll need to protect myself."

"You will have a husband or your father to do that. Let's go home now."

"No, I'm hungry. I want some gumbo."

The two made their way down the street, and just as they reached a cafe where Chantel had eaten with her father several times, she saw Neville coming down the street.

"Neville!" she said, and ran to meet him. "I'm glad to see you."

"Why, I'm glad to see you, too. You're out shopping?"

"Yes. This is Elise."

"Oh, yes, I remember you," Elise said. "You came to the house once with your father, Mr. Oliver, did you not?"

"Yes, I did. I'm glad to see you again."

"We're going to eat," Chantel said eagerly. "Do you want to join us?"

"Why, as a matter of fact," Neville said with a smile, "I was on my way to get a bite myself. This is a fine cafe." He followed them inside. It was a small shop with only eight tables, all of them filled but two. The proprietor came over and greeted Neville. "Ah, Mr. Harcourt. It's good to see you again."

"I have guests today, Nicholas."

Nicholas beamed and bowed at the waist. "Come this way." He seated them and said, "What will it be today?"

"I want some gumbo," said Chantel.

"I think I'll have shrimp. What about you, Elise?"

But Elise was looking across the room at a young man who was smiling broadly at her. He arose and came over and said, "Good morning, Elise."

"I'm glad to see you, Charles."

"I don't want to interrupt your party, but perhaps you'd care to join me."

Elise looked flustered, and Chantel came to her rescue. "You may go if you want to. Neville and I will stay here."

"I suppose that will be all right," Elise said.

As soon as the two had left and seated themselves across the room, Neville said, "I've missed you. I haven't seen you riding lately."

"Papa's been out of town a lot, and I can't go unless Robert takes me—and Robert usually goes with Papa."

"So, what have you been doing, besides going to school?"

Chantel stared rebelliously across the table. "I've been very bad. This morning I threw a book across the room and broke a very valuable vase."

Neville pursed his lips, turned his head to one side, and asked, "What made you angry enough to do that?"

"It's my schoolwork. They're making me do stupid things."

"I had the same problem in school. I suppose everyone feels the same way at times. What was it in particular that upset you?"

"My literature class. Sister Jane is making us read poetry, and next Monday morning I've got to recite a foolish poem and tell everybody in the class what it means."

"Well, that doesn't sound too bad," Neville remarked.

Chantel continued her lament while they ate.

"What is the poem? Have you memorized it yet?"

"Yes, I have," Chantel said, enjoying the gumbo. It was delicious, hot and spicy the way she liked it, and she quoted her poem rapidly around mouthfuls of food.

> Nuns fret not at their convent's narrow room:
> And hermits are contented with their cells;
> And students with their pensive citadels;
> Maids at the wheel, the weaver at his loom,
> Sit blithe and happy; bees that soar for bloom,
> High as the highest peak of Furness-fells,
> Will murmur by the hour in foxglove bells:
> In truth the prison, into which we doom
> Ourselves, no prison is: and hence for me,
> In sundry moods, 'twas pastime to be bound
> Within the Sonnet's scanty plot of ground;
> Pleased if some Souls "for such their needs must be"

Who have felt the weight of too much liberty,
Should find brief solace there, as I have found.

Chantel scraped the bottom of her bowl and looked up with disgust. "Isn't that a silly poem?"

"Why did she give you that particular poem to work on?"

"I think because it's about nuns."

Neville was looking neat as usual. He had on a dark gray suit, and his shirt was gleaming white. His hair was brushed, and his eyes were warm as he studied the girl. "I don't think it's really about nuns," he remarked.

"Why, what *is* it about then?"

"You know, Chantel, poems usually say one thing and mean something else."

Chantel stared at him and then snorted with disgust. "Why don't they just say what they mean?"

"Because we don't want things always to mean what they say, and sometimes you *can't* say what a thing means."

"Why can't I? If you ask me how many apples there are in a barrel, I'd just say 'six.' I don't start making rhymes and talking about them as if they were something else."

Neville smiled. "Yes, but you can remember other things that you couldn't find words for. For example, a time that you were so happy that you couldn't possibly tell anybody so that they'd understand—or perhaps so sad that you couldn't express it."

Instantly Chantel's head dropped. She thought of the time after her mother and her sister died. She had not been able to say to anyone how she felt. "I guess that's true. But this old poem talks about nuns."

"Take it a line at a time. 'Nuns fret not at their convent's narrow room, and hermits are contented with their cells.'"

Chantel stared at him, astonished. "You know that poem? Do you have it memorized?"

"As a matter of fact, I like it. Now, what do those things have in common?"

"Well, it's about nuns who are in a room."

"What kind of a room?"

"A narrow room."

"Right. And where are hermits?"

"They're in cells."

"And what's a cell like?"

"Well, it's small."

"Right. So, we're talking about small, narrow rooms and small, narrow cells. And the next line talks about students. They also are usually in a confined space."

"Well, what about maids at the wheel, and the weaver at his loom?"

"Well, when maids work they are confined. They have to sit for hours at their spinning wheels. And the weaver, he's tied to that loom. He may have to sit there as much as twelve hours a day. But notice the next line. These maids, and these weavers and students and nuns and hermits, how are they sitting there?"

Chantel thought for a moment. "They sit blithe and happy."

"That's right. So, even though all of these individuals are in rather confined and sometimes hard circumstances, they're happy. Now, think about the rest of the poem and tell me what that sort of thing has to do with the rest of the details."

"Well, let's see. It says that bees will soar, but they'll murmur by the hour in foxglove bells."

"A foxglove is a small flower, Chantel. And a bee will get inside of one. It'll be not much larger than the bee itself, but the poet Wordsworth says that the bee will murmur by the hour there. So, that's where the poet is leading us. Now look at the next line: 'In truth, the prison into which we doom ourselves, no prison is.'"

Chantel listened as Neville talked about the poem, his face glowing. She was fascinated that he found so much pleasure in it, and she found herself caught up in it.

"Actually, although there is a nun in the poem and there is a hermit, it's really about the sonnet. That's what this poem is."

"Sister Jane told us that. It has only fourteen lines."

"And what does the poet say about the sonnet?"

Chantel thought and then replied, "Why, he says the sonnet's scanty plot of ground is a pastime."

"That's right. He found pleasure in working in a very small area. So, I think the poem talks about being happy and content even though we don't have the whole world. Maybe we have a very small job or a very small circle of acquaintances. But being big doesn't mean a thing is good. Can't you remember some whole weeks, Chantel, that were not nearly as good as one hour?"

"Yes, I can," Chantel said. "Lots of them. Like when Papa would take me riding. I lived for that. I'd wait for weeks, and then finally he would come. And that was good."

"Well, life is like that. Perhaps you could point this out to the other students. And at the end of the poem there is a strange expression. Wordsworth speaks of people 'who have felt the weight of too much liberty.'"

"I don't understand that. I don't have enough liberty."

"I think all of us need some sort of bounds. For example, you are getting to be a grown-up young lady. When a young lady is not married, she can see any number of men. But after she's married her attentions have to be concentrated on her husband. And that's a good thing."

"I should think it would be." Chantel suddenly laughed. "Why, this was fun, Neville!"

"I think so too."

"You'll have to help me with more poems. I don't have the vaguest idea of what some of them mean."

"Maybe so. Ask your papa if I can come by some evening and go over some of your work with you."

"I will. I really will." She looked over suddenly at Elise and laughed. "Elise tells me about the men who come calling on her. She's thirty now, but is still so pretty lots of them come. I think she enjoys teasing them."

"I hope you never do that, Chantel."

"Me? They'll never come chasing after me the way they do Elise. I'm not pretty."

Neville suddenly reached over and took Chantel's hand. "You're growing up. You're going to be a lovely woman some day, and I think you're pretty right now."

A warmth suddenly seemed to grow inside of Chantel, and her face grew red. She murmured, "Thank you," and when he released her hand, she knew that his compliment would stay with her for a long time.

The door opened, and Chantel, who was sitting in a chair, jumped up and ran to her father. She dropped a book on the floor as she went, and when he had kissed her and released her, she bent to pick it up.

"What book is that?" Cretien asked curiously.

"This is a present that Neville gave to me. Papa, listen. He helped me with the poem that Sister Jane assigned me to memorize and teach to the class." She told him how Neville had explained the poem to her. "He's so smart about poetry and I'm so dumb," she concluded. "Can he come by some time and help me some more?"

"I don't see why not." Cretien looked at the book and said, "But what book is that?"

"It's a Bible. Look, he signed it for me. It was the first day, when we went to his father's office. You remember? And he took me out to buy me something to eat. We went to a bookshop, and he bought it and gave it to me."

Cretien Fontaine was not overly religious, but what religion he had was tied up completely with the Catholic faith. He shook his head, saying, "If you want to know anything, you should ask the priest. He is qualified to interpret Scripture."

"Oh, yes, Papa, but it was a present, and Neville signed it."

"Well, I suppose you may keep it, but I would rather you did not read it."

It was not a direct command, so Chantel did not argue. She said instead, "Papa, I saw what I wanted for Christmas."

"Good. What is it?"

"It's a pistol. I found it in a shop while Elise and I were out at the square."

Cretien stared at this daughter of his. She was growing up so fast that he could hardly keep up with her. Now he suddenly laughed and said, "No, you may not have a pistol. Certainly not! Now, you pick something else."

"All right," Chantel said. But inwardly she thought, *When I'm a grown woman I will buy a pistol for myself.* "Can we go riding today, Papa? We haven't been in a long time."

"No, I have to take Collette to the doctor."

Chantel looked up quickly. "Is she sick?"

"No, she's not sick." Cretien came closer and let his hand drop on the girl's shoulder. When she turned and looked up at him, he was struck, for the moment, at how much her eyes brought back the memory of his first wife. He could not speak for a moment, then he came around and said quickly, "No, she's not sick, but she's going to have a baby."

He watched the girl's face and saw doubts flicker in her eyes. "Aren't you happy about having a brother?" he demanded.

"Yes—but, Papa, it may be a girl."

"No," Cretien Fontaine said firmly, "it will be a boy! You will have a brother—and I will have a son."

Chapter eleven

August brought a terrible heat wave to New Orleans. As Oliver Harcourt sat at the dinner table, sweat poured down his face. Taking out a damp handkerchief, he mopped the perspiration away and then said, "I'm not happy with your attitude, Neville."

The dinners that Neville shared with his father were not the most pleasant times for either of them. The food, of course, was very good, because Oliver Harcourt would have nothing but the best. The room was attractive and pleasant, with fine pictures on the walls and a rosewood buffet and a snowy white tablecloth with fine china, but there was more to a dinner than a room and a fork.

"What's wrong, Father?"

Oliver chewed a bite of the thinly-sliced baked ham and said, "You just don't have enough drive. That's the main problem. I've told you before that the law is not an easy master. When we have a case, we have to fight as a soldier fights against an enemy. Our opponents are our enemies, Neville. You go around trying to be nice even to people like the Barnleys."

"I feel a little sorry for the Barnleys," Neville replied. The Barnleys were an older couple, almost helpless, who were being sued by one of their clients. The man was determined to ruin them. Neville had winced when his father had struck out with all of the power of his sharp legal mind at the older couple.

"They made their bed, and now they'll have to lie in it. And I want you to prepare a brief that will finish them off."

"I think you could do it better than I could. I don't really believe in this case."

"You're soft like your mother!"

"I think you're right about that, Father. I'm not much like you. I never have been."

Oliver Harcourt stared at his son. It was as close to a rebellion as he had ever seen in the young man, and his eyes grew half closed as he studied him. He had never spoken of his disappointment that Neville was, indeed, like his dead wife. She was a gentle soul, but there was no room for gentleness in the courtroom.

Neville looked a great deal like her as well, having rather classic features and being of a relatively small stature. Oliver would have preferred that his son be six-foot-four, as he himself was, and burly as a wrestler.

He had no other children, and all his hopes were tied up with this young man. He had not learned that one sometimes must deal with youth a little differently from the way he dealt with an opposing lawyer in a courtroom. For some time he spoke, driving his point home by smashing his fist into his palm.

Suddenly he remembered something. "By the way, what's this about your giving a Bible to Mr. Fontaine's daughter?"

"Why, yes, I did. You remember the day he brought Chantel to our office? You asked me to take her out and buy her something to eat. She was interested in something in the Bible, so I bought her one."

"Well, it was a fool thing to do! Those people are Catholics. Didn't you know that?"

"I suppose I knew it."

"Well, Catholics don't read the Bible; only priests do. I wish you wouldn't read it so much yourself."

Neville suddenly sat up straight and said, "I'm sure you don't mean that, Father."

For just a moment Oliver Harcourt was shocked. Neville was usually so pleasant and soft-spoken, but suddenly he had seen something in his son's eyes that he rarely saw—something close to anger and determination.

"There's nothing wrong with reading the Bible, son," he said quickly. "For yourself, I mean—but giving a Bible to a young Catholic girl, especially one of our clients, is different."

"Did Mr. Fontaine lodge a protest?"

"He mentioned it. The girl's very impressionable."

"I've been helping her a little with her lessons. I stopped by the house twice. She's having trouble with her literature class."

"I'm not sure that's a good thing. It's good business to be nice to clients, but you don't want to get involved with their home lives."

The two ate silently, and then Oliver said, "I don't understand you at all. This unhealthy interest you have in religion troubles me."

"I don't think it's unhealthy."

"Why, going down to the docks and talking to men about God and handing out religious tracts to them! That's not your place, Neville."

"Well, whose place is it?"

"The ministers'."

"Can you imagine our minister doing that?"

"No, I can't, and I don't appreciate your doing it either! It doesn't look good. Now, why can't you just do your duty? Simply go to church and give money."

Neville touched his lips with the linen napkin, then put it down. He said carefully, "I think God wants me to do more than that, Father."

"What do you mean?"

"I've been thinking God might want me to serve Him in a more active way."

The older man stared at his son. "You don't mean you're thinking of entering the ministry?"

"I have thought of it. It's been on my heart for some time. I couldn't speak to you of it because I knew you wouldn't be sympathetic."

"It's foolishness, Neville! You have a fine career ahead of you. You can serve God and be a lawyer at the same time. I do."

Neville resisted the impulse of saying what was on his mind at that moment, and simply replied, "I've been thinking of it a great deal. I should have told you before."

"Well, it's foolishness, and I won't have it! It would be the waste of a brilliant career! You'd throw everything out the window for nothing."

"I wouldn't call serving God in the ministry 'nothing,'" Neville said gently.

Oliver Harcourt stared at his son. It was as if he had been walking along and had abruptly run into a wall that wouldn't give. The light of determination in Neville's dark blue eyes unsettled him, and he said no more. The memory of this scene, however, rankled the older man.

"Well, you *are* filling out. Look at you now!"

Elise had just helped Chantel get dressed, and the new dress did indeed reveal that the beanpole was beginning to develop some curves.

Chantel stared at herself. She had been aware of the growth in her body, of putting on weight. She was still tall and thin, but now, at least, she was not a skeleton as she had felt herself to be. She turned to Elise, her eyes wide with hope. "Do you really think I'll fill out some day?"

"You've already started to be a nicely shaped young woman. And your hair is so pretty."

Chantel reached up and touched her auburn hair, the golden glints caught in the light. She turned then and said quietly, "I don't know what I'd do without you, Elise. You've been such a friend to me."

Elise was pleased. She loved her young mistress fiercely, and pride came to her as she thought of how the young woman was maturing.

"You'd better go to your father," she said. "He has a surprise for you."

"A surprise?"

"Yes. Go see him."

Chantel finished dressing quickly and left the room. She started to go down the hall when her father stepped out of the bedroom he shared with his wife.

"Papa, good morning."

Cretien came to her, and there was a smile on his face and a joy that she had rarely seen. "What is it, Papa?"

"The baby came last night."

"Last night? And you didn't tell me?"

"You'd already gone to bed, and we had to rush to get the doctor here."

"Is it a boy or a girl?"

"A fine boy!" Cretien's eyes glowed, and happiness emanated from him. "And your mama is fine. Come along, but be quiet. She's asleep and very tired."

Chantel tiptoed into the room and saw that Collette was asleep. Her face looked pale and wan.

Chantel's attention went at once to the special bed that her father had built. It was low enough that when she went over and looked inside she could see the red face of the newborn infant.

"He's beautiful, Papa. May I pick him up?"

"Yes, but be very careful."

Chantel gently picked up the baby. She cuddled him in her arms and stared down. "He's beautiful, Papa, just beautiful!"

"He is, isn't he? A fine boy!"

"What is his name?"

"He will be Perrin Covier Fontaine."

Chantel held the baby, crooning to it. She looked up, and there were tears in her eyes. "It will make up a little for losing my sister, Papa. I hope we will be very close."

"Of course you will, Chantel. Brother and sister. You will love him, and he will love you." Cretien saw the affection in Chantel and was pleased. "You will not be lonely now, for you will have a brother to love."

"So you have a new baby brother, Chantel?" Damita was lying under a huge live oak tree sucking on an orange. Flanking her were Simone and Chantel. "Well, you can say good-bye to any attention you'll get from your parents."

"Oh, I don't think so!" Chantel answered. "We all love the baby."

Simone rolled over on her back and stared at the huge limbs of the live oak tree, some of them as big around as full-grown trees. "Damita's right," she remarked. "A new baby gets all the attention."

Chantel didn't argue, for indeed, she had received little attention from her father since the birth of the baby. Instead, she tried to change the subject. "Where's Leonie? I haven't seen her all day."

"I think she's ironing her dresses." Simone yawned. "I'd hate to have to iron my own clothes. Makes me all hot and sweaty."

Chantel sat up and said, "I think we ought to do something for Leonie."

"Do what?" Damita asked. She tossed the half-eaten orange to the ground and got to her feet. "You mean help her iron?"

"No, not that." Chantel knew there would be no volunteers to help Leonie do this tiresome task; she alone among the Four Musketeers was poor. Damita's father was one of the richest men in New Orleans, and Simone's family had plenty of money. Leonie was a charity girl, a student that the convent took in from time to time from among the poor. She was an orphan, the daughter of an unmarried French actress who had died giving birth to Leonie. The Ursulines had taken her in, but she had nothing except what was furnished by the convent.

"She doesn't have any nice clothes, and she never has any sweets or good food to eat to keep in her room," Chantel said. "We all have so much! I'd like to buy her some new clothes and a few goodies."

Damita, who always had everything she needed and more, was not prone to noticing what others needed—but she had a generous heart. "That's a good idea, Chantel. I've got some money. How about you, Simone?"

"I've got enough to buy her a dress." Leaping to her feet, she said, "It'll be fun! Come on, let's surprise her."

"I'll ask Sister Martha for permission to go to town," Damita said.

Fortunately, school had ended early, and the girls had a half-day holiday. They obtained permission to go into town from Sister Martha with little trouble. Damita didn't give her the real reason for their visit, but said, "We'd like to buy a few things to give to the poor, Sister." Sister Martha was pleased, and the girls went at once to find the object of their good works.

They burst into the workroom, and Leonie was taken by storm. "Come on, Leonie," Damita cried, and took the iron away from the surprised girl. "We're going to town."

"But—I need to finish my ironing!"

"You can do that later," Simone grinned. "We've got things to do!"

With Leonie completely mystified, the four left for town. Their first visit was to a dress shop, and when Damita said to the clerk, "This young woman must have a fine new dress! Now, let's see what you have!" Leonie was taken aback.

"I can't buy a dress," she whispered. "I've *never* bought a dress!"

"Well, it's about time." Chantel smiled. "You're going to buy one now, maybe more."

The three girls had a wonderful time, insisting that Leonie try on a number of dresses. They each liked different dresses—except Leonie, who was too dazed to even speak—but finally they agreed on a blue dress that looked wonderful on Leonie.

"We'll take it!" Simone said with satisfaction. She walked around Leonie examining the dress, and nodded. "Wrap it up for her."

"But—it costs so much!" Leonie said, a worried look on her face.

Damita came over and put her arm around Leonie. "Don't even think about the cost. We've got the money and we're going to buy lots more things."

All three of the girls were shocked to see tears well up in Leonie's eyes. She swallowed, tried to speak, but could not. "I—I don't know what to say," she finally managed.

"Say—'Let's go buy another dress!'" Chantel cried. "We've got a lot of shopping to do!"

When the four girls returned to the convent, they were burdened with packages. They had bought some things for the poor, which would satisfy Sister Martha, but the bulk of their plunder was for Leonie. They entered her room giggling and squealing, and asked

Leonie to try on everything again. The purchases included two dresses, a heavy coat for winter, a warm fur cap, a pair of gloves, two pairs of shoes, underwear, and stockings. In addition to this was a wealth of sweets of all kinds.

Leonie stood in the middle of the floor, looking at her three friends who were all admiring her—and helping themselves to the sweets. "I—never had any real presents before."

The three girls grew quiet, for all of them felt somewhat shamed. All three had grown up in prosperous circumstances, and the words of Leonie brought a feeling of guilt to each of them. Damita got up at once and went to Leonie. She put her arms around the small girl and said, "Well, you've got some now—and three sisters to look out for you."

Simone got up, and she also kissed Leonie. "That's right. We're the Four Musketeers, aren't we?"

And then Chantel, whose heart was filled with joy, joined them. "One for all—and all for one," she said. She hugged Leonie, and a thought came to her. "I want to tell you all something," she said. "As long as we live, if I can ever do anything for any of you, I'll do it!"

Damita Madariaga had been pampered her whole life and wasn't accustomed to serving others, but something in Chantel's words touched her. "That's the way it is with me. Come to me if you ever need help."

"And I feel that way, too," Simone said. "I'll never say no to any of you!"

And Leonie, who had nothing—except perhaps the largest heart of the four—whispered, "I don't see how I could ever do anything for any of you, but I'll love you all my life!"

The four girls were quiet, touched by what had happened, and then Chantel cried, "All for one—and one for all!" And the other three echoed her words.

Chapter twelve

Chantel looked up as her father spoke, hearing a trace of anger in his voice. They had nearly finished breakfast, and, as was his custom, Cretien was scanning the pages of the morning paper.

"This fellow Jackson, he's nothing but a rude Kaintock!"

"You mean the man who's running for president?" Collette asked. She was, as always, beautifully dressed, for she spent a great deal of her time and her husband's money on clothing. Her dress this day was exceptionally ornate. It was made of light green silk with a fine gold brocade around the off-the-shoulder neckline, the tight bodice, and the hem of the full, floor-length skirt. Its full sleeves billowed out at the shoulder and grew very tight at the elbow, and the skirt was cinched in at the waist by a sash and had six small bows of white silk down the middle.

"That's the one. Why, he's had several duels already!"

"Duels over what, Papa?" Chantel asked. She really cared nothing about Jackson, but she always listened to what her father had to say.

"He'll be president. No doubt of that, and the country will go straight to the dogs. What America needs is a good aristocracy." Cretien continued to flip through paper. "Well," he said, "I see they finally outlawed suttee in India."

"Suttee? What's that?" Collette asked as she nibbled at a section of grapefruit.

"In India, when a man dies, they put him on a pile of wood and cremate him. The law says his widow has to be burned with him."

"You mean burned *alive?*" Collette demanded. "How awful!"

"Oh, I don't know." Cretien grinned and winked across the table at Chantel. "I know a few wives that might justify such a policy." He laughed then and said, "Not you, of course, my dear."

"Papa, I read that a man named Burt has invented a new machine."

"A machine? What kind of a machine?"

"You don't have to write anymore with a pen. You use this machine, and it prints the words just as they appear in a book."

"Nothing will ever come of that. It would be too complicated. Like this—" He thumped the paper. "Those crazy Englishmen have invented a steam engine. There's a story here about something they call a steam locomotive named *The Rocket.*"

"What does it do, Cretien?" Collette asked.

"They build iron tracks for it, and it runs along them, I understand. Nothing will ever come of that, of course. Horses, that's the thing."

Breakfast was almost finished, and Chantel said quickly, "Papa, Neville is going to come to my party today." She had taken special care with her appearance this morning, for it was her sixteenth birthday.

"How did that happen?" Cretien was not pleased at the attention that Neville Harcourt showed to Chantel. Ever since he had discovered that the young attorney had given his daughter a Bible, he had been suspicious. He shook his head, his displeasure evident on his features. "I hear disturbing things about Neville."

"What sort of things, Papa?"

"Why, he's become some sort of a preacher now."

"A preacher?" Collette looked up with surprise. "But he's a lawyer."

"Oh, I don't think he's left his law practice. His father's not doing too well, you know. His health isn't good. I'd admire the young man if it weren't for this preaching."

"Where does he preach? In one of the Protestant churches?"

"I don't know the details. I just know his father told me that he was furious with Neville, and I don't blame him."

Chantel knew that Neville had become a lay preacher of some

sort. She, of course, had never heard him preach, and he did not speak of his activity often. But she did not like the fact that her father was displeased and was glad when suddenly their attention was taken by Perrin.

"Want seet roll!"

Perrin, at the age of two, had become a tyrant in the Fontaine household. His parents doted on him, and neither of them could deny him anything. The result was a two-year-old who demanded his own way under every circumstance. Now Perrin, who was seated in a specially built high chair, was frowning at the egg that had been placed in front of him.

"No egg! Want seet roll!"

"Eggs are better for you than sweet rolls, Perrin," Chantel said. "And they're good, too."

But her words did not assuage the child. He began screaming for sweet rolls, and almost at once Cretien called out, "Ann—Ann, bring Perrin some sweet rolls!"

"Yes, sir, right away." The maid scurried away and soon came back with a plate with two sweet rolls on it. She placed them in front of Perrin, who grabbed one with both hands and began tearing at it as if he were starved.

"Don't bolt your food, Perrin," Collette warned. But her words had no more effect on him than they ever had.

Collette urged him to drink his milk, and Perrin gulped it down, almost choking in the process. He was overweight and ate almost constantly only the sweetest and most fattening of foods. Chantel had tried to speak to her parents about her brother, but they were both so happy to have a son that they paid no attention whatsoever.

After breakfast Chantel moved to the drawing room, where she sat for some time reading a book that Neville had given to her. It was called *The Last of the Mohicans,* and she found it fascinating. Neville had good taste in literature, and knowing her love for the romantic element, usually tried to steer her toward the more acceptable novels. He himself appeared to have read everything. Chantel was sure that he knew more than all of her teachers at school.

As she plunged into her book, more than once she felt tears rise to her eyes. The plight of the Mohican chief moved her greatly. How terrible, to think of an entire tribe perishing.

Suddenly she heard the sound of Perrin's footsteps, and without warning her book was snatched from her hand. She gave a cry as the boy took a page and tore it out. Leaping forward, she grabbed the book and slapped his hand. "No, Perrin, you mustn't tear books! That's a bad boy."

Collette had followed on Perrin's heels, and she said angrily, "Don't you ever strike your brother, Chantel!" She snatched up Perrin, who was crying at the top of his lungs, and cuddled him, saying, "Now, don't cry, Perrin. Your sister didn't mean to hurt you."

Chantel stared at the two and said, "Mama, Perrin has to learn discipline. He can't destroy people's property."

"It's only a book," Collette said. "Now here, I want you to go to town for me. Here's a sample of the thread that I need to finish my project." Chantel understood that Collette made demands like this to exercise control over her.

"But I need to get ready for my party."

"You'll have plenty of time for that. It's not until four o'clock. Hurry along now." She turned her attention to Perrin, who was still sulking. "And remember. Never strike your brother again."

Chantel was glad to get away. She loved Perrin, and at times he could be very sweet. But any child that is given his own way constantly and never rebuked is bound to develop bad character traits, and Chantel worried about him.

Her father could see only that the dream of his life had been fulfilled—he had a son. He was planning Perrin's future already, even making arrangements for schools when the child was old enough. He had once mentioned that he had picked a university for him to attend in France.

Leaving the house, Chantel hurried to town. It was a warm day in May, and the streets of the city were busy. She went into the shop, found the thread that her mother needed, then decided to go visit Neville's office, which was only two blocks away.

She made her way along the busy streets, and as she moved, she paid particular attention to the women she passed. She still felt herself too tall and awkward, and she admired women who were small of stature and had pronounced curves. She had developed somewhat, but the long-seeded idea that she was ugly and ungainly was hard to shake off.

When she reached Neville's office, she found the two clerks working in the outer office. One of them, a short, fair-haired man of some twenty years, smiled at her. "Well, Miss Fontaine, I hope you haven't come to see Mr. Harcourt. He's not in the office today."

"You mean Mr. Neville?"

"Oh, no, Mr. Neville's here. His father, I meant. He's not too well."

"I'm sorry to hear it."

"I'll tell Mr. Neville that you're here." The clerk knocked on the door, listened for a response, then stuck his head inside to announce her. He turned to her and smiled. "Go right in, Miss Fontaine."

Chantel entered the office and found Neville rising to greet her with a bright smile. "Well, this is a welcome break in a dreary day."

"I just came by to remind you of my party, Neville." Chantel smiled and said, "I want you to dress up and look your very best. You'll meet all of my friends."

"I don't know why you want to invite a Methuselah like me to an event filled with attractive young people."

"Don't be silly! You're only twenty-one."

"And you are sixteen. Happy birthday, Chantel, and may I say you look quite lovely today."

Neville's compliment brought color to Chantel's cheeks. He was always quick to compliment her, but not so often on her physical appearance. "This isn't my party dress," she said quickly.

"Well, you look very nice. Come and sit down. Let's have some coffee."

Chantel always enjoyed talking to Neville because he knew so much and was witty. She studied his appearance as he spoke of a case that he had had in court. *He's not very handsome,* she thought, *but some people think he is.*

He was no more than five-foot-ten but was very trim and athletic. His hair was light brown, almost auburn, and had a curl to it. It was crisp, and he kept it cut rather shorter than most men. His eyes were a warm brown, and he had eyelashes that were no doubt the envy of many women. His eyes were his best feature, always alert, and Chantel often wondered if he had any sweethearts. He never spoke of young women, but she knew that he occasionally escorted them to the opera or the theater.

Finally Chantel rose and said, "I must get home. I've got a thousand things to do before my party."

"I'm going to be a little bit late, I'm afraid."

"Oh, Neville, you promised to be there!"

"I know, but an appointment came up that may run a little long. But I have your present, and I'll give it to you now. It won't get lost in a group of other gifts."

"It would never do that."

Neville walked to the desk, opened a drawer, and pulled out a small package wrapped in brown paper. He came over and handed it to her. "Happy birthday, Chantel."

"Oh, thank you, Neville."

"You don't know what it is yet."

"Whatever it is, I'll love it."

"Well, I spent too much money then. I should have given you a rock."

Chantel carefully removed the paper and found a box inside. She opened it, and for a moment stood speechless. "Neville, they're absolutely beautiful!" She laughed with delight and stared down at the green earrings. "Are they real jade?"

"Of course they're real. Do you think I'd give you a cheap imitation?" Neville grinned. "They're almost the color of your eyes. Put them on and give me a preview."

Chantel put the earrings on with excitement and demanded a mirror, which Neville produced from his drawer. She stared at the earrings and cried, "Oh, they're absolutely beautiful, and they do match my eyes!" She whirled around and threw her arms around Neville and kissed him on the cheek.

"Here now! We can't have this. Young ladies don't rush up and kiss strange men."

"You're not a strange man."

"Well, you're too old to be kissing fellows—even an old fellow like me."

But Chantel was utterly taken up with the earrings. She could not stop staring at the small mirror. Finally she said, "It's all right for me to kiss you, Neville. You're my big brother. You always have been." She came over and put her hand on his cheek. Even at sixteen she was almost as tall as he was. She hoped that she would never be any taller. "I've got to go now. I'll see you at the party. Don't be any later than you can help."

Neville walked her to the door, and when she had left, he closed it, came back, and went to the window. He watched her figure as long as he could see it among the milling crowd below. Long thoughts ran through him, and he recalled the first time he had met her in this very office. She had been a long-legged, thin, rather homely child with enormous eyes. Now he realized, not for the first time, that the years had done something to her. He stood still for a moment, thinking of how beautiful her eyes were and how the stones set them off. Then he shook himself and turned back to his work.

The party was a success as far as most people were concerned. Eleven people were there, mostly her close friends from the convent. The most noticeable of them was Assumpta Damita de Salvedo y Madariaga. Her dark eyes sparkled, and her black hair shone, revealing her Spanish blood. Not surprisingly, she dominated every group she found herself a part of.

"So, your sweetheart gave you those earrings. They are beautiful. He must love you very much."

"Oh, no, Damita!" Chantel said, feeling her cheeks turning red. "Just a good friend of mine. He's actually our family lawyer."

Damita shook her head. "I'll never believe that a cold-blooded lawyer gave you such beautiful earrings. Come now." She winked across at Simone.

"I think she's hiding something, Simone. She tells you everything. Find out who gave her those earrings."

Simone smiled. Her blonde hair was swept up on her head, wisps of curls falling around her face. She whispered, "You can tell me after the party's over. I know you've got a secret admirer. No lawyer would give you a beautiful gift like that."

The fourth member of the quartet, Leonie Dousett, said, "Don't tease Chantel. You're embarrassing her."

Damita laughed. "It's good for her to be embarrassed. She outdoes us all in our studies, so I have to find some way of getting back at her."

They were interrupted then by a tall, striking young man, Roger Devorak. His father was a cotton farmer, and Roger's good looks, along with his family wealth, had many mothers looking to him as a possible husband for their daughters. At seventeen he had already had several rather exciting romances. He came now to stand before the four girls.

"Well, the Four Musketeers again. I'd like to be a fly on the wall in your rooms and hear what you ladies have to say."

"You would be shocked," Damita said, smiling boldly. "I wouldn't have you know what we say for the world."

"Oh, don't pay any attention to her, Mr. Devorak," Leonie said. "You wouldn't be shocked at all."

"In that case I'll have to get the secret out of Miss Chantel." He stepped forward and took her hand, then bent over and kissed it. "A very happy birthday to you, Miss Fontaine." He looked very handsome with his shiny black hair and large, lustrous eyes. He held her hand a moment longer than necessary and whispered, "Now that you're a full-grown sixteen years old and can call yourself a woman, I'll be calling on you."

"I don't believe that," Chantel said.

"And why not?"

Chantel laughed. "Because you're working your way down through the young women of New Orleans alphabetically, and you haven't even gotten through the B's yet. Those of us who have names beginning with F have to wait our turn."

Roger laughed with the young women but shook his head. "You accuse me of being a philanderer, but I will show you that it is not true."

The time went by pleasantly enough, but Chantel was not able to throw herself into the merriment. There was music and several of the better singers entertained the group. There was a cake with candles and opening of presents, but during all of this Chantel was looking constantly at the door. She tried to make herself smile.

When finally the party ended, and just as the last guest left, Neville came rushing up. "I'm sorry to be so late. I couldn't get away."

"That's all right, Neville. Come in," Chantel said.

"Am I too late for a piece of cake and some punch?"

"No, of course not." Chantel tried to smile.

Neville was escorted over to the refreshments.

"Let's go into the parlor, Neville," she suggested, "while the maids clean up."

Neville sat down beside her on the sofa and listened to her tell about the party. Always sensitive to Chantel's moods, he asked her, "What is it, Chantel? You're disappointed."

"Oh, no, I'm not."

"Why, of course you are. I can see it. You're not a hard person to read. What's wrong?"

"Oh, my father didn't come, and I—I thought he'd be here."

"I'm sure he was held up."

"I suppose so." She appreciated the warmth of his hand as he held hers and tried to assure her. "When I was a little girl he missed a party of mine that he had promised to come to. It was a birthday party just like this one. He didn't come, and I cried myself to sleep. But that night," she said, "he came and got me out of bed and took me out to the front of the house. And there was a pony. Lady was the first horse I ever had. So maybe he'll come late, just as he did then."

"I'm sure he will, Chantel."

Neville sensed that she was not in a talkative mood and soon rose to say his good-byes. "Suppose we go riding tomorrow. Can you come?"

"Oh, yes, that would be wonderful. I'll meet you at the park at two o'clock."

"I'll see you then."

He reached out and put his hand on her shoulder. "I'm glad to have you for a friend."

His kind words brought more moisture to Chantel's eyes. She

blinked the tears away and said, "Thank you, Neville. Your gift was the best of all. I'll keep these earrings always."

Cretien stopped abruptly. He had stepped inside the front door and found Collette waiting for him. "I'm sorry to be so late—"

"I'm sure you are!" Collette stepped closer and could smell the liquor on him. "You're drinking too much."

As a matter of fact, Cretien had drunk too much, but he defended himself at once. "I only had a little—"

Collette glared at him. "And that perfume I smell on you. Did you only have a little of that woman you were with?"

"That's no way to talk."

"I'm supposed to ignore this sort of thing? What if you found that I'd been seeing a man?"

"That's entirely different!" Cretien said stiffly. "Don't speak of these matters."

"You should have been at the party! Chantel was watching the door for you all day and all evening," she said, adding more venom to her anger.

Cretien blinked.

He had forgotten the party, and now a sense of deep shame came over him. "I'll make it up to her," he said lamely.

"You can't go back and do things over. Now, let's go to bed."

The next morning Chantel had just gotten dressed when she heard a knock on her door. "Come in," she said. When she saw her father standing there, she said nothing, but waited until he came over to stand before her.

"Are you very angry with me, daughter?"

"No, of course not."

"I wouldn't blame you a bit, but wait until you hear why I didn't make it." He reached into his inner pocket and pulled out a gift. "I had this especially made up for you in Baton Rouge. I had to go over and get it, and it wasn't ready. By the time I got home it was very late. Happy birthday, daughter."

Chantel took the small box with fingers not quite steady. When she opened it, she gasped at the diamond ring that caught the light and glittered and flashed with blue fire.

"Papa, it's so beautiful!"

"I am so sorry I didn't get here sooner," Cretien said. "But how about this. Suppose we have another birthday party, just the two of us? We'll go out and have dinner, then we'll go to an opera. There's a new one called *William Tell.* I know it's a day late, but I want you to have a good birthday."

Chantel's heart seemed to swell. "That—that would be wonderful, Papa."

Cretien reached out and took her hands. He held them for a moment then said, "This makes two of your parties I've missed."

"No, you didn't miss this one, Papa. It's not too late." She laughed and held her hand up, admiring the ring. "I'll never take this off, Papa—never."

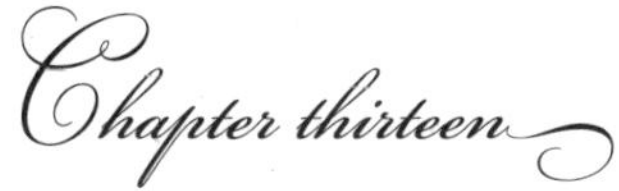

The classroom was cold, and Chantel drew her blue wool coat closer around her. This did not help with her feet, however, which were numb. She looked around and saw that the other girls were just as uncomfortable as she was. Indeed, Leonie's lips seemed to be blue. The coat she had on was thin, and Chantel thought, *I've got to give Leonie a warmer coat. I can give her my brown one. It'll be too large for her, but at least she can keep warm.*

The droning of Father Laurent's voice nearly put her to sleep. The class he taught on church doctrine was enough to bore anyone to death. She dreaded it, and so did the other girls. Their academic subjects were sometimes good, sometimes boring, but never as tedious as Father Laurent's lessons. As far as she knew no one ever paid the slightest attention to what he was saying except to be sure they could pass the examination that would follow.

Two tall windows on the east side of the room admitted the cold winter light of November. Chantel watched the long, slanting rays of pale light as they fell on the faces of her fellow students. She noticed the motes that danced in them and wondered suddenly if God knew the location of every mote. It was the sort of thing that came to Chantel from time to time. She thought of asking Father Laurent, but she knew he would think such a question frivolous.

She rubbed her hands together and paused to admire the diamond ring she wore on the ring finger of her right hand. Every day since her birthday she had taken time to admire it and to think of the second birthday party. She had had a marvelous time with her father. They had gone out to the most expensive restaurant in New Orleans, and while they had eaten her father had amused her with his talk.

Afterwards they went to the opera, and although Chantel did not like opera as well as drama, she was stirred by the music and by the story of William Tell. The scene where he shot the apple off of his son's head was exciting, and she had found herself grasping her father's arm with all her strength. He had laughed quietly at her and said, "Don't worry. I don't think he'll hit the boy."

After the opera they had chocolate and sweets, and Cretien again apologized for missing her party. "I promised you once that I'd never miss another one, but I failed you. Now I promise you again, *chère.* I'll never miss another one of your parties."

"Thank you, Papa. This has been the best birthday I've ever had, even if it is a few hours late."

"Then I'm happy, and I hope you like your gift."

"Yes, more than anything."

Chantel was reliving that scene when suddenly she heard her name called and blinked, drawing herself back to the present. Father Laurent, a large man with a reddish face and pale blue eyes, was staring at her. She heard Damita giggling and knew she had been asked a question.

"I'm sorry, Father Laurent. I didn't hear."

Whatever reprimand Father Laurent was about to deliver was never heard, for just then the door opened and Sister Alice came in.

"Father Laurent," she said. "Chantel is wanted in Sister Martha's office at once."

A shock of surprise came to Chantel. She had never been sent for like this, but when someone was called out of class it usually meant trouble. She waited until Father Laurent dismissed her, then rose and left the room. All the way to the office she wondered what she had possibly done that would call for this type of action.

When she entered the office, she found Sister Martha standing beside her desk. "Yes, Sister Martha. What is it?" Chantel asked.

"I'm afraid I have bad news for you, my dear."

"Bad news, Sister Martha?"

"Yes, it's—" The nun hesitated, then said, "It's your father. He's had an accident. You must go home at once."

"Is he all right?"

"I don't know the details, but I think you'd better go right now."

Chantel stared at the nun with fear running along her nerves. Then she wheeled out of the room. Not even stopping to get her heavy coat, Chantel ran out of the building into the cutting wind, but she paid it no heed.

The distance from the convent to her home was only a few blocks, but she ran so hard she was out of breath when she pushed through the black iron gates and ran up the steps. She opened the door and almost fell inside.

"Chantel!"

Chantel saw Collette, and cried out, "What happened to Papa?"

Collette came over, took Chantel by the shoulders, and looked up into her face. "I'm so sorry, dear," she said. Her eyes were red and wet. "Your father was riding his stallion, and the horse fell going over a jump."

"But will he be all right?"

"Chantel—your father is . . ."

"I want to see him!"

"We put him on his bed in the bedroom, but—"

Chantel tore away from Collette's grasp and ran up the stairs, taking them two or three at a time. She ran down the hall to her father's room.

There on the bed she saw her father lying in the most awful stillness she had ever seen. Her throat closed up, and the room seemed to tilt. She walked stiffly to the bed and looked down on his pale face, then suddenly fell forward across his chest. She held to him, crying, "Papa—Papa!"

Finally she felt hands raising her up and heard Collette say, "Come away, dear."

Chantel rose and looked down at her father's face. Through the tears the features seemed to waver, and a sudden sense of loss came over her.

PART THREE

· 1831 ·

Neville

Spring brought beautiful weather to New Orleans. The sky overhead, as blue as could be imagined, was broken by fleecy white clouds that drifted slowly by. The date was May 15, 1831, and a warm breeze blew across the crowd gathered for the ceremony. The faculty of the Ursuline Convent was gathered together on a small platform that had been erected in the courtyard. The black robes of the priests and nuns, highlighted by blinding white collars and hats, made a startling contrast to the colorful dresses of the family and friends of the graduates. As Chantel glanced around, she thought, *It looks like a tulip garden with all the beautiful colors of the dresses.*

Indeed, the women in the predominately Creole gathering had worn their best—gowns of pink, blue, green, and yellow that caught the sparkling sunlight. The air was light, the final speech had been made by the bishop, and now the diplomas were being handed out. Chantel moved forward, listening to the names of her fellow students. Finally she heard her own name called out, then a slight pause and the words "Summa Cum Laude."

A sound of applause came to her, and she flushed as she reached forward and took the diploma from Sister Martha. The nun smiled at her and whispered, "I'm proud of you, Chantel."

"Thank you, Sister." Grasping the diploma as if it were a precious jewel, Chantel turned and flashed a smile at Neville. To her surprise, he kissed his hand and waved it at her.

As she made her way back to her seat, a wave of memory swept over her. She thought of the past months that had come and gone, and sadly wished that her father could be here to share this day. She continued to live at home with Collette and Perrin, but the house had become a torment for her. It was Cretien who had made it a special place for her, and every time she entered the door it was with a pang of grief. She thought of the lonely nights when she had wept herself to sleep, and after all these months her loss seemed to grieve her even more.

She made her way to her seat, glancing once again at Neville. He wasn't looking at her at that moment, and she saw his profile and thought of how his friendship had helped her endure the recent struggle.

Chantel sat there until the ceremonies finally came to an end. They stood to their feet, graduates and guests alike, and the bishop said a brief prayer. Then the graduates went to their families.

Collette and Elise smiled at her and kissed her, but it was Elise who was the warmest.

"You did the best of all, *mon chère!*" She beamed and hugged Chantel again so hard that it almost made her lose her breath.

"I'm very proud of you—and your father would be so proud, too," Collette said. She was wearing a light, summery blue dress and looked very pretty as she stood there. Collette had never been unkind to Chantel directly, but since Cretien's death she had been preoccupied. It hurt Chantel that her stepmother seemed to grieve so little at the loss of her husband.

Nevertheless, she managed a smile and said, "Thank you, Mama."'

"Aren't you going to give me a present, Chantel?"

Chantel laughed and bent over to ruffle Perrin's hair. He was three and a half years old now and resembled his mother more than his father.

"You're supposed to give *me* a present," Chantel teased.

Perrin scowled at her and then shrugged. "Okay. You can have one of the toys that I'm tired of."

"That's not very generous, Perrin," Collette said. She turned to

Chantel. "You've worked so hard, dear, but now, perhaps, you can rest a little."

Elise was still excited over the honor Chantel had won. "You were the very best!" she said. Then she laughed and shook her head. "I thought I'd never get you raised."

Collette gave Elise a hard look, for it grated on her nerves that a servant was in many respects closer to Chantel than she was.

Chantel started to answer, but at that moment Sister Martha came up and in an unusual gesture put her arm around Chantel and squeezed her. "Well, I'm going to miss you around here."

"I'll miss you, too, Sister Martha. But we'll only be a few blocks away. I'll come and visit you."

Sister Martha shook her head and gave a slight laugh. "I doubt that, but it would make me very happy if you would. When our students move away we rarely see them again. Now, what are you going to do with yourself? Get married, I suppose."

"Oh, no, nothing like that!"

"What? Not ever? Perhaps," she said, "you'd like to stay on and become a nun." Her eyes twinkled as she said, "But I don't think that is your calling."

At that moment Neville appeared and said, "Good afternoon, Sister Martha. Are you proud of your prize student?"

"I certainly am. But I must say that I occasionally suspected that some of her essays were assisted by another hand." She stared hard at Neville and said, "I call no names, you understand."

Neville flushed and said, "Well, I did give her some help from time to time."

Sister Martha nodded and said, "You would make a good Catholic, Mr. Harcourt."

"That's quite a compliment, coming from you, Sister."

"You must come and see me. I believe I could enlighten you if I just had time enough."

Neville laughed and said, "I'm afraid of you, Sister. You're too good an evangelist to suit me, but I appreciate your offer."

Sister Martha went to speak to the other graduates, and Neville said to Chantel, "I've come to take you away to celebrate."

But at that moment, Chantel was surrounded by a trio who wore the same costume of graduation. "Chantel! You won! I'm so proud of you!"

"Thank you, Leonie." Chantel took the shy kiss from the girl, then said, "Are you ready to face the world now?"

"Well, *I* am!" Simone was beaming as she came to exchange hugs with Chantel. "I'm so glad to be out of this place I could scream!"

"The sisters are saying the same about you, Simone." As usual Assumpta Damita de Salvedo y Madariaga dominated the group. She held up her hand to flaunt an enormous diamond ring that looked like blue ice. "How do you like my graduation present?" She laughed. "Father never thought I'd make it. I wouldn't have if it hadn't been for you three!"

"Congratulations to all of you," Neville smiled. "I'm not sure the world is ready for the Four Musketeers."

Damita went directly to Neville. "Don't you have an expression of congratulations for me, Neville?"

Neville looked flustered but gave Damita a quick kiss on the cheek. "Is that the best you can do?" Damita mocked. "Chantel, teach this crude fellow how to express himself!"

"Come along, Neville," Chantel said, taking his arm. "This brazen woman will eat you alive." She turned to leave, but then stopped and called back, "Remember, one for all and all for one!"

Antonio's Restaurant was absolutely gorgeous—at least Chantel thought so. She sat across from Neville, feasting her eyes on her surroundings: enormous ornate mirrors framed in curved, French gold-leaf frames, chandeliers that shed their light in brilliant cascades over the tables adorned with white tablecloths, fine china, and silver flatware polished so highly that she could see her reflection in the flats of the knives.

"This is wonderful, Neville, but isn't it awfully expensive?"

"Well, I've got enough to pay my share. I'm sure you do too." Neville stared at her without expression and then burst into laughter when he saw her expression. "I was only teasing," he said. "This is my treat."

Their waiter came, a tall, thin man with Gallic features, who apparently spoke only French and assumed that his customers did as well.

"May I recommend the shrimp and andouille omelet, sir. It consists of sautéed shrimp and andouille sausage and wild mushrooms folded in a fluffy omelet and touched with a spicy Creole sauce."

"Does that sound good to you, Chantel?" Neville continued in French.

"No, I would like fish tonight."

"In that case, mademoiselle, we have fresh fillet of snapper, grilled over an open flame. It is served with sour-cream mashed potatoes and a spicy smoked tomato beurre blanc. It is accompanied by a salad tossed in sherry vinaigrette."

"Ooh, that sounds good. I'll have that."

Neville studied the menu and then ordered oven-roasted duck. "Is that good?" he asked the waiter.

"Certainly, sir. We serve only the finest food here. This is a deboned, crisp, oven-roasted duckling served on a field of peas and hickory-smoked bacon ragout with green onion mushroom rice. And what wine shall I bring?"

"Just coffee, if you please."

"No wine?"

"No, we're trying to quit," Neville said.

Chantel giggled and said, "Water will be fine for me. Thank you very much."

After the waiter left Chantel said in English, "Neville, you were teasing him."

"He looks like he needs a little teasing. As a matter of fact, he looks like he has a bad stomachache."

"Neville, what a thing to say!"

When the food came Chantel threw herself into it.

"I'm eating like a field hand!" she exclaimed. "It's a good thing I'm so tall."

"You mean it's better to be tall and fat than it is to be short and fat?"

"It's not easy for me to gain weight. I don't think I'll ever get fat. Neither will you. My mother was never fat, and your father wasn't either."

Neville's father had died six months earlier of a sudden heart attack, and now she asked rather timidly, "Do you miss your father a great deal, Neville?"

"Oh, we weren't as close as most fathers and sons—but, yes, I do miss him."

"I still miss my mother and father dreadfully. I suppose I always will."

"It gives us something in common. We're both orphans."

"I wish you wouldn't use that word. It makes me sad. But it's true enough, I suppose, and it does make us closer, doesn't it? You're my best friend, Neville," she said suddenly. "I don't know how I would have gotten through these last months without you."

Neville was touched by her words. "We are best friends," he said. "I want you to know that if there is anything I can do for you, you can always count on me."

They finished their meal and then chose for dessert deberg cake, a vanilla sponge cake moistened with rum syrup and layered with strawberries and lemon-butter cream and topped with a dark chocolate ganache.

As Chantel ate with great enjoyment, she asked, "When are you going to get married, Neville? You're getting to be an old man."

"I guess twenty-three is fairly old to seventeen. But soon you'll be eighteen, and I think, according to all the laws of such things, you'll be classified as an old maid."

"I think it's better to use the term *maiden lady.*"

"Well, as long as the thing doesn't sound bad, I suppose it's all right." He sipped his black coffee, then put the cup down and grew serious. "What do you want to do now that your education is complete?"

Chantel folded her hands and leaned forward. "I want to move back to Fontaine Maison. It's gone downhill since we left there, and I want to build it up again. I always loved it so, Neville."

Her eyes glowed, and she did not realize what an attractive picture she made. Elise had fixed her hair in a French roll. Her skin, as always, was her best feature—creamy, perfect, and smoother than anything imaginable.

Neville toyed with his coffee cup, then shrugged slightly. "Sometimes it's hard to go back to old times that we liked so much. Things aren't the same."

"But it will be the same for me. I just know it will."

"Have you talked to your stepmother about this?"

"Yes. She doesn't care."

"Well, financially it would be possible. Your father left you a separate trust so that you'll be independent. At least you will be, in a few days."

"I've been wanting to ask you about that, Neville. Isn't it unusual for a man to leave a daughter a separate trust?"

"As a matter of fact, it is. Most men are afraid women aren't to be trusted. One of my clients left his daughter a fortune, but she didn't get it until she was thirty-five years old. He didn't think any woman younger than that would be able to handle it."

"Why do you think my father did this for me?"

Neville squirmed a little in his chair and ran his hand over his hair.

"You did it, didn't you, Neville?" she insisted. "You talked my father into this."

Neville shifted uncomfortably. "Well, I did use what influence I had with him, but he wasn't really hard to convince. He loved you very much, Chantel, and he wanted you to have the good things in life. Or what he considered the good things."

Chantel took Neville's hand. "That was so sweet of you," she said. "If you hadn't done that, I wouldn't be able to go back to the plantation."

"Well, it belongs to the three of you—but Perrin won't be a full owner until he's grown, of course."

"You're always looking out for your little sister, aren't you?"

Neville gave her an odd look and lifted his eyebrows. "You're not my sister," he said.

"Well, not really, but I like to think of you as my brother."

Neville studied her for a moment, then suddenly grinned. There was an impish look in his eye. "I have a graduation present for you."

"Oh, you shouldn't have done that! This dinner is present enough."

"Of course I should." Reaching into his inner pocket, he pulled out a package. "Congratulations. And please accept this little gift as a token of my admiration."

It was a small package, no more than five or six inches square and an inch-and-a-half thick. Chantel removed the paper wrapping, then lifted the lid of the box. She gasped and then put her hand over her mouth with shock. "Neville, what a beautiful pistol!"

"It's the one you wanted when you were just a little girl."

Staring down at the pistol, she touched it and said, "It's plated with silver."

"Yes. It wasn't very attractive before. I thought a silver-plated derringer might do for more formal occasions."

"Neville, you're crazy!" She picked the gun up, and Neville uttered a muffled grunt and leaned forward. "Please don't wave that thing around in here. I'll teach you how to load it and shoot it—but not in a restaurant."

"It's just what I wanted," Chantel said. "Thank you so much."

"Well, I hope you don't have occasion to use it."

"I promise to shoot only young men who become too familiar."

"Good idea. Now, I expect I'd better get you home."

⌒

Chantel took Neville's hand and stepped out of the carriage. As she walked up to the iron gate that kept the courtyard secure, she fumbled in her reticule and found the key. He took the key and opened the gate, then Chantel turned and said softly, "Neville, this has been so wonderful! I will never forget it."

"Won't you?"

"No! You've made it a perfect graduation for me."

Neville was watching her carefully. They were almost the same height, and a shock ran over him as he realized that the young girl he had known was gone forever. The girlish figure had disappeared. Her hair was glossy in the moonlight, her lips stirred with a pleasant expression, and there was a light of laughter in her dancing eyes.

"Chantel, I'm about to break a promise I made to my mother when I was much younger."

"You shouldn't do that, Neville."

"I'm afraid I'm going to have to."

"What promise did you make her?" Chantel asked.

"I said I'd never kiss a young lady until she was at least eighteen."

Chantel giggled, expecting that he would kiss her on the cheek and make a joke of it. But Neville leaned forward, put his arms around her, and kissed her full on the lips. Chantel was unable to move, so surprised was she, and then she felt an unexpected pleasure. He had a clean smell about him, and his lips were firm against hers.

She had thought often about being kissed, but now that it had come it had caught her completely off guard. She found herself kissing him back.

Neville drew back, a startled expression in his eyes. He cleared his throat. "Well, you can shoot me with that pistol now."

"No, I won't do that." Chantel put her hand on his arm and whispered, "Good night, Neville. It was a wonderful evening. And thank you for your gift."

Chantel shut the gate and watched as he walked back to the carriage.

Chapter fifteen

"Why, you've grown up! You're a fine young lady now!" Simon Bientot and his wife had come to greet Chantel, who got out of the carriage and stood before Fontaine Maison. Marie came to embrace her, and Simon shook her hand.

"You're all grown up!" Marie echoed, admiration glowing in her eyes.

"Well, I hope I won't grow up any more. I'm too tall now."

"Nonsense. You are just right," Simon said stoutly.

"I'm five-feet-ten. Most men aren't much taller than that."

Chantel had reached a separate peace over her height. For a time she had tried to stoop over to make herself appear shorter, but Elise had kept at her until she finally straightened up, and now she had a fine carriage. She wore a gray traveling dress that outlined her figure well, and the fading rays of the sun caught the golden glints in her auburn hair.

"Let me get your bags, and you go in, Miss Chantel," Simon said.

"All right, Simon, but tomorrow I want to see everything."

When she stepped inside an eerie feeling came to her. It was as if she had stepped back in time, for just the appearance of the foyer took her back to her earliest memories. She knew that Marie was standing beside her, and Elise, who had accompanied her, was waiting, but for one moment she could almost hear her father's voice calling her name. Quickly she shook her shoulders and said, "I'm anxious to see my room. I've missed it so much."

"I haven't changed a thing," Marie said quickly. "I just cleaned it and aired it out."

Chantel stepped into her room, and the sense of the past was even stronger than it had been in the foyer. The very wallpaper, patterned with tiny pink dancing horses, made her catch her breath. Her father had let her pick it out herself, and she had loved it with all her heart. Her bookcase was filled with books from childhood and some later ones. The four-poster bed was turned back and looked inviting. She moved around the room and shook her head. "I have thought of this room so often. I'm so glad to be back home."

"You can change your clothes, and then we will have a good dinner."

"Thank you, Marie. I am hungry."

Elise came forward and began unpacking. She was somewhat subdued, for she had not wanted to leave the excitement of New Orleans life for the rural scene. Chantel went over to her and gave her a hug. "You and Charles will like it around here, Elise." Chantel had grown fond of the man Elise had married months earlier—Charles Watkins.

"Charles will like the hunting, but there's so little to do!"

"Yes, there is. We'll be busy getting this place together and making it like new again."

After Elise left to go unpack her own clothes, Chantel pulled her diary out of her reticule. She sat down and noticed that the same pen that she had used as a child was still on the table. She also saw that someone had thoughtfully refilled the inkwell. She smiled as she dipped the pen into it and began writing:

June 15, 1831

I am home again! Elise is sad because she hates to leave New Orleans, but I am so glad to be here! To be able to ride over my own fields and see the workers and live the life I want to live!

It's all possible only because of Neville, and I'm so thankful to him . . . I made him promise to come and see me, and I think he will. But I can't wait until tomorrow. Simon's going to take me over all the plantation, and I'm going to make a list of everything that needs to be done to the house. It's so good to be home!

She dusted the writing with sand, blew it off, and tucked the journal under her clothes in the lower drawer of the armoire, just as she had done when she was a little girl.

Rising early, Chantel put on her riding dress and went down to a fine breakfast. Clarice Debeau was there, broader and seemingly shorter than when Chantel was a child, but still the same Clarice. Her voice was loud enough to break china, or so Simon declared. But the cook had a genuine affection for Chantel and after hugging her, she then sat her on a stool while she made breakfast—fluffy eggs, crisply fried ham, and biscuits that melted in the mouth. Chantel ate in the kitchen instead of going to the dining room, listening as Marie and Clarice brought her up-to-date on the latest gossip.

When she was finished, she went over the first-floor plan with Marie.

"I want to do so much. Some of the paper needs to be replaced, and the furniture needs to be refinished. And I want to enlarge the kitchen and put in a larger stove."

Marie smiled at the exuberance of the young woman. "You'll be too busy going to balls and having parties for all of that."

"No, I won't. I came back to make this the finest plantation in Louisiana, and I'm going to do it, too. You just wait and see, Marie!"

Chantel wandered over the rest of the house alone, coming at last to the room that had belonged to Veronique. She opened the door and stepped inside. The curtains were drawn, and it was dark. She stood for a moment until her eyes grew adjusted to the gloom, and then she went over and opened the curtains, letting the light in.

She turned and saw the small bed that had belonged to her infant sister. Brutus had made it out of black walnut, and it still had the rich gloss and sheen of fine wood. Chantel ran her hand along the bed, then reached down and touched the pillow, which was covered with a fine linen pillowcase. How often she had come to this room and held her sister close. Dear little Veronique, with the strawberry blonde hair and striking violet eyes.

Chantel found herself missing her sister as she had not for a long time. Finally she tore herself away and left, closing the door. She would keep the room exactly as it was, as long as she was alive to see to it.

"He's a fine-looking animal, monsieur," Chantel said. She walked around the steel-gray stallion, noting the perfectly arched back and strong hindquarters. She ran her hand over the muscles of the chest, and when the stallion turned to her, she reached up and held her palm out. He touched it with his velvety nose, and Chantel laughed. "He likes me already."

Simon had brought Chantel to Fremont's stables only a week after she had returned to Fontaine Plantation. She expressed her desire to Fremont clearly. "I want the best you have, monsieur."

"I think this is too much horse for you, mademoiselle." Fremont was a short, barrel-shaped man with steady brown eyes, and he had a reputation for breeding the best horses in the area.

He looked at Simon and gave his head a shake as if to say, *Help me here. She doesn't need this horse.*

Simon attempted to put in a word. "Miss Chantel, this is a man's horse. You need—"

It was the worst thing he could have possibly said.

Chantel gave him an indignant look. "I can ride him!" She turned to Fremont and said, "I'll try him out."

Fremont started to protest, but when he saw her determination he sighed, "It is your responsibility, mademoiselle."

"Of course. Now, have him saddled."

Simon offered a hand to help Chantel up. She took her seat, held the lines, and touched the withers of the gray. "What's his name?" she asked.

"We call him Bravo."

"Come on, Bravo," Chantel said. She was an excellent rider, but the strength of the horse was somewhat intimidating. She held the lines firmly, but she knew that with his strength, he could pull them out of her hands if he chose. Nevertheless, he seemed eager to run. She brought him to a trot, then a gallop, and finally a dead run.

Simon stood watching her and shaking his head. "I can do nothing with her," he said.

"Well, she's a fine rider. Maybe she can handle him."

"She has a great deal of determination. I found that out when she was just a child."

"You go ahead in the buggy, Simon. I'll ride Bravo home."

"But we need to go by the store and pick up a few things."

"You can do that. I have an errand I want to go on."

"All right, but be careful of that horse. You don't know him yet. He may have a trick or two in him."

"Nonsense. He's a perfect gentleman." Chantel leaned over, patted the smooth hide of the horse, and then laughed as he nodded his head up and down. "You see? He agrees with me. Come, Bravo. Let's go."

Chantel pulled up at the cemetery and slipped out of the saddle. She had taken her things out of the buggy and put them in the black leather saddlebags. Now she tied the horse firmly to a thick sapling at the edge of the cemetery and patted him. "You wait right here. I won't be long, Bravo." She smiled as he lowered his head and studied her, then expelled his breath with a slobbering sound. "I'll give you an apple when we get home. You'll like it."

Moving through the cemetery grounds gave Chantel the same feeling she had sensed when entering the house. It brought back the past in a vivid fashion indeed. She recalled her mother's funeral and saw herself as a young girl standing beside her father as the two of them watched her mother's body being put into the vault.

And then her thoughts shifted, advancing until she saw herself again standing beside Collette and Perrin as her father's body was placed beside that of his wife. She remembered wondering what

Collette thought about such an arrangement, for the vault had been made for just two inhabitants.

Now it was almost dusk, and already the swallows that lived in the old church were turning in acrobatic flight above the cemetery. Several bats suddenly seemed to erupt from the steeple and made black marks against the darkening sky. Chantel did not like them; bats always gave her a strange feeling. Tearing her eyes away, she moved over to stand before the vault. She stood for a long time, and finally she knelt and placed her hands on the cold granite. She prayed for the souls of her father and her sister and her mother.

It disturbed her still to think of purgatory. She had stubbornly resisted all efforts to implant such a doctrine in her head. Sister Martha had once remarked, "Well, if she has no heresy worse than this in her life, it will be well."

Chantel had often come here as an adolescent and knelt at this very place, often staying away until a servant was sent to fetch her. Now there was no one to tell her what to do or when to return, and she felt the loneliness of her life more than she had in a long time.

She knelt there, lost in thought, then suddenly she heard the sound of footsteps. Before she could rise, a hand gripped her arm, and she found herself pulled to her feet. She turned quickly and found herself facing a rough-looking man, large and with a terrible scar across his broad cheek. He had thickset features and wore a cotton cap pulled halfway down over his ears. He wore a shirt with the sleeves torn off, and his arms were thick and muscular.

"Well, what do we have here? What a beauty, Ned."

A second man, this one smaller and thinner framed with hazel eyes, said, "What do you got, Jackie? Well, now, ain't she a pretty one!"

The burly man glanced around. "Let's take a walk over in them woods, pretty. I'll show you what a real man's like."

Terror flooded through Chantel. She opened her mouth to scream, but her voice was cut off by a rough hand over her face. She smelled the stench of the man, unwashed and feral. He pulled her toward the woods, and when she tried to fight, he simply picked her up off the ground as he would a child. She kicked at him, but he merely laughed. "I like a woman with spunk. You see what's in them bags on that horse, Ned, while me and my sweetheart have a little fun."

"I get my turn then, right?"

"Right you are."

The two men laughed and made crude jokes, and Chantel knew fear as she had never known it before in her life. She suddenly managed to wrench her head away from his hand and screamed out, "Help! Somebody help me!"

"That won't do, sweetheart. There ain't nobody to hear except maybe a priest, and he'd better not stick his head out of that church."

Chantel fought with all of her strength, but to no avail. She wished that she could die rather than be attacked by such a brute.

"All right, you, let that woman go!"

Chantel heard the words and felt her captor's grip loosen. The smaller man, named Ned, was running toward them, and now she turned frantically to see who had spoken.

A tall man wearing brown trousers, half boots, and a dark blue coat stood before her. His voice was strong as he said, "Turn the woman loose and be on your way!"

"Well, Ned, we've got us a hero here. Wot do yer think of that?"

"I think we'll just see what he's got in his purse," Ned said. He moved to one side, and as he did, pulled a wicked looking knife from his belt. He grinned and said, "Come now, bucko. Hand over your purse, and maybe I won't cut your bloomin' throat."

Chantel saw the tall man spread his hands out, holding them to one side in a strange manner. When Ned made a slash at him, his hand shot out, and he struck him a blow that sent him reeling backward. Stooping over, the newcomer picked up a small branch that formed a sort of club. He did not speak again, but when Ned came at him, he parried the thrust in an expert fashion, then brought the improvised weapon down on his wrist. Ned let out a squeal, and the knife dropped.

Chantel staggered backward. The big man surged forward, releasing her arm. He also had a knife and began slashing her rescuer. She heard him cry out, "Gotcha that time!" and saw that Ned had recovered his knife and that they had surrounded their opponent from each side. Armed with only a club, he would have no chance.

A sudden thought came to her. She whirled and saw Bravo tied only a few yards away. Quick as a flash she ran to him. He sidled away, but she said, "Be still, Bravo." She lifted the flap of the saddlebag, pulled out her reticule, and reached into it for her pistol. She grasped it and ran back. She could plainly see blood running down her rescuer's arm. "Stop!" she cried.

The man named Jackie turned and said, "Wot's that?"

"Both of you get away from him, or I'll shoot you!"

Jackie laughed brutally. "With that little pop gun?" He came toward her, and Chantel lifted the pistol. She aimed at him and pulled the trigger.

He reached and grabbed his shoulder. Chantel could see the scarlet blood gushing out, and she said, "You get away! And you, too!" She aimed the weapon at the smaller man, and when he stared at her, she said, "I'll shoot you if you don't."

"Come on, Ned," the big man said. "I'm bleedin' to death! You got to do something."

"All right. Come on, Jackie."

The two left at a half run, and Chantel turned to see her rescuer suddenly drop to one knee. She ran forward and said, "Are you hurt?"

He turned his face to her. "They cut me pretty bad."

His arm, she saw, was bleeding freely. She said, "Here, sit down." When he was sitting, she pulled his shirt out, tore a strip off, wound it around the cut, and tied it. "We'll have to get you to a doctor."

"I don't think I can walk too far."

"Get on the horse. I'll get up behind you. It isn't far to my house."

It took both of them to get him into the saddle. Thankfully Bravo did not budge, but stood like a rock.

She pulled herself on behind him and spoke. "Come on, Bravo. Home, boy!"

"I think he's going to be all right," Marie said. She straightened up and looked at her handiwork.

"He looks pale to me," Simon said.

"He's lost a lot of blood. You'd better go for the doctor, Simon."

"Right. I'll get him here as soon as I can."

Chantel had watched as Marie had bound up the wounds of the man. He had a long, deep cut on his left arm, another not so deep on his chest, and one along his ribs on his right side. The arm had been the bloodiest, and Marie had insisted on sewing it up. She had been the doctor of sorts at Fontaine Maison for years and had grown adept at such things.

Chantel stood looking down at the pale face of the man. His eyes were closed, and she thought, *He's got to be all right.* He had dark brown hair and a handsome, tapered face. His body was trim and fit. "Are you sure he'll be all right, Marie?"

"Yes, but he's lost much blood and will be weak for a time."

"I'll take care of him. You and I, we'll see to it, won't we, Marie?"

Marie Bientot looked at the young mistress and lifted one eyebrow. "Of course, *chéri*. We will take care of him. He saved your life, didn't he?"

"Yes, he did." Chantel laid her hand on the man's forehead and moved a lock of hair back. She stared at him in a dazed fashion. "And then I guess I saved his."

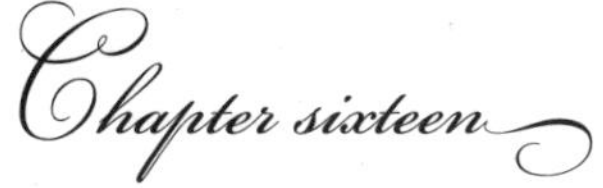

Chapter sixteen

Doctor Leo Compare resembled an actor more than he did a physician. Of Creole blood, he had glossy black hair with a pronounced curl, eyes so dark they seemed like ebony, and a smooth, olive complexion. He was happily married with four children, though he was only twenty-five years old, and half of the young women of the parish had feigned illness just to get a call from the good doctor.

Now as Doctor Compare straightened up, he turned his head to one side and looked at Chantel, who stood on the other side of the bed. "This is a tough one, Mademoiselle Fontaine. If he had lost another pint of blood, I think he would be in his tomb."

Chantel had watched as the doctor removed the stitches from the arm of Yves Gaspard. She had spent considerable time with her patient during the three days since he had rescued her, and now she smiled. "He's going to have a scar on that arm."

"It doesn't matter," Gaspard said quickly. "At first I was afraid it would affect my hand. It's my painting hand, you see. I could do without the left but not the right."

Gaspard was a handsome man, well over six feet tall and lithely built. He had dark brown hair that lay neatly along the back of his head, long enough to touch his shoulders. His eyes, a light brown, were well-shaped. His face was wedge-shaped and his mouth wide. He had a thin, dark mustache that he had kept trimmed rather awkwardly with his left hand for the past few days, but otherwise he was smooth shaven.

He turned to the doctor and smiled. "My hostess saved my life, Doctor Compare." He shook his head in wonder. "I heard a legend once of some tribe in South America. They had a custom. If someone saved the life of another, that person belonged to his savior."

"Oh, I'm not a savior! Don't be foolish. And it was you who saved my life first."

Doctor Compare turned and packed his supplies in his bag. He studied the two for a moment, then nodded. "You are well enough to do whatever you please. Just be sure you don't put extra strain on that arm."

"But a little painting will not hurt, no?"

"No, not a little. Be sure you feed him well, mademoiselle. When one loses that much blood, it takes a while to build the strength up again."

"I'll certainly do that. Thank you for coming, Doctor Compare."

When Compare left the room, Chantel said, "Why don't you come into the dining room, and we'll have breakfast together."

"That would be good. This is a lovely room, but I need to get around." Gaspard stood up, and for a moment seemed to sway. At once Chantel stepped forward and took his arm. "Are you all right, Mr. Gaspard?"

"Just a little dizzy. I think the good physician is right. I do not believe I will try any strenuous exercise." He smiled down at her, and she realized, not for the first time, how much he resembled her father.

Gaspard was a much taller man, but the eyes were the same shape, as were the lips. And when Yves Gaspard smiled, it was the smile of her father all over again. Something about the curvature of the mouth, the set of the lips, was exactly the same.

"Come along," she said. "Lean on me."

"I hate to be dependent."

"This is different. I've been very worried about you."

Gaspard had his arm over her shoulder and held it there lightly. He was wearing the clothes he was wearing when he came to Chantel's rescue—a pair of light gray trousers and a maroon-colored shirt open at the throat, with long, full sleeves. The right sleeve concealed the wound that the doctor had bandaged. He wore shoes of glossy black leather.

When the two entered the dining room, Marie Bientot met them. "Sit down," she said. "Breakfast is ready."

Chantel moved to her place, and the tall man sat down across from her. As he did, he said, "I appreciate your sending your servant out to get my painting things. I was most worried about them."

Indeed, upon regaining consciousness that had been Gaspard's first request. He had been painting in the cemetery when he heard Chantel's cry for help. "I would not have liked to have lost them."

"I've got them in a spare room any time you're ready," Chantel said. "I love the painting you were working on."

"It is not finished."

"No, but I see what it's going to be."

The painting was little more than a sketch, but already the strong lines were clear. Its subject was one of the large statues of an angel that had always intrigued Chantel.

"Why did you decide to paint an angel?" she asked.

"I am very interested in angels."

"Really? Why is that?"

"I can't say, but I believe in them strongly. I believe everyone has his own angel. I think there's a verse in the Bible that says something like that. In any case, it pleases me to think that there is a strong, mighty angel looking over my shoulder, always ready to help me when I get into trouble. As a matter of fact"—he smiled and leaned forward—"I think maybe one or two angels were watching over us in that cemetery."

"What a nice thought!"

"Yes. There's much evil in the world, but there is much good, too."

At that point Clarice brought in a huge tray, accompanied by Marie with the silver coffeepot. The two women laid out an excellent meal—poached eggs, fresh bread, butter straight from the dairy, currant jelly, and slices of savory ham. When it was all on the table, Gaspard said, "I have an odd habit of saying thank you to God before every meal."

"It's not odd at all," Chantel replied.

She bowed her head, and Gaspard said with enthusiasm, "Our good God, everything comes from You, so I am thanking You for this wonderful food and for the hospitality that I have found. Bless this house and all that are in it. Amen."

"Amen," Chantel said. "You must be a devout believer then."

"Not at all," Gaspard said. "Perhaps I shall be one day."

"You're not a Christian?"

"I am sad to say that I am not—but I will be one day. I think the Lord is after me, and one day He will catch me."

Chantel laughed. "What an odd thing to say. You should be pursuing God, not the other way around."

They ate their breakfast, and more than once Chantel was struck at the strong resemblance she found between Yves Gaspard and her father. She studied him surreptitiously. He was fine looking, although not typical. His hair was longer than most men's, but she found this attractive. He had traveled much in Europe and over the United States and told stories both humorous and informative.

"Well, where is your home, Monsieur Gaspard?"

"Please, could we not call each other simply Chantel—which is a lovely name indeed!—and Yves?"

"I'd like that very much."

"Good. My home is in New Orleans."

"And your family?"

"My parents are living, but I am the only surviving son." He had been drinking coffee laced with chicory, and now he held the tiny, fragile piece of china in his hand and rolled it slowly around. It looked very small between his fingers.

She noticed that his hands were long and strong looking but not bulky. *The kind of hands an artist ought to have,* she thought.

"I am a disappointment to them I am afraid, Chantel."

"Why in the world would you say that?"

"They expected more of me." He hesitated, and a sadness seemed to cross his face. "My family was prominent at one time. It still is socially, I suppose, but my father had unfortunate business reverses, so that all we have left now of what was once a sizable fortune is a fine house, old and rapidly going downhill for lack of means to repair it and keep it up."

"Well, that is sad. But your painting—surely they're not disappointed that you're an artist."

"I'm afraid they are." Yves sipped the coffee, and his smile was somewhat sardonic. "You have heard tales of starving young artists, I suppose. Well, you're looking at one now, Chantel."

"You haven't sold any paintings?"

"Very few. It is a very competitive world, the world of art. People buy according to name, not according to beauty. When one has a name, it is very simple. No matter what you paint people will buy it. But for those of us who are on the outside it is difficult."

"But I'm sure you're a great painter."

"That makes two of us who think so."

"But really. I can tell from that one painting you have talent."

"Talent is not the most important thing in art."

Chantel stared at him with surprise. "It isn't?"

"Oh, no, indeed! Shall I tell you what is the most important thing in the life of an artist? I think of any artist—painter, sculptor, singer."

"Yes," Chantel said, leaning forward. "What is it?"

"It is—timing. You see, if I paint a beautiful picture, and I take it to a show and exhibit it, if it so happens that a wealthy man or woman goes by and sees it and likes it and buys it, they buy it because they're there. If they were not there, it would not be bought. When this happens often enough, time after time, the artist becomes famous. No, Chantel, it is not talent that counts the most. Talent is important, but you know who I think of as the greatest artist who ever lived?"

"Rembrandt?"

"Naturally you would think so, but I think not. It was probably someone who had far more talent than Rembrandt, but he was trapped in a place where he could never develop his talent. The timing was wrong. He was born in the wrong place at the wrong time. A farmer, perhaps, and his hands grew rough with handling a plow and grubbing with a shovel, so he never painted. But he would have been greater than Rembrandt if he had had Rembrandt's chances."

"I'm sure your work will sell. I will buy your angel painting myself when it's finished."

"Good." Yves smiled, and his dark eyes flashed. "I will charge you five times what it is worth."

After breakfast they went out to sit on the porch, and he admired what he could see of the plantation. "I love the country. It's so beautiful here. But I'll try to get out of your way as soon as possible."

"Nonsense. You must stay until you are fully recovered. And you must finish the picture of the angel. Then I will buy it."

"Well, I don't know what you think about this fellow, but I do not think he is good for Chantel."

Marie and Simon were sitting in their kitchen finishing up their evening meal. Simon stared at his wife, then took a long pull at his glass of wine. He licked his lips and set the glass down. "He seems to be a good enough fellow."

"He's been here a week, and he is strong enough to go," Marie said firmly. "But he doesn't."

"What's wrong with him?"

"I think Chantel is smitten with him. He's fine looking and has good manners, but he has no money."

"He's fine looking, no doubt of that. As to his talent, I know nothing of such things."

"If he were good, he would be making money. Chantel told me herself—although she didn't mean to—that he is poor and his family has nothing."

Simon leaned back in his chair, balancing on the two legs, and studied his wife. "You worry too much."

"You men, you have no sense whatsoever! Don't you know she's a beautiful young girl with a fortune? And what is he? Poof! He is a nobody! A pauper. A painter who drinks too much."

"How do you know he drinks too much?"

Marie sniffed and stared at him with disgust. "All painters drink too much! Artists, they are not good people. They are immoral."

Simon laughed and reached across the table and captured her hand. He held it tightly, though she tried to pull it away. "And how many artists have you known?"

"I have read about them, and everyone knows that they are immoral."

"I do not know it."

"You know nothing about men and women!"

Simon squeezed his wife's hand and grinned at her. "I knew enough to get me a fine wife."

Marie frowned, then suddenly her face broke into laughter. "You always know how to get around me, but I am right. You will see."

"She's a young girl. Naturally she likes to be admired."

"She should marry someone like Francis Taubin."

"Why, he's the dullest man I've ever met!"

"But he has a good plantation and lots of money. Romance is very fine out in the moonlight, but when the bills come due, what good is it?"

"Perhaps Gaspard will be going soon."

"I hope so. It would be better for Chantel if he did."

At the moment when the Bientots were speaking, Chantel and Yves were at the river. He liked to paint at sunset, and now the last colors were fading. Chantel watched with admiration. She had never found a man so interesting.

The breeze was warm, and from time to time the surface of the water echoed with the splash of a fish. Chantel watched as a turtle crawled out on a log and stretched his head out as if seeking food. She watched him until finally he went into the water with a *kerplunk!*

"It's getting late. You can't see to paint."

"I know, but it's going well. Funny about painting. One day you're doing well, and the next day you can't start again. You've lost it."

"It's going to be a good painting, isn't it?"

"Who knows? You paint a bad painting the same way you paint a good painting."

Chantel came over to stand beside him. He had started a picture of the bayou and had centered on a great blue heron. The bird, of course, was not there now, but he had been drawn in, and he would come last, Yves had said. But he had caught something of the late afternoon in a Louisiana bayou. The sky overhead was just beginning to grow dark, and the huge cypress trees lifted themselves out of the water, dangling bundles of Spanish moss like huge birds' nests. "It's a good painting," she said. "You got it just right." She watched the even strokes of his brush and finally said, "I may want to buy this one, too."

Yves turned and smiled. "I'll just stay here and paint pictures of the bayou, and you can buy them all."

Chantel smiled back at him. It pleased her that she had to look up. It made her feel small and fragile—a rare thing for her. "I wish we could do that."

He began to clean his brushes, and as he was gathering them all together, she said, "Why have you never married, Yves?"

"I'm too romantic."

"Too romantic! But that's a good thing."

"Well, my parents wanted an arranged marriage. In fact, they tried that several times. One of their choices was a very beautiful woman. Well, not beautiful, but pretty enough. But she hadn't a brain in her head. I can't talk about bonnets all my life."

"No, I suppose not." She saw he was finished, and she turned to take one last look at the river. "I hate this river," she said quietly.

"Hate it? Why, I think it's beautiful."

"Well, I suppose it is, but—" She broke off and then turned and walked away from him. She folded her arms and looked down at the ground.

She was surprised when he came up behind her and turned her around. "What's the matter?"

She hesitated but something kept her going. "It's my mother and my sister. They drowned in this river."

Yves looked at her for a moment, then drew her over to a huge cypress that had fallen. "Sit down," he said. Sitting down next to her, he put his arm around her and said, "Now, tell me about it."

Chantel did not like to talk about her loss, but she found the weight of his arm comforting and his silence also. He did not interrupt until she had told the whole story.

He whispered huskily, "I'm so sorry, little one."

"Little one?" She turned and looked at him, her eyes glistening with tears. "No one ever called me that. I'm too tall."

"No, you're not too tall." He pulled her up and said, "You're just as high as my heart."

Chantel could not speak for a moment, then she finally whispered, "What a sweet thing to say."

"I probably read it in a poem. But it's true enough. Don't worry about your height. You will marry, and you will have a husband and children, and they will fill your life."

"I doubt that I'll ever marry."

"Yes, you must marry. I hate to see a woman wasted." He leaned down suddenly and kissed her, just a light kiss, but it was on the lips. It shocked her and at the same time gave her a sense of security and comfort. "Just stay away from starving artists like me."

"If I do marry, it will be because I love a man. Money doesn't matter."

Yves suddenly laughed and then shook his head. "I must talk to your stepmother—or this lawyer friend you have mentioned. You're too innocent to be left alone."

"I am not!"

"Yes, you are. There are selfish men who would love to find a girl like you with beauty and money." He reached out and put his hand on her cheek. It felt warm and strong, and she covered it with her own. "But I will help you, *mon chère.* Bring all your sweethearts to me, and I will tell you if they are worthy or not." He laughed and then shook his head. "Come. I'm hungry. Let's go home and get something to eat."

As they made their way home, Chantel could not help replaying the scene in her mind. *You're just as high as my heart.* No one had ever said anything poetic or beautiful to her before. *Even if he did get it from a poem,* she thought as they made their way homeward, *it was a beautiful thing to say.*

Chapter seventeen

Neville had been laboring over a particularly knotty case, struggling with the stacks of paper spread out on his desk. He stared at the date on his calendar—August 5—then ran his hand through his hair. Finally, in desperation, he grabbed it and seemed to try to lift himself out of his chair. "Blasted idiots! Why do they have to take this thing to court?" he muttered.

Finally an interruption came when Jenkins, his clerk, stuck his head in the door. "Miss Fontaine to see you when you have time, sir."

"Why, send her in at once," Neville said. His face brightened, and getting up from his desk, he walked around it. He greeted Chantel warmly, and when she put her hands out, he took them and held them. "Thank heaven you've come," he said. "I'm about to go crazy."

"I'm so glad to see you, Neville."

"When did you get into town?"

"Just last night. It was very late, but I've come to take you out to lunch."

"Good! I'm starved."

"I have a friend I want you to meet."

"Oh, who is that?"

"Come along, and I will tell you on the way."

Neville left the office, and as soon as they were outside and in the carriage, he got the full story of Yves Gaspard.

"Do you know him, Neville?"

"No, I don't. I've heard of the Gaspard family, but I've never met any of them."

"He is a wonderful artist."

"Really?"

"Yes. I bought two of his paintings that he did right on the plantation." Neville listened as she spoke with animation, her eyes glowing. Cautiously he tried to find out more about the man that had so stirred her, but soon they were at the Royale Restaurant, and she said, "We're supposed to meet Yves here."

When they entered they were greeted by a waiter, and when Chantel asked if anyone had reserved a table, he nodded. "Yes, Monsieur Gaspard, I believe. He said you would be coming. Would you step this way, please."

Neville followed Chantel, and when the two got to a table along the wall, a tall man stood up, and Chantel introduced them. "Yves, this is my best friend and my attorney, Neville Harcourt. Neville, I'd like for you to meet Yves Gaspard."

The two men made a half bow and then shook hands. Yves said, "I've heard so much about you, Mr. Harcourt. You've been a good friend, indeed, to Chantel."

"We've known each other a long time."

The three of them sat down, and Yves looked around saying, "I've eaten at this place several times. The food is exquisite."

The three of them ordered, and after the waiter left Neville said, "I understand you're a painter."

"Well, the jury is still out on that. *I* think I am, but the world has not beaten a path to my door."

"I'd like to see your work sometime."

"Naturally I would be proud to show it to you. I have a studio at our family home."

Chantel wanted the two men to like each other, but she soon discovered that Neville was up to something. Without appearing to do so, he was eliciting information about Yves. *He's acting like Yves is a criminal under suspicion. I wanted them to meet as friends.*

Finally she said, "Really, I think both of us owe Neville a debt.

The pistol that I shot that man with was a gift from him."

Yves grinned, his teeth very white against his olive complexion. "Very fortunate for both of us that you did. Yet a rather strange gift to give a lady."

"Oh, I'd always wanted one," Chantel said quickly. "And Neville got it for my graduation."

"Are you still carrying it?" Neville asked.

"Yes, I have it right here, but I don't think I'll need it in the restaurant."

The meal was pleasant enough, but when they were through, Yves rose and said, "I have an appointment. It's been good to meet you, sir."

"And you, too, monsieur."

Yves turned to Chantel and said, "I'll pick you up early. Perhaps we can have something to eat after the opera."

"That will be wonderful, Yves."

Chantel watched the tall form of Yves as he left—and noticed that an attractive woman seated near the door also turned her gaze on him. "Do you like him, Neville?"

"He seems a very nice fellow, and he did you a great service. I have to like him for that." Neville toyed with his spoon and then said, "I take it he hasn't been very successful in his profession?"

"Not yet, but there's time."

Neville put the spoon down, then folded his arms and stared at Chantel. "You like him, don't you?"

"Very much! And not just because he saved my life."

Neville shook his head slightly. "I've got to warn you about men, Chantel. You're attractive, and you have money."

"Oh, so men would want to marry me only because I have money?"

"Not only because of that, but—"

"Well, you don't have to worry. Yves warned me about the same thing."

"Oh, really?"

"Yes. He said to bring any suitors I have to him, and he will tell me if they're fortune hunters." She laughed and shook her head. "He told me to be careful of him because he is a starving artist, and if he got hungry enough, he might even stoop to fortune hunting himself."

What a clever fellow! Neville thought. He saw that Chantel was infatuated with the man, and it did not surprise him. She had led a sheltered life, and Gaspard was a romantic man if nothing else. He had good looks, charm, and wit, and the very idea of his being an artist must appeal to any impressionable young girl.

"Well, I will make you the same offer. I'd like to look over any prospective suitors you have."

"Why, certainly," she said and gave him a teasing look. "Don't worry, Neville. I'll have any man who wants to marry me ask your permission, just as if you were my father."

Somehow this did not sit well with Neville, but he nodded. "I think that would be very wise." He managed a smile and said, "You're engaged tonight. What about tomorrow night?"

"I'll see if I'm free and send you a note."

Neville knew this meant she would see if Gaspard had anything planned. He covered his disappointment and said, "That will be fine."

⌣

A month had passed since Chantel had come to New Orleans. She had at first intended to go right back to the plantation, but somehow this plan failed to materialize. Almost every night she was at the theater, at the opera, at an exhibition—and almost always with Yves Gaspard.

Neville was troubled, although he never let it show to Chantel. Three times that month she had gone out with him, but one of those times Gaspard had been with them, so it had not been what Neville had wished. He was more worried than he liked to express.

One afternoon in the early days of September he came to the Fontaine home and was greeted by Collette. She seated him and offered him tea, and then said, "Chantel has gone back to the plantation."

At Neville's look of surprise, she continued, "You didn't know? I thought she must have told you."

"No, she didn't say a word."

Neville felt a deep disappointment, but he wanted to know more. "What made her decide to go back?"

"I think it was more Yves's decision. He wants to paint scenes around the plantation, particularly in the bayou. And Chantel, of course, loves the place."

"You thought it appropriate for her to go on a trip with a man?"

Collette shook her head. "I'm afraid she's falling in love with him, Neville. They've been inseparable for the past month."

"Yes, I know. I'm worried about it."

Collette shrugged. "His family is respectable. His mother came from the Defoe family, quite prominent. They were into shipping."

"But I understand they don't have any money now."

"That's true enough." She cocked her head to one side and said, "This bothers you, doesn't it, Neville?"

"Yes, it does. I feel responsible for Chantel."

"She could do worse. Yves seems like a good enough man, from what I understand."

"I don't think it's a good thing for Chantel," Neville replied. "She's young and impressionable, and she hasn't gotten over the death of her father yet."

"No, I don't think she has. Perhaps she never will. She's that kind of girl. But I can't forbid her to see him. She's independent." She smiled archly and said, "You saw to that when you talked Cretien into giving her a trust fund."

"Yes, I suppose I did." Neville rose and said, "Well, I must be going. Thank you for the tea."

"I'll be writing to Chantel. Shall I give her any word from you?"

"Just my good wishes. Good day, madame."

For two days Neville was unusually sharp at the office. His clerks learned to avoid him, and one of them said, "I don't know what's eating on him, but he's not himself. He's gotten to be as mean as a cottonmouth!"

Indeed, Neville was troubled, and he knew that it centered on Chantel Fontaine. His own feelings for her were confused. At times he thought of her as a child, but he remembered the kiss he had taken and how, when he had held her briefly in his arms, it had not been a child but a mature woman who kissed him back. He knew many sad cases of women who had rushed into marriage precipitously with men who were selfish, and although he could not make this charge with any certainty against Gaspard, he could not get the matter out of his mind.

The next Thursday he was having a conference with a man by the prosaic name of Smith whose family was prominent in society. When the business was done, Neville gathered the papers together and said, "I met a man recently named Yves Gaspard. Do you know the family?"

"Oh, certainly. As a matter of fact, I've met the young man. He's some kind of an artist fellow, isn't he?"

"I believe so. How do you know him?"

"I had some business once with the family. His father, Giles, married Jeanne Defoe when she was what was called a 'maiden lady.'" He smiled and shook his head. "She was in her late thirties, and her parents thought she would never marry."

"Was it a good marriage?"

"In some ways, I suppose, but Giles Gaspard was a very poor businessman. He made terrible investments and ran through the money that she brought to their marriage. They live now in an old mansion in the Garden District. They keep up the front somehow. You see them at balls now and then."

"What about the son?"

"Well, he has promise, I suppose. He couldn't make up his mind about a profession. He tried law, I think, and that didn't suit him. Now he's painting pictures."

"And he never married. That seems odd."

"Well, he's tried to marry into money, more than once, I think. Of course the parents are behind that. He almost made a match with the Littleton girl, but her parents shipped her off to Europe to get her away from him."

"I have a personal reason for asking, Mr. Smith. Is there anything you can tell me about Yves Gaspard, I'd like to know?"

Mr. Smith shrugged his shoulders mildly. "I understand the man has led a pretty wild life—but you know artists." He smiled in condescension. "No morals whatsoever."

After Smith left the office, Neville sat for a long time staring out his window. An idea began to take shape in his mind, and finally he called to his clerk. "Charles!" When the clerk came in, Neville said, "I'm going to take some time off. Arrange my schedule so that I can be gone for a week at least."

"Yes, sir. It will be a little difficult. You need a partner."

Neville shrugged. "Maybe you'll grow up one day, and I can take you into the firm. Work on this right away, will you. I'm anxious to get away for a while."

Chapter eighteen

"If you don't stop turning about, Miss Chantel, I'll never get you dressed!"

Chantel, who had been twisting around with excitement, forced herself to stand still as Elise held a dress in front of her. She was wearing ankle-length pantalets and a white muslin petticoat over steel hoops fitted with tapes. She held her arms out, saying, "All right, I'm ready!" As Elise worked the dress on, Chantel held her breath until it slipped into place. Then as Elise fastened the back, she stood looking at it.

The dress was made of blue-green silk overlaid with blue lace flounces. On the chair beside her lay a sheer blue stole, a pair of white kid gloves, and an ivory and silk fan. She stood for a moment staring at herself and then tugged at the dress. "Elise," she whispered, "it's too—it's too low!"

"It's not too low! You've got a good form and beautiful skin. Now stop pulling at it!"

Elise fastened a corsage of green leaves and blue-green blossoms at her bosom and fitted a smaller one in her hair, which was fixed in long rolls that framed her face.

"Turn around now and let me see you."

Chantel obeyed, and the dress swirled outward. "I used to hate these hoop skirts, but I must admit the style is graceful, isn't it?"

"It is, and it shows off your small waist, too. Now, sit down and let me finish you off."

Ten minutes later Elise pronounced her mistress ready for the ball, just as the door opened and Bertha, one of the maids, put her head in. "Your mister is here, Miss Chantel."

"Oh, I've got to go!" Chantel murmured. She went to the door and sailed down the stairs, where she found Yves waiting for her. He was wearing a yellow silk vest, high-button coat, and a pair of tan trousers from under which peeked shiny brown boots. Most men wore high collars and bows, but he had a bright green scarf knotted around his neck. It brought out the color of his eyes.

He stepped forward and said, "You look beautiful, Chantel!"

"You do, too—I mean, you look very nice."

"Are you ready?"

"Yes." Chantel turned to Marie, who was watching with disapproval in her eyes. "We'll be in late tonight."

"Very well." Marie sniffed and turned away.

"It would appear Marie doesn't like me," Yves said as he handed her into the carriage.

"Oh, she's that way about anybody I like."

When they were inside, Yves mounted the seat, took the lines from Brutus, and spoke to the horses. They moved forward briskly, and he turned to look at her more closely. "You'll be the prettiest girl at the ball."

Chantel wanted to say, *And you'll be the most handsome man,* but that did not seem proper. "I doubt that," she said. "Just the tallest."

~

The ball was a complete success. All of Chantel's friends were green with envy, she could tell, for Yves was, indeed, the best looking man there. He towered over most of the others, and it gave her the greatest of pleasure to look up at him as they waltzed.

She protested however. "You really should dance with some of the other ladies."

"Why should I do that when I have you?"

"Because I really must dance with some of the other gentlemen."

"But why would you want to do that when we're the best company for each other in the room?"

Nevertheless, Chantel did make sure that she danced with several other young men, and when she did, Yves had no trouble finding partners. But no matter whom she was dancing with, she found herself watching him.

Once, toward the end of the ball, he brought her refreshments and leaned close to her. She could smell his shaving lotion—a deliciously masculine odor.

"You'd better be careful of that fellow, Beecham," he said.

"Leon Beecham? Why, he's an old friend."

"No, he's not. You know I'm commissioned to steer you away from unsuitable matches. Beecham has a look in his eye that I don't like. I refuse to let you dance with him anymore."

"Don't be foolish. He's perfectly harmless," Chantel said. But it gave her pleasure that Yves would show such a protective manner.

"Well, the lights are still on even if it is after midnight. I expect Marie is waiting to cut a switch to me."

Chantel laughed at Yves's words. "I knew they'd be up. Marie and Elise at least."

Leaping out of the carriage, Yves helped her down and then took her to the door.

"I wish you could come in, but it's very late."

"I wish I could, too. It's been a marvelous evening."

"Oh, it's been great fun! Come in for a cup of coffee, anyway."

The two ascended the steps, leaving Brutus to unhitch the team. As soon as they entered the door, Chantel stopped in surprise, for Neville Harcourt stood in the foyer watching her.

"Why—Neville!"

"Good evening, Chantel—or I guess good morning would be more appropriate."

Chantel was embarrassed, and was glad when Yves said, "Why, it's good to see you again, Harcourt. Have you been here long?"

"I got here about nine o'clock."

"If I had known you were coming, I would have made you come earlier, and you could have gone to the ball with us," Chantel said. She stood for a moment, waiting for Neville to tell her why he had come, but he said nothing, and she could feel a mounting tension that made her nervous.

"Marie, did you fix a room for Mr. Harcourt?"

"Yes, he's in the green room."

Yves was watching Neville closely. Abruptly he said, "Well, I'm danced out. I'll see you in the morning. Good night, Harcourt." He turned to Chantel, saying, "Good night, Chantel. It was fun."

As soon as he left, Neville said, "I came down to see the place and what you're doing to it."

Chantel began talking rapidly.

"I'm sure you'll like the improvements I've made. I'll show you everything tomorrow. And I do need to talk to you about some of the finances."

"And Gaspard. What has he been doing with himself?"

"Oh—he's doing some painting."

This sounded false in her own lips for, indeed, Yves had done practically no painting. He had made some efforts at first, but as the days had passed, they had spent them riding and visiting and simply enjoying each other's company.

"I see." Neville hesitated, then said, "Well, I'll see you tomorrow. Good night, Chantel."

Chantel said in a small voice, "Good night, Neville. I'm—I'm glad you came."

She went to her room, and as Elise helped her to undress and get ready for bed, she mechanically answered her questions about the ball. But she was thinking, *I wonder why Neville really came.* She pushed the question away, and when she had her nightgown on, she said good night to Elise and got into the large four-poster bed. Elise arranged the mosquito netting, and for a long time Chantel lay there listening to the frogs that bellowed forth a rough symphony from the pond. She finally went to sleep, but it was a troubled sleep, unlike that which she usually enjoyed.

Chantel spent considerable time with Neville for the next two days. He was indeed interested in the plantation and spent an equal amount of time with Simon, going over the accounts of the operation. Chantel appreciated his interest, but somehow there was still a tension in the air. She knew it was primarily between Neville and Yves. Not that there were any hard words or signs of ill feeling, but, nevertheless, it was there. *It's just that they don't have much in common,* she told herself.

Once she and Yves went riding and paused beside a field of sugarcane. The green stalks were waving in the breeze, and he turned to her abruptly and said, "You and Harcourt have been friends for a long time."

"Oh, yes. He's been the best friend I've ever had." Chantel saw a smile touch Yves's broad mouth. "What are you smiling at?" she demanded.

"It's more than that."

"What's more than that?"

"It's more than friendship. He's interested in you."

Chantel felt her cheeks suddenly warm. "Don't be ridiculous. He's not interested in me like that. I'm like a child to him, and besides that we're so *different.*"

"Yes, you are. But I'm not sure he appreciates that."

"Don't you like him at all, Yves?"

"Why, I have no strong feeling about him." Yves rested his hand on the saddle in front of him and watched her for a moment. "But I think I can see when a man is interested in a woman. You're right when you say he is different. He has an analytical mind. Not much romance about him, I'd say."

"Well, not really. He's had to work hard all of his life, and the law is not very romantic, I suppose."

"Well, you told me to warn you about fortune hunters, and he's certainly not that. I assume he has money."

"Yes, he's very well off, I think. But anyway, you're wrong about him."

Yves shook his head, smiled again, and then touched his heels to his horse. "Come along," he said. "We'll race to those pines over there."

The next day, right after breakfast, Yves said, "I've got to get back to New Orleans, if I could borrow one of your horses."

"Well, of course, but must you leave?"

"Yes, I have business there."

Later on Chantel walked out to the stable with him. He swung into the saddle easily and then leaned down and took her hand. He lifted it to his lips and kissed it. "Good-bye for a while."

"Do you really have to go, Yves?"

"Yes, your friend wants me out of the way so he can talk about legal matters—and other things."

"Yves, you're so foolish!"

"We'll see. I'll write you from New Orleans, and I'll come back when I can. Will you be coming to town soon?"

"Perhaps. I'll write you back, and we'll see."

Walking back to the house, Chantel felt a disappointment. She had grown accustomed to her talks with Yves. He was teaching her about art, and she felt that she was growing in a way. She also knew in her heart that she was falling in love with him, and it was a wonderful feeling. She had had so little contact with men and none at all with anyone like Yves.

When she walked inside, she found Neville in the study.

"Is he gone?"

"Yes. He just left."

Neville put down the pen and flexed his fingers. "I can't say I'm sorry. I think he's been monopolizing you." He laughed suddenly and said, "And that's what I came down to do."

"What would you like to do, Neville?"

"Well, today, anything you like. Tomorrow I have an engagement."

"An engagement? But tomorrow's Sunday."

"I know. I've been asked to preach at a church close by. The Methodist church with the tall spire on it."

Chantel stared at him. "How did that happen?"

"The pastor there is a good friend of mine. When he comes to New Orleans, we usually meet. He's a fine man, but he had to be out of the pulpit tomorrow so he asked me to fill in for him."

Chantel knew that Neville spoke at churches sometimes, but she had forgotten. "I wish I could hear you, but we're not allowed to go to other churches."

"I can't understand that." Neville shrugged. "I'd feel perfectly free to go to a Catholic church if you invited me."

"You never told me that."

"Well, I'm telling you now. After all, we're all Christians no matter what the sign says out in front of the church."

Chantel flushed. She knew that her own priest would never permit her to go to a Protestant church, and she changed the subject abruptly.

They had a good day riding over the plantation. Chantel kept a close eye on Neville, waiting for him to hold her hand or try to kiss her, but he just wanted to know about sugar production and new methods and storage barns. He talked about enlargements to the house, and she was vaguely disappointed.

I told Yves there was nothing to his crazy idea. Neville would never be interested in me. He knew me too well when I was nothing but a child.

That night Chantel tossed and turned restlessly. Slowly an idea began to take shape within her mind. She had always had this sort of imagination, where an idea would come much like a single grain of corn and then begin to grow and swell until finally it was a full-fledged scheme. At first the thought seemed ridiculous, but as she lay there listening to the symphony of frogs, it came together so perfectly that finally she said aloud, "I'll do it!" A mixture of fear and excitement came to her, and she nodded firmly. "Yes, I'll do it!"

The service had evidently already started as Chantel moved up the steps of the small white church with the steeple. She could hear the singing of the people, and for just one moment she took counsel of her fears.

I must be crazy! It will never work—someone is sure to recognize me.

Still, she stood there wearing the black satin dress with the black hat and the veil that covered her face almost down to the chin. The idea of disguising herself and coming to hear Neville preach had seemed wild and fantastical at first, but as she stood there she determined not to listen to her fears. She had no idea what to expect inside the doors. Still, she could not see any wrong in it. Neville's admission that he would be glad to go to her church came to her, and she thought, *If he can come to my church, I can go to his!*

Lifting her head, she stepped forward, and as she moved toward the door, a man wearing a white linen suit nodded pleasantly to her. "Good morning, ma'am. We're glad to have you visiting with us." He hesitated, then said, "I'm sorry about your loss."

Chantel murmured, "Thank you." He opened the door, and she stepped inside. Another man came toward her at once and said, "There's a seat halfway to the front, ma'am. You can hear everything from there."

"Thank you." Chantel followed him down the aisle and sat down. She was aware that people were looking at her, and she kept her head down. Only when she was seated did she look around.

The church was not large, but the ceilings were high. She was fascinated by the stained glass windows that portrayed what she supposed were biblical scenes. The pews were made of some sort of hardwood, polished to a high sheen, and the floors were hard pine glistening clean.

The people who sat in the pews were singing out of books, and she had never heard the song before. A book was lying on the bench, and a man handed it to her and said, "It's page twenty-nine, ma'am."

Turning to the page, she began to follow along. The words struck her in a way she could not explain:

Alas! and did my Savior bleed
And did my Sovereign die
Would He devote that sacred head
For such a worm as I?

Was it for crimes that I have done
He groaned upon the tree?
Amazing pity! grace unknown!
And love beyond degree!

Well might the sun in darkness hide,
And shut his glories in,
When Christ the mighty Maker died
For man, the creature's sin.

But drops of grief can ne'er repay
The debt of love I owe:
Here, Lord, I give myself away
'Tis all that I can do.

The words did something to Chantel. She had never heard a hymn like this, and she began to think of Jesus in a way that she had never thought before.

The congregation sang several more songs, and then an offering was taken. Finally the choir sang a special song, and by this time Chantel was very uncomfortable. She could not explain why. Just being in a church other than her own seemed wrong—and yet there was joy and excitement on the faces of the worshippers.

She was also struck by the informality of the service. Her own service in the Catholic church, of course, was highly formal, choreographed almost with the precision of a minuet. Very rarely was her heart touched in such a service. But here, somehow, the spirit of God was very real.

Finally she saw Neville stand and come to take his place behind the pulpit. He had a Bible in his hand and looked out over the congregation calmly. There was an ease and assurance about him, and he told the congregation that he was glad to be there and worship with them.

Then he said, "I can speak of nothing other this morning than Jesus and His amazing power to take us all to be in heaven with Him. Turn in your Bible to the twenty-third chapter of Luke to the story of the death of our Lord Jesus. We will read from the Scripture beginning with the thirty-ninth verse:

> *And one of the malefactors which were hanged railed on him, saying, If thou be Christ, save thyself and us.*
>
> *But the other answering rebuked him, saying, Dost not thou fear God, seeing thou art in the same condemnation?*
>
> *And we indeed justly; for we receive the due reward of our deeds: but this man hath done nothing amiss.*
>
> *And he said unto Jesus, Lord, remember me when thou comest into thy kingdom.*
>
> *And Jesus said unto him, Verily I say unto thee, To day shalt thou be with me in paradise.*

Chantel had read this story more than once since Neville had shown it to her so long ago. It never failed to move her. She followed the sermon closely, forgetting her fears and her nervousness.

Neville was a fine speaker. She had known that he must be, since lawyers had to plead cases in court, but somehow preaching brought out a new dimension that she had not seen in him before. The last part of his sermon was clear. "I will remark in closing that this poor, dying thief went directly to be with Jesus. There was no intermediate state. Despite what some may believe, there was no purgatory. There was no more suffering for sins, for Jesus had suffered for sins."

Despite Sister Martha's best efforts, Chantel had resisted the idea of her mother and her sister and lately her father going from this life to a place where they would be tormented for an indeterminate time. Now Neville had reassured her again, saying that the instant one died, that moment they were in the arms of the Lord Jesus—all pain gone, no more tears, no more sorrow.

Neville stepped out of the pulpit and held his Bible high, extending his other hand toward the congregation. Chantel found herself trembling as she listened to his words. "What did Jesus mean when he said, 'It is finished'? Why, He meant that He has finished your salvation. Look to Him and be saved. That is all you must do. He is the only salvation. This morning just one look, just one cry, 'Be merciful to me,' and forever your place in heaven is reserved. As we stand and sing, I'm going to ask you to come forward this morning if you want Christ to wash away all your sins and make your place forever reserved in heaven."

The congregation stood, but Chantel found that her legs were weak, so weak they would hardly hold her. She held the book in her hand, but she could not see it, for her eyes were bleared with tears. She saw people going forward, and when they reached the front, they knelt for prayer. Chantel desperately wanted to get away, and the instant the service was dismissed, she went to her buggy, got in, and drove off.

As she left the church behind, her heart was beating fast. She could not understand what had moved her so. She knew one thing—that she did not know Jesus the way that Neville spoke of. And this frightened her so badly she could hardly drive the team.

Chapter nineteen

Chantel had been so disturbed by her visit to the Methodist church that she did not sleep well. The next morning she got up before dawn, put on one of her oldest dresses, and went down early to breakfast. She was surprised to see Neville sitting in the kitchen, eating a biscuit and talking to Clarice.

"Well, good morning," Neville said, turning to her. "You're up early."

"So are you. Why did you get up this early, Neville?"

"Oh, I like to get up before daylight and just get ready for the day. I'll prowl around the house at home. I call it the cobwebby hours of the morning."

"You sit down, and I'll cook you some eggs," Clarice said. "Do you want bacon or ham or sausage?"

Chantel sat down, but she ate little. From time to time she glanced at Neville, who seemed at ease speaking to Clarice about a trip he had made to New York. She listened with interest as she moved about the kitchen doing her work.

As soon as Chantel had finished the meal, she said, "I've got to go over the plantation today. It's time to matalay the cane."

"Matalay? What's that?"

"Come along, and I'll show you."

The two left the big house and went by the slave quarters. Neville knew very little about the actual work on a sugar plantation, and he was interested in every detail. They found Simon, the overseer, getting the workers ready to cut the cane.

Chantel explained, "They're going to lay all this cane out on the ground and cover it with a layer of dirt. It will sprout pretty soon, and we'll get next year's seed cane to grow the new crop."

Next the two moved toward the sugarhouse, a large, open structure consisting mainly of a roof with a huge chimney that was already sending billows of black smoke into the sky. When they moved inside, Neville was interested in the massive rollers powered by a steam engine. As the workers shoved the cane into the rollers, it forced the juice out into vats. These vats were then heated until the water content evaporated. What was left was unrefined sugar.

"We pack this sugar into wooden barrels to be shipped to market."

"It's a noisy place, isn't it?" Neville said, shouting over the roar of the engines.

"Yes, and it's dangerous, too. Someone's always getting hurt from that steam—and broken rollers can injure the men who work on the machines."

As the day wore on, they made several visits to different parts of the field and then would return to see what was going on in the sugarhouse. The noise of the machinery often reached deafening levels, and the operation gave off a sweetish odor that wafted over the entire plantation.

Chantel pointed out the dark patch in the bottom of the vats, left over from the raw brown sugar.

"That's molasses," she said. "You've had it on biscuits, I suppose."

"Yes, but I didn't really know where it came from."

At noon all the workers stopped to eat lunches they had brought in small cloth bags. A water boy went around taking fresh water to them.

While they ate, Chantel and Neville sat under a large oak tree heavily laden with Spanish moss. She didn't talk much, and Neville himself felt under a strain. As he studied her, he tried to sort out his feelings for Chantel. He knew he had a love for her, but what kind of a love? He could remember the first affection he had felt when she was only a child and lonely from the loss of her mother and her sister. Then, as she had grown up, he had helped her with her lessons, still with the affection of a grown man for a child.

But he knew something had changed. Even in her old dress she made a winsome sight as she sat there under the tree, her legs drawn up under her. There was still something childlike about her, an innocence that he found most appealing. But since the night he had kissed her and held her, he no longer thought of her as a child. Now as they sat there, he thought again of Yves Gaspard, and the thought worried him.

He tried to engage Chantel in conversation, and she responded, but he knew she was troubled. Finally he asked her, "What's the matter? You seem a little out of sorts today."

"Oh, nothing."

"Come now, Chantel. I can tell when something's wrong."

Chantel wanted to ask him to tell her more about heaven and what he really felt about his religion. She knew that it was a very personal thing with him, that his whole heart was in it. She longed for such a feeling herself, but did not know how to ask. So she put him off, and the moment passed.

Evening came, and the slaves were down in their quarters. From their rocking chairs on the front porch, Neville and Chantel could hear the sound of their singing. They listened for a while to the mixture of their songs with that of the crickets and the frogs.

"I like it at night like this, sitting here and just listening to the singing," Chantel said. She had bathed and changed clothes, and Neville smelled the fresh cleanness and the slight fragrance of lilacs that she always wore. She was looking out over the grounds, and her profile was turned to him. He admired the clean lines of her jaw and the firm roundness of her neck. Her hair was down, and he knew that she had washed it, for he could also smell the sweet freshness of the soap she had used.

Neville Harcourt was not a man of impulse. He had developed an analytical mind, a necessary piece of equipment for the practice of law. But there was another level to him, as there is to every man, which goes beyond reason and explanation. He had been trying to reason with himself about his feelings for Chantel Fontaine for days now, and had arrived nowhere. The more he tried to approach it as a fine point of law or a mathematical problem that could finally be solved, the more confused he became. Now as he sat beside her,

Neville suddenly realized that he would never be able to figure out his feelings as he could analyze a case before a judge or a jury. He gave up on analysis. Instead, he reached out and touched Chantel's arm. When she turned to him, her eyes were open wide with surprise. He knew that there was only one way. He had to speak what was in his heart.

"Chantel, I want to ask you something."

Chantel knew he had been troubled, for he had said little, and she wanted to help if she could. "What is it, Neville? Is there something I can do?"

"Yes, I think there's something you *must* do."

Chantel put her hand over his as he clasped her forearm. "You've been so kind to me. Anything that I can, you know I would do."

Neville Harcourt felt suddenly like a man on a high perch with a body of water down below, trying to make up his mind whether to dive or not. If he did not dive, he would be safe. If he did launch himself out, there would be no turning back. He might be badly hurt if he did not hit the water right.

Finally he said, "Chantel, I want you to think of me as a man—" He hesitated slightly and then said, "As a man you might marry."

Chantel had not been expecting his request. She stared at him, conscious that her heart was beating faster. Her head swarmed as she thought of all the years that he had been so kind to her, but she knew her answer was going to hurt him. She had more admiration for this man than any she had ever known, except her own father, and now she understood for the first time what it meant to be a young, attractive woman who men would come to.

Finally Chantel moved her arm so that his hand fell away. "Why, Neville," she stammered, "I—I've never thought of you that way. And I'm sure we're more like brother and sister."

"Perhaps so when you were a child, but you're not a child now."

Frantically Chantel tried to think of some way to ease the shock of the blow, and she grasped onto something that had been on the edge of her consciousness.

"I'm not in love with you, Neville, and I don't think you're really in love with me. But even if that were true, we could never marry."

"Why not?"

"Because I'm a Catholic and you're a Protestant. You know better than I how those two would mix."

Neville, of course, had gone over and over this, and he had no ready answer for her. He said quietly, "I know that's a problem, but if two people love each other, they will find a way to make things work."

"Would you become a Catholic?"

"No," Neville had to admit, "I never could."

"Well, I've been a Catholic all my life. You can't expect me to change either. This is too big a gap, Neville." She said gently, "You're such a fine man. You've been my best friend, and you've helped me in so many ways. But there are too many differences, and, really, I don't love you. Not—not in that way, Neville."

A numbness came over Neville, then he felt the pain of rejection. He tried to speak and could not for a time. Finally he turned to her and said, "I'm not taking this as the final answer."

"Oh, but you must, Neville! You really must."

And then out of his pain, Neville felt a sense of something very much like anger. It was not anger exactly, but more like fear, not for himself but for Chantel. He knew he had to speak, and he knew that what he said would not be well received. But he was not a man to shirk his duty.

"I must say this to you, Chantel. Yves Gaspard is not the man for you."

Instantly Chantel stood up. "I wouldn't think you'd do that, Neville—attack a man when he's not here."

"I would say exactly the same thing if he were standing right beside you." Neville stood up and caught her by the shoulder. "You don't really love him. I know you don't."

"You don't know anything of the sort. Let me go!" Chantel turned and left the porch, walking almost blindly. Tears had come to her eyes, for she knew that she had lost something this night. *Why did he have to say such a thing? Now we can never truly be friends again.*

A hundred thoughts raced through her mind, and she ran to her room and threw herself across the bed.

Back on the porch Neville simply stood, bitterness and hurt contending within him.

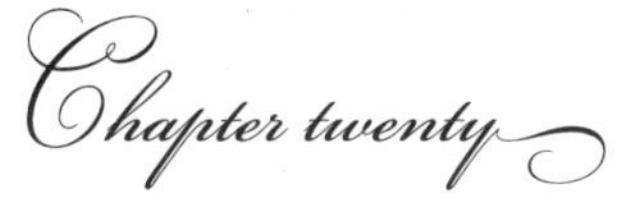

Chapter twenty

Chantel listened and took in the paintings arranged on the wall of the large room. She had come to the exhibition at Yves's invitation.

"You must come!" he had urged her as soon as she returned to New Orleans. "I may even sell some paintings, and it doesn't hurt to have an attractive woman standing there looking at them. It'll draw men as honey draws flies."

Chantel had been glad for the distraction. She had been ill at ease ever since Neville had asked her to marry him. He left early the next morning, and for two weeks she had gone about the work of the plantation, trying to bury herself in the activities of restoring the house. But work had not been able to accomplish very much. She could not help going over the scene again and again in her mind. She was naturally tenderhearted and knew that she had given him a severe blow, but there was nothing she could do about it.

She returned to New Orleans to the town house, and at once Yves had welcomed her back and drawn her into the busy world of life in the city. Now she stood at the exhibit listening to him talk about his paintings. Yves wore a colorful costume, which he was able to carry off. He had cream-colored trousers, glistening black boots, and a white shirt with an emerald green neckerchief knotted around his neck. His dark hair glistened and his white teeth flashed as he spoke.

"This fellow here, his name is Martin. He is not a good painter, but he is a good salesman. I wish that I were."

"I'm sure you'll be able to sell some paintings. They're so good. Especially those of the bayou at Fontaine."

Yves nodded. "I hope you're right. I would like—" Yves did not finish what he was going to say, and the expression that crossed his face caused Chantel to turn to see what had attracted his attention. She saw a petite but well-shaped woman in a striking blue dress that fitted her form admirably. She was smiling as she approached.

"Dominique," said Yves, "I'm surprised to see you."

"It's good to see you, Yves."

"May I present Mademoiselle Chantel Fontaine? Chantel, this is Madame Dominique Sagan."

"I'm glad to meet you," Chantel said, nodding. The woman was striking. There was a boldness about her looks, and she exuded an aura of sensuality that even an inexperienced young woman like Chantel could feel.

"I came looking for you," Dominique said.

"I hope you will buy all my paintings," Yves replied, his eyes fixed on the woman. Suddenly he was aware that Chantel was studying him carefully. "Dominique and I are very old friends," he said.

"Yes, we are. Before I was married, we were very close friends indeed."

The words were innocent enough, but something in the woman's tone caught at Chantel. She listened as the two spoke, and knew she was being left out of the conversation. Then Yves was interrupted by a man who came up and said, "Gaspard, I'd like to talk about buying one of your paintings."

"Certainement!" Yves said instantly. As he turned to follow the man, he said, "I'll be back as soon as I gouge this fellow for all he's worth."

As soon as Yves was gone, Dominique Sagan turned her attention on the younger woman. "You have known Yves for a long time?"

"No, not very long." For some reason Chantel did not want to speak of Yves with this woman.

"Poor Yves, he will never be successful."

"Why do you say that?" Chantel said, hurt by the remark.

"Oh, Yves has talent—but he lacks determination. I'm sure you've noticed it if you've known him for long."

Until that moment Chantel had never admitted this, nor would she allow herself to think of it. But suddenly she recognized that Yves was not a hard worker. He talked about painting a great deal. Indeed, nothing pleased him more than talking about it, but day after day had passed without his touching his brushes at all. He worked spasmodically, sometimes for almost a whole day without stopping. Then he would leave his work and not go back for many days.

"But if he has talent—"

"Ah, my dear Miss Fontaine, talent is very common. It is determination and tenacity that matter."

Chantel suddenly remembered that Yves himself had said something like this to her. But now she was on the defensive. "But if he had a chance, don't you think he could succeed?"

"Perhaps with enough hard work he could, but who is to support him while he's learning to apply himself?"

Chantel did not answer, and suddenly the woman smiled and said almost gently, "You don't know about us? About Yves and me."

Chantel did not want to hear what Dominique Sagan was about to say.

"We were very much in love once. He was younger, and I helped him. I had very little money, but I worked so that he could paint." Dominique saw the question that formed itself on Chantel's lips but refused to be spoken. She answered it almost off-handedly. "Yes, we were lovers."

Chantel had never met a woman who would confess such a thing so lightly. She tried to think of some response but nothing would come.

"Why didn't you marry?" she finally asked.

"Because we had nothing. And besides that, his family didn't approve. They wanted him to marry a woman from a wealthy family."

Chantel could not think clearly. She looked across the room to where Yves was talking to his prospective buyer and thought how happy she had been in his presence. She had suspected he had known other women, but now the proof of it was right before her.

"Why are you telling me this?" she said, giving Dominique a direct look.

"Because I think it is always best to know the truth. I knew the truth about Yves. I know it now, but I think you do not."

"I don't want to hear any more of this!"

"I'm sorry if I've offended you. I meant well."

"Do you want to marry him now? You're obviously very prosperous."

"After we separated," Dominique said, "I married a much older man. For his money, of course."

Once again Chantel was shocked. She knew that such matches were made, but she had never heard anyone confess to it.

"My dear, you're young and very romantic. Be careful."

Dominique turned and left, leaving Chantel in shock and dismay. She stood there, wondering if she should leave, but as she struggled, Yves suddenly returned.

"Well, he bought the painting. We'll have to go out and celebrate." He broke off suddenly, saying, "What's the matter?"

"Oh, nothing."

But Yves knew at once what had happened. "I suppose Dominique told you about us."

"Yes, she did."

"I wanted to marry her, but I had no money."

"Was it you who broke off the affair?"

"I think both of us knew that we could never marry." He hesitated, then shook his head. "I cared very much for her once, but, as I say, it was a long time ago."

For Chantel the charm of the day was gone. "I must go home now," she said.

"What about our celebration?"

"I'm not feeling much like celebrating, Yves."

He reached out and took her hands and held them for a moment. "I know this is hard for you, Chantel," he said gently. "You've led a sheltered life, and I've had a hard one. Part of it I could not help. A man cannot help being born poor. Some of it I'm not proud of, but men can change. And you have become very precious to me."

Chantel would have welcomed those words an hour earlier, but now she could not help but think of Dominique Sagan. A jealousy that she had not known before lay in her, and now it began to manifest itself. "Do you still love her, Yves?"

"When two people really love each other, I don't think you ever lose all of it," he said carefully. "But she is married now, and that's the end of it." He watched her face and saw that the light had gone out of it. "I'm sorry that you're hurt."

Chantel met his eyes. "I would rather not go out tonight. Some other time."

Yves had been losing steadily for the past hour. He had lost all the money he had gained from the sale of his painting and had signed a note for two hundred dollars.

A voice said, "Could I speak to you privately, Monsieur Gaspard?"

He looked up and found Neville Harcourt standing beside the card table. Ordinarily Yves would have complied with Harcourt's request, but now he had a good hand and was anxious to try to recoup his losses. He knew Neville did not like him, and he felt little affection for the lawyer.

"This is good enough. Say what you have to say."

"It's a private matter."

Yves studied his hand and tried to concentrate, but Neville pressed him. "It's rather important."

"I know what it is. You're jealous of Chantel."

Neville suddenly straightened up. "If you were a gentleman, you wouldn't mention her name in a place like this."

"Go away, little man! You have lost. Chantel cares for me, not you."

"You're a scoundrel, Gaspard, and a liar!"

Yves Gaspard had a temper that was a fiery, deadly thing—though he had been careful to keep it hidden from Chantel. He threw the cards down and turned with his face flaming. "No man calls me a liar!" He suddenly reached out and slapped Neville's face. It was not a hard slap, but it left the print of his fingers there. "There. That gives you the right to choose the weapons for our meeting."

The room had grown quiet, every man at the table staring at Neville, awaiting his reply. No self-respecting man would take a slap from another man, not in Creole society. The dueling code was strict, and according to every man's thinking Neville had but one choice.

Neville shook his head. "I don't believe in this stupid dueling business. I've delegated all fighting to my dogs. Stay away from the lady! You hear me?"

He turned and walked out, and Yves suddenly laughed. "He's a coward. I wouldn't dirty my hands on him." He sat down at the cards and won the hand, and within an hour had gained back his losses and won some extra besides. He thought, *When Chantel hears of this, she won't think so much of him.*

The next day Yves found out exactly how tough Chantel could be. He went to her and told her of his encounter with Neville, embellishing the affair and ridiculing Neville for being a coward.

Chantel listened without saying a word. Her first feeling was that she was embarrassed for Neville, for she was well aware that among men duels were the common way of settling matters, but she said nothing of that. Instead she looked at Yves and asked quietly, "Did you use my name in that place?"

"Why—only after he gave me provocation."

"What provocation could cause you to bring up my name among men like that?"

Yves saw that he had made a tactical error and at once came to take her hand. "You are right. I should not have done that. I am very sorry, Chantel."

"I'm disappointed in you, Yves. I thought better of you."

Yves began to elaborate on his apology, but she said firmly, "I'll have to ask you to leave."

Yves wanted to press his case, but he suddenly found that this soft, gentle woman had some steel in her. He saw in her eyes that further apologies were useless, and he bowed slightly. "I'll come back. You will forgive me. You're too generous to do otherwise."

Chantel said, "Good day, Yves." She waited until he was gone, and then the shock of it hit her. She was disappointed in Neville but more so in Yves. She had no desire to see either of them, yet staying at home seemed intolerable. She needed to get out where she could think.

She put on her cloak and hat and walked toward the plaza. As usual it was filled with merrymakers and visitors from outside the city. She stopped and watched a juggler and put a coin in his hat. Another man had a trained dog that could do marvelous things. It took her mind off of Yves and Neville's encounter for a moment, and she gave another coin and patted the dog, which licked her hand gratefully.

For over an hour she wandered, occupying herself with watching those who strolled by. New Orleans was the most cosmopolitan city in the United States. One could see almost any nationality if he sat long enough, and she forced herself to take note.

She turned to go home when suddenly a huge crowd seemed to appear out of nowhere. It was a wedding party, and the parade gave evidence of a wealthy family. Chantel stood well back from the curb, peering around people who lined the street. As the procession passed, the crowd of onlookers shifted, and through an opening in the crowd she saw something that caused her to freeze. Across the way stood a Cajun family, obviously from the country, judging by their rough dress. Although the father and mother were dark and stocky, the girl with them had strawberry blonde hair and violet eyes!

She appeared to be no more than nine or ten. She wore no hat and just a simple dress, but when she turned to face the street, Chantel had a clear look at her. And the sight ran through her like a jolt of electricity. The girl was the image of her dead mother.

Chantel had imagined her sister as a growing child thousands of times, refusing deep in her heart to believe that Veronique was dead. Now here was a child with the impossible violet eyes and the exact strawberry blonde hair and the same bone structure as her own mother!

It must be Veronique, by some miracle of God!

At once Chantel tried to cross the street, but at that moment the crowd surged to make way for another parade. The people cheered as the street filled with a marching band.

Chantel struggled, saying, "Please let me through!" A woman pushed her back, saying, "You can't have my place. Stay where you are."

Chantel moved to her right, but the crowd was dense, and she could not make her way through. Finally she reached the street and tried to get through the parade, but she was nearly run down by a horse. A tall man grasped her and yanked her out of the way. "Are you crazy, woman?" he demanded. "You're going to get killed!"

"Let me go!"

"You'll have to wait until the parade's over."

"Let go of my arm!" Chantel cried. When he released her with a look of disgust, she ran back down the street until she found a gap. She walked rapidly in front of the crowd, searching for the trio.

But there was no sight of them. In desperation she walked back and forth, pushing her way, but it was hopeless.

The parade passed and the crowd dissolved, more or less. Chantel continued to search for the small figure that had imprinted itself upon her mind. *Veronique. It has to be you! It has to be!*

Finally, however, she saw that it was hopeless. She turned slowly homeward, but a new resolve had birthed itself in her.

I know that was Veronique. She didn't die in the flood. She was found by these people, and now I must find her.

She was filled with hope and at the same time despair, for she had no idea where to look. She uttered a prayer, without realizing she was speaking aloud, and people turned to stare at her.

"Oh, God," she cried, "let me find my sister!"

Chapter twenty-one

Chantel slept very little the night after she saw the young girl on the streets of New Orleans. She tossed and turned and finally got up. She put on her robe and went to the balcony, where she stood looking out over the now-empty streets. The sounds of the city were still there, but she could only think of the child with the violet eyes.

It has to be Veronique! No one else could have violet eyes and hair like that and look so much like Mama!

For a long time she stood on the balcony, and finally she knew that, whatever else she did with her life, she would have to find her sister. For many years she had felt a sense of loneliness, and since her father had died this had grown even worse. Her heart cried out for a family, and there was none but Perrin, whom she felt quite sure would never be close. But now there was hope.

From somewhere far away came the sound of music—the faint, thin, reedy sound of a piano. She did not know the tune, but it was a haunting melody that she could barely hear. Finally it faded away, and still Chantel stood there. She found herself tensing her muscles, yearning to do something. What she wanted was action, but what action could she take?

In the silence Chantel bowed her head and began to pray. "Oh, God, I can't pray as I should. I don't know You as I want to, but I ask You to help me find this girl. If it is my sister, we need each other. Help me, for I am desperate, O God!"

The Mass brought Chantel little sense of peace. She had been praying with all of her heart, but it seemed that the heavens were made of steel and that her prayers could not go through.

Now as the Mass droned on, Chantel was aware of it in a very mechanical way. But her heart was still crying out. Finally the priest stood up and gave the homily.

Usually this was a very dry, brief sermonette of sorts, in which the congregation were enjoined to do good deeds. But Chantel turned her attention to the priest, Father Mohr. He was a tall, thin man with ascetic features and a dry voice that seemed to rustle as he spoke. He emphasized nothing really, and his homilies usually had a soporific effect on his hearers. But Chantel was desperate for wisdom or guidance of some kind, and she listened as the priest read a Scripture from the book of Genesis. It was rather confusing to Chantel, for she was not familiar with this story.

"This Scripture speaks of Abraham, the man of God, who had grown old. He wanted a bride for his son, but the land in which he lived was filled with idolatry. So he called his servant and sent him back to his own home country to find his son a bride among his own people.

"The servant went back, but when he reached his destination, he was in a quandary. How could he find exactly the right girl to be a bride for the son of his master, Abraham? He did a very peculiar thing, and one that I would not ordinarily recommend. He devised a circumstance and asked God to work in the middle of it. First, he took his camels to a well one evening where the women came to draw water. Then he began to pray. Let me read it for you from the book of Genesis:

And let it come to pass, that the damsel to whom I shall say, Let down thy pitcher, I pray thee, that I may drink; and she shall say, Drink, and I will give thy camels drink also: let the same be she that thou hast appointed for thy servant Isaac; and thereby shall I know that thou hast shewed kindness unto my master.

Chantel had never heard of anything like this, and she listened as the priest said, "Many times we want to find the will of God, and we cannot. Here this servant of Abraham made a very dangerous experiment. He set up a condition for God. My children, I would not advise you to try this. It is true that in this instance once it proved to be the right thing to do, for the young woman did come, and she said exactly the words that Abraham's servant had requested. And so the servant found the will of God, but in a most unusual way. But I warn you that though God did answer the prayer of Abraham's servant, He did so to fulfill His redemptive plan. This is not an instruction for believers today; we should not try to force God to work in our lives in this way." Chantel thought hard on this. When she got home, she found her Bible. Not knowing where the story was, she had to read almost the entire book of Genesis before she found it.

Chantel read the story several times, then, feeling rather foolish, she got down on her knees, folded her hands, and put her forehead against them.

"God, I need someone to help me find my sister. And I pray that you will send someone." She hesitated, then said, "I hope you won't be angry with me, O God, but you did this once for one man. I ask you, let the next person who comes to me and says, 'I will help you' be the person to help me find Veronique."

This was a different kind of praying for her. Always before she had prayed "Our Father" or "Hail Mary" or the traditional written prayers. She was shocked to discover how difficult it was to speak directly to God. It gave her an odd sense of the vastness of God and the smallness of her own being.

After she had prayed the prayer she felt even more foolish. She got to her feet, looked around the room uncertainly, then shook her head. "It can't be," she said aloud. "I will have to do it for myself."

Four days passed, and every day Chantel did little but think of Veronique. She dressed each morning and searched the French Quarter, where she walked the streets hopeful of catching another glimpse of the girl she believed to be her sister. She also thought about the prayer she had prayed. At times she felt it was the most foolish thing she had ever done. She even scolded herself, saying, "You can't back God into a corner and force Him to do something. He's God and you're nothing."

Still, the thoughts would not leave her mind, and she found herself praying every day, "Lord, send someone, and let him say 'I will help you.'"

As the days went by, she kept expecting a stranger to come up and say the words to her, but nothing happened.

Finally, on Friday evening, Chantel was sitting in the parlor. Her heart was heavy. She tried to pray, but there was no answer.

A sound came to her, and she turned as the door opened. "It's Mr. Neville," Elise said. "Do you want to see him?"

"Yes. Show him in, Elise."

Chantel rose, and as Neville entered the room, she searched his face nervously for signs of anger. She saw none, however, for he smiled and came over to her at once.

He put his hand out, and before she could speak, he said, "I know I've troubled you with my offer, Chantel. But I came to say that I want to be your friend. If that's all I can be, I'll be satisfied." He lifted her hand and kissed it. "I want you to be happy. That's my fondest hope." He hesitated, then said, "I will help you with anything I can."

Suddenly Chantel's eyes filled with tears. He had said the very words! *I will help you.* She held onto his hand and whispered, "Oh, Neville, I'm so glad you've come. Come and sit down. I have something to tell you!"

PART FOUR

· 1831 ·

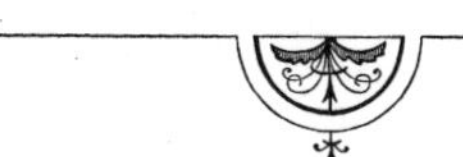

Veronique

As Chantel looked at him with pleading in her eyes, Neville felt a great pity for her begin to form in his spirit. Her eyes were wide, and there was a tremulous quality in her lips that spoke of the turmoil taking place in her soul. She whispered, "I'm so glad I've got you to talk to, Neville. There's nobody else."

Reaching out, Neville took her hands in his and felt the unsteadiness of them. "Don't be disturbed, *mon chère.* Come and sit down. You must tell me everything." Leading her to the couch placed against the wall, he pulled her down beside him. She did not try to free her hand. "Now, tell me all. We have plenty of time."

Words tumbled from Chantel's lips, and Neville listened intently. She spoke first of the time when her mother and sister were lost in the flood. He could tell that that day was still as clear as crystal in her mind, for she gave precise details. She even recalled that the dress she had been wearing was blue.

"But I never believed them when they said that Veronique was dead, Neville—never!"

"I suppose that's natural enough, since her body was never found."

"It was more than that—although, of course, that had something to do with it. Something in me would not admit that I had lost my sister. Everyone tried to tell me otherwise, my father the most of all.

He didn't want me to have false hopes. But I knew deep in my heart that she was alive."

Neville listened as she spoke of her grief and her loneliness. She had a fear of being alone that was almost pathological. Finally she told him about her experience in the Quarter where she saw the young girl.

"There couldn't be two girls of that age with strawberry blonde hair and violet eyes. Neville, I've never seen anybody else with violet eyes. Have you?"

"No, not that I can think of. And she looked to be the right age?"

"It's hard to say with young girls, but I know it's Veronique. But I couldn't reach her. You know how the streets are when the parades take place. I tried to push my way through, but people grew angry and wouldn't open a way. By the time I was able to pass through the middle of the parade, they were gone."

"What sort of people did they appear to be?"

"Very rural people. Veronique was wearing a plain dress with rough-looking shoes. And the man and the woman that were with her—oh, Neville, they couldn't have been her parents. She was so fair and her hair so light, and they were very dark."

"Olive complexion?"

"Yes. Their hair was black and their eyes were dark. I remember once my mother told me that dark eyes always predominate."

"That's usually true," Neville admitted. "If the father and mother are both dark, the chances of a child having light hair or violet eyes are very slim."

"And the child had very fine features, Neville, so like my mother! These people have rounded features, both of them. Their faces were wide, and they were thick-bodied and short. This girl's figure was like mine when I was that age—tall and very thin."

Neville felt Chantel's hands squeeze his own, and he returned the pressure.

"Neville, I don't know much about the Lord. Not like you do."

Neville blinked with surprised, for it was the first admission that Chantel had ever made that there was something missing in her own spiritual life. He remained silent as her words poured out.

"I know that God is almighty, and He does great things. And I know the story of Abraham's servant who went to find a bride for his son, Isaac. If God could bring that young woman to that well at the exact time that the servant arrived, He could bring my sister to New Orleans at the exact time that I would be there. Couldn't He, Neville?"

"Of course He could. Anything is possible with God."

"Do you believe what I'm telling you, or do you think I've lost my mind? I know that's what everyone else would say."

Neville hesitated. He did not want to raise false hopes, and yet when he saw the hope and fierce desire in Chantel's eyes, he knew he had to encourage her. "Of course it's possible, and we must find out. And I will help you."

"Oh, Neville, thank you!" Chantel threw her arms around Neville's neck and clung to him, and he held her for a brief moment.

"Now then," he said. "We must see what is to be done."

"What can we do? How can we possibly find her?"

"Well, there is one thing that we must do, and that is ask God to help us. Without His help, I do not think it will be possible. We don't know the names of these people. We don't know where they're from. We know nothing about them."

"Yes, let's pray together. I know God will hear your prayer."

"He'll hear *our* prayer. Scripture says that if any two of you will agree on anything, it will be done."

"The Bible says that?"

"Yes, it does. So, I want us to pray right now that God will help us in our search." He saw Chantel bow her head; then he bowed his own and prayed aloud, "Father, we are helpless in this matter. There is no way humanly speaking that we can find the one we seek. But, Lord, You know everything. You know the exact location of every human being on the face of the earth. You know the secret thoughts of each one of us. We're not asking anything impossible, for with You, O Lord, nothing is impossible. I pray in the name of Jesus that You will open the door that will help us to find this young woman. Amen."

"Amen," Chantel whispered. When she looked up, her eyes were brimming with tears. She could not speak for a moment. She brushed them away, then fumbled for a handkerchief. Finally she turned her face toward Neville and asked, "What will you do now?"

"I'll have to become a private detective. In fact, I may have to *hire* one. I must go now." He rose to his feet, and Chantel went with him to the door.

"Good-bye, dear Neville. God go with you."

Neville touched her hand, then turned and left. As he walked toward his horse, his mind was swiftly organizing all the facts. For a moment he was daunted, for he knew how slim the chances were of finding anyone as obscure as the people Chantel had described. But he straightened his shoulders and said under his breath, "Lord, it's up to You now!"

Collette sat still, her eyes fixed on Chantel's face, listening with growing astonishment to the story her stepdaughter had to tell. She said nothing until Chantel said, ". . . and, Mama, Neville is going to help me. He may even hire a private detective to help find those people."

"Chantel, I wish you hadn't gone to strangers with a story like this." Collette's voice was sharp. "Do you realize what you've done? If he goes out and hires a private detective, the word will get out that we're looking for a girl who died ten years ago."

"But, Mama—"

"I know what you're going to say. You've never accepted Veronique's death, and I always thought it was bad for you. I think it's tragic that her body wasn't recovered. If it had been, this would never have happened. You see, my dear, that's one value of a funeral. When you see a body lying in state in a coffin, and you see that coffin put into a grave or mausoleum, there's a finality about it, and your mind can accept it. But when someone simply disappears, it's very difficult to really believe that they're lost. I don't think what's happened to you is at all unusual."

"But, Mama, weren't you listening to me? Her face was *exactly* like my mama's face, and she was built exactly like me. And she looked nothing at all like those people she was with."

"You're not thinking clearly, Chantel. I realize those circumstances are unusual, but they're not unheard of. Children don't always resemble their parents. My own father was only five-feet-eight-inches tall, but my youngest brother was six-feet-two, and he looked nothing at all like any of us. He did, however, look like my great-grandfather, who was the same height. Perhaps this young girl resembles someone back in her family. A grandmother, or an aunt."

Collette's words had a chilling effect on Chantel, but only for a moment. She shook her head, and pressed her lips together. "I know she's my sister."

"I know you want to think that, but think also of this. If she were your sister, and we found her, what problems would come of it!"

"Problems? What do you mean? How could it be a problem to find her?"

"She's ten years old. She's been raised by a poor, ignorant family. She knows nothing else. I doubt that she can read or write. My dear, even if you could find this child, you would be doing her no favor to try to bring her into your life. Can't you see that?"

"No, I can't, Mama. We could give her a good life."

"You are mistaken, Chantel. Her character is formed by this time. She would never be able to adjust to such a different way. And besides this very real problem, have you considered that you would have to share your inheritance with her? Do you realize that? And Perrin would be the loser."

At that moment Chantel realized why her stepmother did not want this girl to be found. The truth brought such pain that she could not speak for a moment. She did realize, however, that further talk with Collette was useless.

She simply said, "I'm sorry you feel that way, Mama, but I must do this." She got up and left, and as she closed the door to the study it felt as though she was closing the door on something more than just a room.

As Chantel spoke to Yves she was very calm, for after her interview with her stepmother two days ago, she had forced herself to think clearly. She had spoken with Neville only once since then, and that very briefly. He had simply come by to say that he had engaged a firm to help him in his search.

"They are not very hopeful," he had said. "But you and I know that there's more to this than they realize. God is on our side."

The words burned into Chantel and gave her hope. She spent a great deal of time praying, sometimes in her room actually on her knees. But whether she was eating or working or going about her business in a usual way, the thought of her sister was never out of her mind, and she prayed quick, silent prayers. It amazed her that she could pray at all. She found herself calling out to God as if He were in the same room with her—which she knew Neville would insist was really the case.

When she told Yves her tale, he ran his hand through his thick hair and shook his head. "I never heard of such a thing, Chantel!"

"You don't believe me then."

"No—no, I didn't say that! There are stranger things in this world," Yves protested quickly. "I am just surprised, as I'm sure you were."

"Indeed. But as I said, I have never believed that my sister was dead."

"And so what is to be done?"

"Neville has promised to help. He has hired some private detectives."

"And I will help also, Chantel. I don't know how to go about it, but I will go look for your sister."

"That's so sweet of you, Yves. I doubt if you will find her by walking the streets. Neville said we must find the family."

"Well, perhaps the detectives will be able to do that." For a moment Yves seemed at a loss for words, then he said, "I have been thinking of the thing that happened between your friend and myself."

Chantel looked up quickly, searching Yves's face, and she saw that he was embarrassed. "And what do you think, Yves?"

"I think I made a fool of myself," he admitted. "He was right to rebuke me for using your name in that place. I have felt so badly about it, Chantel, and I hope you will forgive me."

"Of course I do."

"That's like you," Yves said. He shook his head and said, "I've been ashamed of that, and I will ask his pardon when I see him. In public if he desires."

"He won't ask that."

Yves gave her a careful look. "You're very sure of that, aren't you?"

"I know him very well, I think."

"It's a good thing to know people a long time like that. I've moved around so much I haven't had time to make that kind of relationship."

A thought came to Chantel, and she said, "What about the woman I met—Dominique?"

Yves blinked with surprise. "She was something out of my past. That day in the gallery was the first time I'd seen her for a very long time."

"You haven't seen her since?"

"No. Her husband is old, as I think I told you, and very ill. I understand he requires constant care."

"You haven't forgotten her, have you, Yves? I can hear echoes walking around in your voice when you speak of her."

"It's too late for that," Yves said. Then he shrugged his shoulders. "Just tell me what you want me to do, and I will do it. I know many people in the Quarter. I have friends among the Cajuns. I will go ask them. They will remember such a striking girl."

"That would be good of you, Yves." Chantel gave him her hand as she rose.

He bent over, kissed it, and shook his head. "Strange thing—a very strange thing indeed."

Neville looked up as Robert Martin entered his office. He got to his feet, an eager light in his eyes. "Have you found out something, Martin?"

"I'm not sure."

Martin was a small, nondescript individual. He dressed neatly enough, but his clothes were not stylish. He could have passed for a bank clerk, a tailor, a salesman—practically anything—and one would never notice him in a crowd. Everything about him seemed neutral—his eyes, his hair, and his features were all without any striking difference from hundreds or even thousands of others. Once Martin had told Neville that this was a great advantage in his profession, for he was able to move about without attracting any attention.

"I know you're anxious, so I came at once."

"And what have you found?"

"A lead that will probably come to nothing." Martin shrugged his thin shoulders. "But it's all we have at the time. To make a long story short, I've found a man in prison who says he has seen the girl. He's a Cajun and has traveled a great deal. He wants money for telling you where she is."

"Well, did you give it to him?"

"Why, no, sir! Not without your permission."

"Well, give it to him."

"It may be expensive. He wants a hundred pounds."

"Offer him less, but pay it if he won't come through."

"All right. I'll—"

"No, wait. I'll come with you. Let me get the cash."

"Well, Lord help you, sir! You can't give that kind of money to a criminal for what may be nothing."

Neville ignored the detective's words. "Let me go alone. He may talk more freely to me."

"I expect that's right. He's suspicious of any police. But I warn you. You may be throwing your money away."

"I'll worry about that. You've done well, Martin."

Lamont was a tall, lean man with a sallow face and suspicious-looking dark eyes. "Yes, I have seen this girl three times."

"Where did you see her?"

"Ah, if I tell you that, then you will have no need to give me money, will you, sir?"

"Tell me again what she looks like."

"She is very thin and has very odd-color hair like I never see before. It is red but not red. More blonde. But her eyes! I never forget those eyes. Strange. Not blue but like a little violet out in the bayou. You see such a flower?"

"Yes." A thrill ran through Neville, for the description was exactly what he had hoped for. "All right. I'll give you fifty pounds."

"No, I need one hundred pounds. I will take no less."

Neville studied the eyes of the prisoner and saw an insolence there. He knew he had no other choice. "All right. One hundred pounds."

"I know you brought it with you. You are very anxious."

Neville pulled the money from his pocket. It was in an envelope, and he handed it over. "There it is. Count it." He waited until the man had done so, then said, "Now, where did you see the girl?"

"Do you know the country west of Baton Rouge?"

"Not very well."

"It is not a good country, some of it, but there is a man who lives there named Simon Tubberville. I was in business with him once, and we see each other from time to time. I meet his wife one time, and I see this girl. He brought them to Baton Rouge. He would not let me come to his house. He did not want me there because he did not trust me. Imagine that! Not trusting poor old Lamont!"

I wouldn't trust him with a dollar, Neville thought, somewhat ironically. "Where does he live?"

"That I cannot say. He lives in the Bayou Teche, and I tell you that is one bad place."

"You don't know how to get to their house?"

"No. I tell you about the girl. I swear it on my mother's grave, and I know Simon Tubberville is her father. But that is all I know."

"Well, tell me about that country."

"Very bad people live there. Simon Tubberville is not a good man, just as I'm not a good man. You are a good man. I can tell that."

"Never mind all that. Tell me about the bayou."

Neville listened as Lamont told of the size of the bayou and its lack of trails. And those trails that did lead through it often were underwater.

"You only go deep into the bayou in a boat, but some have gone in who never came out, if you get my meaning. People there are very close. They do not like outsiders."

"All right. I'll find him." Neville stopped and said, "I am sorry for your predicament. I know God could help you."

Lamont stared at him. "No, God gave up on me a long time ago. Good-bye now."

When the door to the town house opened, Neville stepped in and found Yves there with Chantel. It was the first time the two had met since their difficulties, and Yves came forward at once.

"I must ask your pardon. I was totally wrong in that affair we had, and I apologize. If you will go with me to the men that heard it, I will apologize before them."

"That's not necessary," Neville said quickly.

Yves laughed. "Chantel said that is what you would say."

Chantel was glad that the two men had come to this point, but she was anxious. "What have you found out, Neville?"

She drew him into the parlor, where he took a cup of hot chocolate. As he sipped it, he told them what he had discovered.

Chantel was excited, but Yves frowned.

"That's bad country. That criminal told you exactly right. Men have gone into Bayou Teche and never come out again. They are a bunch of cutthroats and robbers."

"Nevertheless, I'm going there."

Yves said at once, "Then I will go with you. I know many people in the Baton Rouge area, even some on the outer edges of Bayou Teche."

"All right, we'll go together," agreed Neville. "Chantel, we'll get word to you as soon as—"

"I'm going with you. No one would know Veronique except me."

Both men tried to dissuade Chantel, but she kept the argument short. "She's my sister, and I'm going with you. That's all there is to it."

"Stubborn as a bulldog." Yves laughed. "All right. When do we leave?"

"First thing in the morning," Neville said. "We'll pick you up before dawn, Chantel."

After the two men left, Chantel was too excited to sleep. She walked the floor, and finally in a gesture of exultation, she lifted her hands above her head and cried, "Thank you, God! Thank you, God! Thank you, God!"

Elise came in. "Did you call for me?"

"No." Chantel smiled sweetly. "I wasn't talking to you."

Chapter twenty-three

Elise protested against Chantel's making the trip with two gentlemen, but she gave up when sharply rebuked. Chantel would not be stopped.

She was dressed and her bag packed when Neville arrived very early in the morning. She had slept little, and when she settled down beside Neville in the carriage, she said, "What about Yves?"

"We'll pick him up, and then we'll be on our way. Have you had breakfast?"

"No, but I'm not hungry."

"We need to eat. It's going to be a hard trip."

Yves was waiting, holding a bag. He climbed into the backseat of the carriage, and Neville drove to a small restaurant that he knew opened very early. When they had finished a quick breakfast, none of them saying a great deal, Yves said, "I hope your horses are good."

"I think you'll find them adequate," Neville said with a slight grin. He was proud of his horses, for they were indeed a prize—a matched set of bays. They were just the right team for such a quick day's journey. "It's fifty miles to Baton Rouge, more or less, and the roads aren't good. But I think these two can do it."

"What are their names?" Chantel asked curiously.

"Castor and Pollux."

"What strange names. What do they mean?"

"Do you know anything about the constellations of the stars?"

"No, almost nothing."

"Well, if it's clear tonight, I'll show you a constellation called the Twins. It's two figures that seem to be holding hands, and the heads of each are almost the brightest stars in the sky some nights. One's called Castor and one's called Pollux. Mariners use them a lot in their navigation."

"We'll have to navigate to Baton Rouge if the roads are bad, and we're bound to be axle-deep in mud with all this rain," Yves said.

His words were fulfilled, for the roads were terrible. Heavy rains had fallen, and they passed by more than one heavy-loaded wagon mired down in the mud. But Castor and Pollux more than justified Neville's boast. They were not the fastest animals, but they were strong and capable of a full day's journey, even under such poor conditions.

At noon they stopped and had a quick meal at an inn, then after an hour's rest for the team, they continued. The rain started to fall when they were an hour out of Baton Rouge, and by the time they pulled into the port city, Chantel was tired, wet, and miserable.

Yves had been watching her closely and said, "We'll stay here tonight. Get a good room, a good meal, and a good night's sleep. Tomorrow we'll go on to Bayou Teche and see what we can do."

The Majestic Hotel was somewhat less than its name implied, but the room Chantel had was very nice. She was able to have a hot bath and afterwards came down to find Neville waiting for her. He was alone and said quickly, "Yves went to see a fellow he knows who may be of some help in our search."

"I'm starving," Chantel said.

"I can't vouch for the food here, but we'll hope for the best."

The meal was good. They had crawfish *étouffée* and filet of snapper and cups of gumbo. When they were finished with the meal, they rose.

Chantel said, "I don't think I can sleep, although I'm very tired."

"Let's sit out on the porch for a while. You'll get sleepy soon."

It was strangely warm for October. They found chairs out on the wide porch and were all alone. The lights of Baton Rouge were faint and dim, for it was a small place compared with New Orleans.

They sat there for a time, and finally Chantel said, "Neville, will you tell me something?"

"If I can."

"Tell me how you came to know God so well."

"Well, it's not a very dramatic story, I'm afraid. I know some men who tell about their conversion, and it's almost terrible how they ran from God, and God had to practically destroy them before they would bow their heads to him."

"How old were you when you found God?"

"I was sixteen."

Chantel smiled. "I'll bet you were one of those very good boys. One that the other boys hated because their mothers would say, 'Why can't you be good like Neville?'"

"Oh, I wasn't all that good," Neville laughed. Chantel's mind amused him. She had an active imagination, and he had thought more than once she would be a great writer if she would put her hand to it. "I had a few youthful sins."

"Tell me about them!"

"No, I certainly will not."

"Pooh, I want to hear!"

"All right. You tell me about your youthful sins."

Chantel laughed, a good sound in the night air. She pulled her coat closer around her and said, "All right. We'll tell those only to God."

"That's a good idea. Actually I didn't get into some of the gross sins that other young men my age got into, and I don't know why. I never had a mother, but I always thought of her in heaven. And since I never seemed to please my father, I wanted desperately to please the Lord. I think I stayed out of trouble in the hope that I could someday see my mother in eternity."

"That's practically what happened to me! After Mama died, I thought about God all the time, and I wanted to know she was in heaven."

Neville smiled at her. "We talked about that the very first time we met. Do you remember?"

"Of course I do. And I also heard you preach about it one time."

Neville was astonished. "How could that be?"

"The time you came and preached at the Methodist church. I put on a black dress and disguised myself as a widow with a dark, heavy veil."

"I remember that! I was coming to speak with you after the sermon, but you vanished. I had no idea it was you, of course."

"Yes. I was ashamed. But I remember your sermon so well."

"Well, that's a compliment. Some people can't remember what I say the next day."

"But how did you find God? Were you in a church?"

"No. I was all by myself. As a matter of fact, I was in the middle of a busy street. I had been thinking about my mother, longing to see her in eternity, and I'd been reading the Scripture. And, of course, I'd heard preaching on the new birth for a long time."

"The new birth?"

"Yes. Do you remember in the third chapter of John the story of the man called Nicodemus?"

"I do remember. I thought it was very strange that this man came to see Jesus by night."

"Yes, he might have been ashamed because Jesus was known as the friend of sinners. Respectable Jews would have nothing to do with known sinners. That's why Jesus disturbed them so greatly, Chantel. He talked with them, laid His hands on them, prayed for them. The so-called respectable religious leaders found that offensive."

Chantel turned to face Neville, her eyes luminous by the light of the flickering lantern overhead. "But that is what I found so wonderful about Him. The love that He had for everyone."

"Yes. That's what I felt, too, and still do. But I do not understand when He told Nicodemus, 'You must be born again.'"

"Perhaps we'll never understand all of it, but the Bible clearly teaches that we have very bad hearts. The book of Romans says, 'All have sinned and come short of the glory of God.' We haven't all sinned alike," he added quickly. "Some have sinned more hideously than others, but that doesn't excuse us. What is necessary is that we understand that we all need God."

"Oh, yes, I believe that!"

"I'd read the Bible before, and a verse had come into my heart that said, 'Whosoever shall call upon the name of the Lord shall be saved.' That verse stuck in my memory. I thought about it night and day, but I didn't know what it meant. I thought I had already called on God. I carried that with me in my head almost like an echo.

"One day I was walking along a busy street thinking about this, people everywhere, all around me, talking and laughing and shouting. And then the verse came again. 'Whosoever shall call upon the name of the Lord shall be saved.' And at that moment, Chantel, I was pretty desperate. And I didn't call out loud, although I think my lips moved. I just said, 'God, I need You, and I'm calling on You. Your word promises that if I call, I'll be saved. So I'm calling right now, and I'm asking You in the name of Jesus and by His blood to save me.'"

"And what happened?"

"Well, this sounds odd, but nothing much really happened. The crowd was still there. I didn't feel any different. There were no flashes of lightning. I went on about my work that day, and I thought a few times about what I had done, but it didn't seem to be any different. But that night when I went to bed, I went to sleep almost at once, and then I had a dream that I was in some place that I had never seen. It was beautiful place, although I can't describe it. I never could remember the details, and then I heard a voice that said, 'Neville, you have called on Me, and you are now in the family of God. You have been saved from your sins.' And then I woke up, and I felt so strange. I got out of bed. I walked the floor. I knew it was only a dream, but it was so real, Chantel! And I determined right then that I was going to believe what I had done was real—and I did."

"But did you ever feel anything?"

"Oh, yes, many times. As I began to pray and study and draw near to God, I felt a peace that I had never known. And then, after a time, joy began to fill me. Just a little at first. But then finally one day, I knew I wanted more of God, so I called on Him again and asked Him simply to fill me with His spirit so that I could worship Him. And this time He answered my prayer right away. I began to praise God, and as I worshipped Him, great joy came to me."

"And is it still there?"

"The knowledge that I'm saved is always there, but sometimes I feel depressed. Even then I know what happened is the most real thing in my life, and I know Jesus is in my heart."

Chantel fell utterly silent, and Neville did not speak. Finally he said, "Are you troubled, Chantel?"

"I—I have nothing like that in my heart. I have always been in church, but I do not know God like you do."

Neville hesitated and then said, "Would you like to?"

"Oh, more than anything in the world, but I don't know how. It sounds too simple."

"As a matter of fact, the Bible says that it is simple. If it were a complex matter that only a genius could understand, I'd be lost and going to hell. But all you need to do, Chantel, is believe that Jesus is the Son of God and He died for your sins. Just ask Him to cleanse those sins and take Him into your heart."

Again Chantel was silent, and finally Neville said, "Would you like to have Jesus in your heart?" She did not answer, and he saw that she was trembling. "I don't believe we can push anyone into the kingdom, but you remember this. I was converted when I was not in a church, and no minister or priest was talking to me—and you can find Him the same way."

Chantel found it difficult to speak. She was frightened, somehow, of his words. Quickly she rose and said, "I think I should go to bed."

"I think that's a good idea," Neville said. "Come. I'll walk with you to your room."

They entered the hotel and walked together until they came to her room. She unlocked her door, then turned to him, and he saw that she was deeply troubled.

"Don't be afraid of Jesus, Chantel," Neville said. "He means only good for you."

"Good night, Neville."

Chantel turned and shut the door. She leaned back against it and knew that she was greatly moved. She wondered at herself and at her response to Neville's words. Finally she prepared for bed, and when she closed her eyes and pulled the covers up, she found herself thinking of Jesus as the Savior, the Christ. She almost cried out as Neville had for Him to come into her heart. Finally she tried to sleep, but the words kept coming back: *Whosoever shall call upon the name of the Lord shall be saved*—and the strange Scripture that she could not forget—*You must be born again.*

Finally she trembled, and fear rose in her, but along with that fear a great desire came. She got out of bed, knelt beside it, and prayed, "Oh, God, I am so confused. You know me, and You know that I really want You. So, I'm going to do what Neville did. I'm going to call on You."

And there on her knees in that hotel room, Chantel Fontaine called on God with all her heart. She never could remember the exact words she said, but for a long time she cried out for God in desperation.

Finally she grew cold. She got back into the bed, and she felt totally exhausted. But somehow she felt satisfaction. *I've called on God, and I've asked Him to save me. That's all Neville did.* She snuggled down into the bed, pulled the covers closer and said, "I'm trusting You, Jesus, to be in my heart." Then almost at once she fell asleep.

The next morning Chantel awoke, and the first thing she thought of was, *I called on the Lord, and I'm going to believe that I will have the same spirit Neville has. I'm going to believe I will know God better every day.* All of her training had been that the more prayers that one said, the better it was. She had her rosary with her, but she did not reach for it. Instead she simply knelt and said, "Lord, I'm believing that You are faithful and that You have saved me, and I thank You for that in Jesus' name."

She got up and began to sing as she got ready to go downstairs. She found herself thinking of her sister, and somehow faith rose stronger in her, and she said, "God, I know You're going to hear our prayers."

When she got downstairs, she found Neville and Yves already in the restaurant. When their food came, she began to eat hungrily, and she listened as Yves spoke of what he had discovered. "I found a man whose name is Broussard—Michael Broussard. He says we're crazy for wanting to go into Bayou Teche and find Simon Tubberville."

"But he'll go with us and show us the place?" Neville demanded.

"He'll go part of the way." Yves shook his head. "This fellow Tubberville, he's got a terrible reputation. He's been in jail more than once, and Broussard says he's a killer. He got into a fight here in a saloon, and kicked a man to death with his boots."

What a horrible man for my sister to be with! Chantel thought. But though the knowledge of such a terrible man frightened her, there was no other option. "When can we go?" she asked.

"Right away," Yves said. "Broussard's waiting for us. I hope you have some money. I had to promise him plenty of it, Neville."

"I've got the money. Let's go."

"How will we actually do this, Neville? I mean—what if he won't let her go?"

"I don't think we can make much of a plan. I hope money will settle it, but if not—we'll do whatever we have to do."

Chapter twenty-four

"This is Michael Broussard. He expects to be paid ten pounds for taking us into the swamp," Yves said.

Broussard was small and very thin but with a wiry strength that was obvious in his bared forearms. He wore a pair of dark blue wool trousers, a gray sweater over a white shirt, and a wool cap perched on the very back of his head. His eyes were quick as a squirrel's as he glanced around.

Neville was inclined to offer only part of the fee, but he knew it was no time to bargain. He took out his wallet, extracted some notes, and handed them over. Broussard stuck them carelessly in the pocket of his trousers and said, "I have to have the money up front, you see, because, well, you may not come back soon."

"You mean we may not come back at all?" Neville asked, lifting his eyebrows.

"That could happen. Personally, I think you are crazy to go in there. Simon Tubberville is not a man who welcomes company. One of his own daughters run off some time ago."

"Do you know why?" Chantel asked.

"I reckon the old man was too rough on her."

"We have to go," Neville replied, "so do the best you can for us."

"Very well. We go now."

By the time they reached the edge of the bayou, the sun was already climbing high in the sky. The road leading west out of Baton Rouge was even worse than the one coming from New Orleans. At times it was nothing but a two-lane track of mud. Broussard led the way on horseback, and once the carriage became so mired that it was all the men and the horses could do to get it free.

The weather was turning colder, and a bitter wind sprang up out of the north. The earth was gray and brown with deadness, and the gloomy overcast seemed to dampen Chantel's spirit. After leaving the main road, they followed Broussard until they were traveling on what seemed to be no more than a path. It was barely possible to get the carriage through.

Finally Broussard pulled up his horse and pointed. "There is my place. We can put the horses in the barn."

The house was no more than a shack, and half a dozen children scrambled out to greet Broussard. He dismounted and hugged them. Then, as Chantel got out of the buggy, he said, "This is my wife, Hannah. Come, if you want to go inside. I will put the horses up."

Hannah Broussard was a surprisingly cheerful woman, not pretty, but with a vivacious air. She fed them a lunch of fresh bread and blue crabs cooked in a way Chantel had never seen before.

Neville insisted on paying for it, and when the meal was over, he looked toward Broussard, saying, "Can we go now?"

"It will be late, but I think it best. I will take care of your horses while you're gone."

He led the way out to the edge of the swamp, where three small, fragile-looking boats were tied up. "We will have to take all three boats, for I am not waiting in that swamp for you. You can bring my boats back here—if you come back at all."

"Cheerful fellow, isn't he?" Yves whispered to Chantel as they approached the boats. He touched one with the toe of his boot and shook his head. "I hope they float."

As Chantel got in, she realized how small the boats were. "What are these things called?" she asked Broussard.

"We call this boat a *pirogue.*"

Chantel got into one of the small boats with Broussard. The two men each got in another, and they all shoved off. Broussard balanced himself, standing up and using a pole to propel along. The other two men struggled awkwardly.

"This is a sorry way to get from one place to another," Yves said under his breath.

"But the only way. We'll just have to learn," Neville said.

They traveled until the sun had passed the meridian. It was a world that Chantel did not know. Cypress trees rose on either side of them, blocking out the feeble sun so that it was twilight under the canopy. From time to time she sensed things alive in the swamp around, but her eyes were not quick enough to catch them. Once a horrible scream came to her, and she started. "What was that?" she asked Broussard.

"A panther. He will not hurt you here, mademoiselle, but do not get caught out alone after dark on dry land."

Finally Broussard pulled his boat onto what appeared to be dry land, as dry as anything could be in this world. He pulled the prow up and held out his hands. "This is where you must walk," he said.

Chantel took his hand and stepped out, and they waited until the men had pulled their boats in.

"Me, I go home. Here, I have drawn this map for you. I am not good at drawing."

The three travelers bent over the map. It was indeed poorly drawn, but Broussard pointed out landmarks. "You will see a big cypress that has grown in two, like a 'V,' you know?" He held his forefinger and his middle finger spread wide apart. "Last time I was there, there were big birds nesting in the top, but maybe not now. The road divides there. You take the left turn. Be sure you take the left or you miss them."

Yves and Neville went over the map several times, asking questions and adding to it as Broussard remembered other things. Finally Broussard said, "I will wait here for you until dark. If you don't come back, I will go on. But I will leave these two boats. You bring them back to my house. Right?"

It occurred to Neville that Broussard might take the boats before they returned. He reached into his billfold again and withdrew some notes. "You can hold this for a deposit," he said. "If we don't come back, the boats are paid for."

Broussard nodded. "If you must go, you be quick and careful. Tubberville has a quick anger, and he sometimes shoots to scare people off. Not to kill. Just to turn them back."

Yves touched the pistol at his waist and said, "I hope it doesn't come to that."

"You will not see him to shoot at him. He is invisible in the swamp. You go now. And may the good God go with you."

The three turned and began their trek down the path. It was hard to follow, as if it were traveled infrequently. Yves went first, followed by Chantel, while Neville brought up the rear. They stopped from time to time to consult the map, and more than once they heard splashing in the swamp.

"I hope those alligators don't come out after us. They're vicious beasts," Yves muttered.

The trail wound in a circular fashion, and once they heard a panther scream faintly and far away. More than once it seemed they were completely lost, but always the map mentioned some landmark that got them back on track.

Suddenly Yves halted. "Look, there's a cabin up there."

The other two hurried forward to stand beside him, where they could see the outline of a cabin on the border of a fingerling of water. Out beyond it there was the white of egrets, and smoke was curling up out of the chimney.

"Somebody's there," Yves muttered. "Do we just go right in?"

"I think we have to," Chantel said.

"What do we tell them?" Yves demanded. "You can't just barge in there and say, 'We've come to take your daughter.'"

"That's right," Neville said. "We'd better think about it."

"How about this. Let's tell them I'm a painter and I'm interested in finding a place to paint in the swamps."

"I don't know. If you start out by lying to them, it may get us in trouble," Neville said.

"It's true enough," Yves replied. "I could get some great paintings out here."

"Let's just see how it develops."

Chantel was fraught with uncertainty as they moved forward. What would they say to whoever was in the cabin? All the descriptions they had had of Simon Tubberville were of a man who would be dangerous to cross. She did not like the idea of deceiving him, but as Yves said, what could they say to the people?

The three had gotten only halfway across the clearing when a woman stepped out. She had a rifle in her hand and raised it, finger on the trigger, although not pointed directly at them.

"Hello," Yves called out quickly. "My name is Yves Gaspard. My friends and I are a little bit confused."

The woman lowered the rifle. She was short and heavily built, with eyes that were dark with suspicion. "Who are you and what do you want?" she said.

They moved closer, all of them keeping an eye on the rifle. Yves boldly said, "I am a painter, madame. I am looking for a place in the swamp to paint things such as the birds and the animals and the setting."

As Yves was keeping the woman's attention, a movement caught Chantel's eyes. She turned her head only slightly and then, without preamble, the girl that she had seen in the streets of New Orleans stepped out. It was the same girl, no doubt about that! Chantel studied her carefully, and her heart suddenly filled as she saw the features so much like her own mother's. The child's hair was dirty and entangled, but it was the same strawberry blonde color, and there was no mistaking those eyes.

She heard Neville clear his throat and turned to see him watching her. She nodded slightly but did not know what to do.

Neville said, "I wonder if you could feed us? We would be glad to pay." He reached into his pocket, pulled some gold coins out, and jangled them.

The woman stared at him and said, "It will not be much."

"Anything will be fine with us," Neville said. "We're very hungry."

The woman moved inside the house. It was filled with the smell of cooking food. The girl followed them in, and the woman said, "Get something for them to eat from, Jeanne."

"Yes, Mama."

The three visitors sat down, all of them watching the girl rather furtively. This was the object of their quest, but how were they to get her out of this place?

The food came, and when it was put before them, the men began to eat. Chantel took a bite or two, but could not have told what she was eating. Her attention was all on the girl who was standing up, watching them out of her strange violet eyes.

"Your name is Jeanne?"

She nodded.

The woman had stepped outside for something, and Chantel said, "I am glad to meet you. My name is Chantel."

The girl was shy as a wild rabbit. She lowered her head and could not speak.

"Do you go out of the bayou very often, Jeanne?" Chantel asked.

"To Baton Rouge—and once to New Orleans. That was not long ago."

Chantel longed to go to the girl and take her in her arms and cry out her true name. She sat there trying desperately to think of a plan, but nothing came to her.

The woman entered the room abruptly. "You have to go now," she said. "My husband does not like people coming here, and it will be dark soon."

"That's right," Yves said quickly, getting to his feet.

Chantel rose and went outside the cabin. She turned at the door and saw that the girl was watching her, her enormous violet eyes dominating her face. The impulse to cry her name was almost unbearable, but she clamped her lips together and turned. Neville followed her, and the three moved down toward the trail. They had not gone more than a dozen steps when a harsh voice halted them dead in their tracks.

"What are you doing here? What's your business?"

The man that Chantel had seen in New Orleans stood off to one side of the path. He had a rifle in his hands and a pistol stuck into his belt. His eyes were fierce, and his face was half concealed behind a grisly beard. Although he was rather short, he was obviously tremendously strong, and his countenance was forbidding.

Yves started to say, "We were looking through the bayou for—"

Chantel interrupted him. "We want to talk to you, sir, about the girl who is living with you."

Instantly the man turned toward her. "My daughter?"

Chantel hesitated, and then she said simply, "I do not think she is your daughter. I think she is my sister."

The man's face grew crimson. He lifted the rifle and aimed it straight at Chantel. "Get out of here! If you come back, I will kill you! She is my daughter! Do you hear?"

"Come along, Chantel." Neville's voice was tense, and he gripped Chantel's arm and practically pulled her away. When they got to the place where the path disappeared into the thickness of the huge cypress trees, Chantel turned. She saw Tubberville standing there glaring at them fiercely, and beyond him she saw Veronique standing in the doorway, her eyes filled with fear.

There was nothing to be done. She stumbled down the path, and Neville held her arm, saying, "It's all right. We found her. God will make a way to bring her out of here."

Chantel turned her head, and Yves said urgently, "God will have to do it. That's a rough fellow there. Come along. We've barely got time to get back to the boats before dark."

They hurried through the falling gloom, and when they knew they were safe and the boats within reach, Yves spoke to Neville. "You're a lawyer. Is there any way to get that girl from him legally?"

"It would be hard. I think they probably found her and took her for their own, but there's no proof or evidence. A court of law always gives preference to the parents, and that's what they're going to claim they are."

Yves dropped his head and studied the ground for a moment. Then he said, "Then you'll have to kill Tubberville. He will never let her go. You saw that, didn't you?"

Chantel listened, and her heart cried out for an answer. But as they all climbed into the boats, she was filled with doubt and uncertainty. Silently she prayed, *Oh, God, we need a miracle!*

Chapter twenty-five

From somewhere far off came a hoarse bellow. Yves straightened up and demanded, "What's that?"

"Just a bull gator." Chantel had heard the sound so often in the bayou bordering Fontaine Maison that she was not disturbed. She slapped at a mosquito making a meal on her arm and looked over at Neville. He was sitting on the porch of the Broussards' small cabin, leaning back against the pillar that held the roof up. "Isn't there anything we can do legally, Neville?"

"I don't think so." Neville had been quiet all the way back from the Tubberville house and had suggested they go back to Baton Rouge. Chantel had absolutely refused, so the three of them had taken another meal from Mrs. Broussard and now were sitting outside, where the smells of the bayou were rich and thick.

Yves said, "But if the girl is not their daughter, how can they keep her?"

"As I've said, we don't have any evidence, Yves. Not a shred. The Tubbervilles aren't about to admit that they found the girl."

Chantel got up and walked over to the edge of the porch. She leaned wearily against the support, which was made of hewn cypress, and peered into the bayou in the direction of the Tubberville cabin. A bitterness rose in her, and she said with desperation, "But we've got to do something! We can't leave my sister there."

A silence followed her proclamation, and then Yves said, "We could kidnap her."

"What!" Neville swiveled around and stared at Yves. "Are you crazy? We'd all wind up in jail."

"This thing is not right. I don't care what the law says," Yves said defiantly. "I say we go back and hide in the woods, and when we see the fellow leave, we go in and take the girl. We get away and dare him to come and get her. He doesn't know our names. How would he find us?"

"We can't do it, Yves," Chantel said.

"Why can't we? You want your sister back. I don't see any other way to get her."

"There has to be a way!" Chantel exclaimed. Turning to Neville, she said, "I don't know anything about the law, but in a case like this there must be something."

"Louisiana is under the Napoleonic law. It's the only state that is," Neville said. "It's a strange sort of code, and lawyers coming in go crazy at first. But I'm telling you that there's nothing in it that will allow us to go in and take a child away from a family. Imagine what would happen if you had a child and someone came in and took him away."

"But this is different. She's my sister."

"I think you're right, but how can we prove it? If I went to a judge with this kind of story to get a court order, why, he'd laugh me out of his office."

From inside the house, they could hear the laughter and chatter of the Broussards' six small children. Neville had been quiet, searching his mind desperately to find a solution, but he knew the law well enough to realize that the door of legal methods was closed. "We'll just have to pray that God will open up a door."

Yves laughed shortly. "I know what that means."

"What does it mean?" Chantel said quickly.

"It means Neville has given up. Doesn't it, Neville?"

"Not at all. Well, perhaps, it means I've given up on any human solutions. But God can do all things."

"I agree with that, of course, but God helps those who help themselves."

"I don't think that's quite right."

"It's in the Bible, isn't it?"

"No, I don't think so. I believe it's in *Aesop's Fables.*"

Chantel said, "But I can see what Yves is saying. Surely God expects us to do something."

"I am sure He does at times, but I don't think that He wants us to break the law to get your sister back. I do believe that if we ask Him, He will show us a way."

Yves suddenly stood up. "I'm tired," he said. "It's bed for me."

"Good night," Chantel said. She waited until he had gone into the cabin. The Broussards had fixed beds for the men in the loft. Chantel would sleep on the floor in the main room of the cabin.

Neville waited for Chantel to speak, and when she did not, he said, "I'm sorry I haven't been more help."

"Oh, don't say that, Neville! I wouldn't have gotten this far if it weren't for you." She hesitated and then said, "I want to tell you what happened to me." She quickly related her experience of calling on God, and when she finished, she said, "I don't know what happened to me in my spirit or in my heart, but I know that I feel so different. I know God has spoken to me. I just don't know what it all means."

"I think it means God has come into your heart. I think you were converted."

"I don't know that word."

"It's simply another way of saying that you're not under the bondage of sin anymore. You asked God to forgive you in the name of Jesus, and He did."

"I hope so. I need God's forgiveness."

"We all do." He smiled at her, saying, "I'm so happy for you!"

The two sat until the sounds within the cabin grew quiet. The door opened, and Broussard stepped outside. "Your bed is ready, miss. It's not much, but it's the best we have."

"Thank you, Mr. Broussard."

The inside of the cabin was murky, but Broussard said, "We leave this lamp on to give you a little light. Good night." He left to go to the rear of the house.

Before Neville went to the loft, he reached out and put his hands on Chantel's shoulders. Turning her to face him, he said, "God is able. We'll get her back for you."

"Do you really believe that, Neville?"

"Yes, I do." He leaned forward and kissed her on the cheek, then without another word turned and moved up to the loft.

Lying down on the quilts that Mrs. Broussard had provided, Chantel touched the place where Neville had kissed her. "Good night," she whispered and then tried to sleep.

"Wake up, Chantel."

Chantel came awake instantly. She had slept no more than three hours, for she could not help going over and over in her mind ways to get her Veronique back. Now she sat up abruptly and saw Neville standing over her. "What is it?" she said.

Neville held out a piece of paper. "It's Yves. He's gone to get Veronique."

"What!"

"Read the note." Neville's face was grim.

I have gone to get your sister. Don't worry about me. I can do this. Yves.

"Oh, Neville, it's not right!"

"It's not right and it's dangerous," Neville said grimly.

"What can we do?"

"I guess all we can do is wait. You and I can't go thrashing around in that swamp."

Suddenly fear came to Chantel. "I know he's doing this for me, but I'm afraid."

They did wait, but not willingly. Mrs. Broussard cooked a breakfast for them of ham and eggs and biscuits, but Chantel could not eat more than a few bites. The coffee she served was so strong it was bitter.

Chantel turned to Michael Broussard and said, "We've got to go out and find him."

"No, you must not do," Broussard said quickly. "It is too dangerous. The bayou itself has dangers, and Simon Tubberville is no man to fool with."

"I think I should go," Neville said, "but you must wait here, Chantel."

"No, we'll both go."

Both Broussard and his wife argued against the mission, but in the end they were forced to relent. The two left the cabin, got into one of the pirogues, and both of them paddled, sending the small craft skimming across the waters. Dawn was coming up now, and finding the way was not difficult, for they had noted carefully the landmarks that they had followed the day before. Chantel's arms grew tired and her back ached, but she did not even consider resting.

"Listen!" Neville said. "Did you hear something?"

"No, I don't think so. What did it sound like?"

"Like a shot—but maybe I was mistaken."

They paddled steadily and had almost reached the landing when Neville said, "Look, there's a boat over there."

Chantel looked, and her heart lurched. She whispered, "Let's go. It's the one that Yves took." She turned the prow of the pirogue around, and as they approached, she stood up.

"Be careful. These things turn over easily."

"Neville, it's Yves! He's lying in the bottom of the boat."

Neville maneuvered the small craft around, and as soon as it was possible, he grabbed the edge of the craft, and Chantel stepped inside.

Yves was lying facedown in the bottom of the boat. He was wearing a thin white shirt, and when Chantel turned him over, she saw that his breast was stained with blood. "Yves!" she cried and reached down to touch his face.

"Is he dead?"

"No, he's breathing. But, oh, there's blood everywhere!"

"We've got to get out of here. Look, let me get in that boat, and I'll paddle him. You take this one."

The exchange was made, and soon Chantel was following the boat in front of her. Neville called back to her, "I think he's going to be all right, but he's lost a lot of blood."

"We've got to get help, Neville!"

"I know. We'll get him to the Broussards'. Then we can clean him up and see how badly he's hurt."

They paddled so hard that both of them were exhausted, but when they reached the landing at Broussards' cabin, their host was there to help. "I saw you coming," he said as he pulled the boat in. "Is he dead?"

"No, but he's badly wounded."

"We'll get him inside. My wife, she is good with hurts like this."

Yves was a large man, and Broussard and Neville were not. They struggled and finally got him inside the house.

As they laid him back, Yves opened his eyes and saw Chantel. He coughed and made a grimace of pain. "Well," he whispered, "that wasn't such a good idea."

"Oh, Yves, I wish you hadn't gone!"

"So do I," Yves sighed, and his face was pale as old ivory. He did not speak again, but after Hannah Broussard had removed the shirt and cleaned the wound, she said, "It is not so bad. See how high the wound is? It missed the lung, but he has lost a lot of blood. He's very weak."

"We'd better take him to the hospital in Baton Rouge," Neville said.

"If you think so, Neville." Chantel leaned against him and felt his arm go around her. She closed her eyes and found herself feeling faint, but then she shook her head. She looked again at Yves's face and whispered, "He was trying to do it for me, but he shouldn't have."

Chantel's brow furrowed, and she said, "Are you sure you feel well enough to make the trip to New Orleans, Yves?"

"Yes, I'm fine. Just weak."

The two of them were in Yves's hospital room in Baton Rouge. He was dressed, and his bag was on the bed. During the entire four days he had been here, Chantel had come every day, and with relief had seen him lose his pallor. But now she was worried. "Why don't you just wait here?"

"There's nothing I can do here."

At that moment the door opened, and Neville came through. His clothes had been wrinkled when they had left the swamp, but now he was impeccably dressed again. "The mail coach is here, Yves," he said. "But I don't think you ought to try this trip. You're still weak."

"No, I'll be fine. Don't worry about me." Yves stared at Neville and said, "I know you think I'm an irreligious dog, but when I went down from that shot, something happened."

"What was it?"

"They say just before you die your whole life flashes in front of you. I always thought that was ridiculous. But something like that happened. Of course, I didn't lose consciousness right away, but as I lay there in that boat bleeding my life out, I thought what a mess I'd made of everything." Yves smiled suddenly and shook his head. "You would have been proud of me, Neville. I called on God. It's the first time I tried to talk to Him in a long time."

"I'm glad you did," Neville said warmly.

"I think I would have died if you hadn't got there and stopped the bleeding. So, who knows? Maybe I'll be in your congregation pretty soon."

Chantel said quickly, "Just stay here a few more days and get stronger."

"No, I must go. Before I leave I want to warn you about something."

"Warn me about what?"

"About a fortune hunter. His name is—" He stopped abruptly and laughed when he saw the two of them hanging on his words. "His name is Yves Gaspard. He's a fine-looking fellow, but don't have anything to do with him."

"That's not true," Chantel said.

"Not now, but I know myself pretty well. If this hadn't happened, I would have tried to marry you. And it would have been a terrible thing for you." He reached out and put his hand on Chantel's cheek and said in a totally serious voice, "You deserve better than me." Leaning forward, he kissed her on the cheek. Then he said, "I'm ready. You'll be hearing from me."

Neville picked up the bag and walked outside. He watched Yves carefully and saw that the wound still pained him. He put down the bag and helped Yves into the coach. Then, taking the bag, he handed it to the driver, who stored it on the top. He turned back and saw that Yves was putting his hand out. Neville shook it and said, "Thanks for what you tried to do, Yves."

"It's up to you now, Neville—you and God."

Neville watched the coach leave, then turned to find Chantel watching from the porch.

"Well, he's gone," she said. "You know, he's a pretty brave fellow."

"Yes, he is. Well, follow me."

"What are we going to do now?"

"We may have to press charges. I don't like it, but it may be the only way to get Veronique." He turned to her, adding, "But God is up to something, and I want to be in on it!"

Chapter twenty-six

The sun had risen by the time Chantel opened her eyes. She sat up and winced, for her muscles were still somewhat sore from the effort of paddling the pirogue. She had slept better the previous night than she had expected and now realized that it was a Sunday morning. Her thoughts went back to that other life she had had on Fontaine Maison, and she realized that she would have been dressing to go to Mass.

She got out of bed and stared around the hotel room for a moment. It was not ornate in the least, but the bed had been comfortable. Quickly she bathed as completely as she could at the basin, then dressed and fixed her hair. She opened the door and stepped outside to find Neville exiting from his own room. "Good morning," she said.

"Well, good morning. I thought you might sleep late."

"No, but I did sleep better."

"So did I. Come along. We'll have breakfast."

"What are you going to do then?"

"Why, I'm going to church."

"May I go with you?"

Neville's eyes opened wide with surprise. "If you like."

Chantel laughed at his reaction. "I know. I told you once that Catholics couldn't go to other services, but I'm going this time."

"I think that's a fine thing. We'll eat breakfast; then we'll hear a good sermon."

The church was not large, but it was filled to capacity. Chantel's heart beat a little faster as she thought of what her priest might say if he knew what she was doing—but somehow things had changed for her. She felt a freedom she had not known existed as she accompanied Neville down the aisle and took a seat with him. He pressed his shoulder against hers, and she turned to him and said, "I think this is a very good thing to do."

"It's always good to go to the house of God."

The singing was not what Chantel was accustomed to, but she followed the words in the book and tried to sing along. Neville, of course, knew all the words and seemed to find great joy in joining in.

But it was the sermon that really got Chantel's attention. The minister was a man of forty, tall and with a pair of piercing blue eyes. When he announced his text, Neville opened his Bible and found it, so that she was able to follow along. He began reading at Psalm 78, which was a record of the dealings of God with Israel in the wilderness.

> *And they tempted God in their heart by asking meat for their lust. Yea, they spake against God; they said, Can God furnish a table in the wilderness?*

The minister lifted his eyes and said, "That is my subject this morning. Can God furnish a table in the wilderness?"

Chantel listened as he spoke of the difficulties of Israel as they wandered. "They were out in a howling wilderness, and in those days, there were no stores. There was no place to buy food. I imagine mothers with their children were worried, and fathers could not imagine what they would do to feed their families in that terrible, barren place. So they made their big mistake. They failed God, and when Moses asked them to trust God, they taunted him, saying, 'Can God furnish a table in the wilderness?'"

Chantel listened intently as the minister laid out the difficulties, impossibilities really, and she thought, *How very like my situation. But probably everyone in this building has hard things that they are facing.*

"You know the story. God did indeed furnish a table in the wilderness. The Scripture tells us that He rained bread down upon them, and He sent quail for meat. And I say to you this morning, if you are facing an impossible situation, remember it's impossible only for you, for nothing shall be impossible with God."

Chantel heard little of the rest of the message, for those words seemed to have been driven into her heart—*God can furnish a table in the wilderness.*

And as they left the church and walked back toward the hotel, she said, "I enjoyed the service."

"It was a fine sermon," Neville agreed.

"What did he mean about fasting and praying when we want something very much?"

"You remember our conversation with Yves when he said, 'Can't we do something?'"

"Yes, I remember."

"Well, I didn't have a very good answer," Neville said ruefully. "There is something we can always do when we're faced with a problem we can't handle. The Bible says we have to fast and to pray."

"Then that's what I think we should do, Neville."

Neville said at once, "I believe you're right. We'll go to our rooms, you to yours, I to mine, and we'll begin to pray."

"And we won't eat until God gives us an answer?"

"We'll pray until God either answers us or gives us a word that we've fasted and prayed enough."

Chantel felt the pressure of the bed against her forehead. She had prayed until she had thought she could not possibly pray another moment. She had prayed standing, kneeling, sitting, walking around the room. She had wept, she had even cried aloud once—but nothing seemed to have happened.

Now she felt physically exhausted—and also besieged with doubts.

This will never work. I feel so—so stupid! God knows what we need. Why do I have to keep on praying?

She had prayed all day Sunday and all Sunday night, and now the sun was coming up. Her mouth was dry, and she felt the pangs of hunger. She could hear people moving around the hotel and knew that they were going down to breakfast.

How long can I keep this up? And why should I keep it up? It isn't doing any good.

Neville had warned her before they had parted that thoughts like these would come. "It's not a glamorous, exciting thing, praying through like this. Your body gets tired, but your mind gets even more tired. Most people can't keep it up. But remember, Jesus prayed in the wilderness for forty days without eating."

Now Chantel shifted her position again on her aching knees. Suddenly she held up her hands and cried, "Oh, God, I don't know how to pray! I've said everything I know. Do with me what you will, only save my sister."

Then even as she knelt there, Chantel felt her mind begin to clear. It was as if a fog had been in it, and now a fresh wind blew it away. A feeling of completion came to her. Somehow she knew that God had heard!

As she quietly waited, a memory came to her very sharply, as clearly as if she were going through the experience again. It had to do with Michael Broussard and something he had said. She had paid little heed at the time, but now as she knelt there, suddenly she knew that this was the answer she had been seeking. She got to her feet slowly and whispered, "Thank you, God."

Then she walked to the door. Going out into the hall, she knocked at Neville's room. When he opened the door, she did not even give him time to speak. "I think God has given me something, Neville," she said, "but you must decide."

"Come in and tell me," Neville said. He pulled her inside and shut the door.

"It's a little thing, but do you remember when we asked Broussard about Tubberville? He told us something that I hardly even took in because I was so worried about Veronique. He said that Tubberville had a daughter who had run away from home."

"I remember that. What about it?"

"If we can find her, she will know that Veronique is not her real sister."

Neville blinked with astonishment. "Of course," he said. "I'm so dense! She could give us the proof we need."

"Can we find her?"

"Yes, we can find her. It's something definite." He smiled suddenly and said, "Fasting and prayer seemed to have worked."

A great joy came to Chantel, and she whispered, "It's the first time I ever really heard from God about something. Come, we've got to get started. We must find her quickly!"

Michael Broussard had not been surprised to see the couple return. "I thought you would come back," he said. "How is Monsieur Gaspard?"

"He's very well. Well enough to go back to New Orleans," Chantel said. The two had reached the Broussard cabin at midday and had talked most of the way about how to find Tubberville's daughter. Now Chantel said, "You told us, Michael, that Simon Tubberville had a daughter who ran away."

"Yes, that is true."

"We need to find her," Chantel said. "Does she live around here?"

"No, she ran away with a man, but I think she would not want her father to find her even now. She was an unhappy girl. I think anyone living in that house would be unhappy."

The words gave Chantel pain, and she said, "If we could just find her, I think we could get my sister back."

Broussard shrugged. "I will ask around. Someone will know."

"Can you find out as quickly as possible?" Neville said.

"I will do my best, monsieur."

Neville and Chantel were impatient, but there was nothing else to do. Broussard had left at once, riding out on his gelding, and they had decided that they would not go back to Baton Rouge but simply wait, no matter how long it took.

Finally they went for a walk. November had come, and a chill was in the air. The sun overhead was white and threw rays that did not contain much warmth. They reached the edge of the bayou, and for a time they simply stood looking out.

A great blue heron was fishing down the way. He moved slowly, almost imperceptibly, then suddenly his beak shot down and he came up with a small fish. He tossed it into the air, caught it expertly, and swallowed it headfirst.

Neville turned to Chantel. "I haven't told you what I want to do with my life."

"Are you going to leave the law and become a minister? I know you've talked about it."

"Not right away. I want to start a work down on the waterfront in New Orleans. I don't know if you've ever been there, but it's filled with derelicts, men and women who have reached the very bottom. They're without hope, and no one seems to care about them."

"How can you help them, Neville?"

"Well, for one thing, see that those who are starving get something to eat and a place to sleep, at least for a night or two. And then, of course, I want to lead as many as I can to know the Lord Jesus as Savior." He went on for some time speaking of the rescue mission that he wanted to start.

"I'd like to help, Neville. I can't do much, but I can give money."

"That's a kind heart speaking. I'm sure if you saw some of those poor men and pitiful women, you'd know that this is a good thing to do."

"I do know it, and I think it's wonderful that you want to do such a thing."

"I'll keep on with my law practice, and my income can build the place. I've been talking to some business associates, and many have said that they'd like to help."

"I want to come and see it when you get started. You'll be preaching, won't you?"

"Unless we can get someone better."

Chantel listened as he spoke, and finally she turned her head. "Listen, I hear someone coming."

"It's Broussard!" Neville exclaimed. "Let's see what he's learned."

Broussard came off his horse, smiling broadly.

"You found out something, didn't you, Michael?" Chantel cried.

"Yes. I found the name of the man Joanna Tubberville ran away with. His name is Romain Billaud."

"Good work!" Neville said warmly. "Did anyone know where they live?"

"His family were fishermen. They lived in St. Charles. That's all I could find out."

"That's enough. Thank you, Michael," Neville said. "Come on, Chantel. The door is open."

St. Charles was a rather dreary village, and both Chantel and Neville were tired from their journey. "The horses are about done in," he said. "I think we're going to have to rest them up no matter what we find here."

"Oh, I hope the woman is here. She could help so much."

"She may not want to speak," Neville warned. "Cajuns are very private people—very clannish. They don't display their troubles for outsiders. But we'll see."

He stepped out of the wagon and spoke to a man who was leaning back in a chair against the outer wall of a storefront. "Excuse me, sir. I'm looking for the Billaud family. Do you know them?"

"I reckon I do." The man was a rangy individual dressed in a heavy brown coat with a broad-brimmed hat pulled down almost over his eyes. "You know the family?"

"We've never met them, but we have business with them."

"Well, you may not have heard, but Frank Billaud died last year. His wife still lives here though."

"Can you tell me how to get to her house?"

"I can."

Neville listened carefully to the directions, said thank you, and got back in the buggy. "At least we found the right family."

They found the house with no trouble, and both of them got out and walked up to the front door. It was a plain white house, not large but with two stories, and was well cared for. When he knocked on the door, a tall woman opened it and waited for them to speak.

"Mrs. Billaud?"

"I am Mrs. Billaud."

"My name is Neville Harcourt, and this is Miss Chantel Fontaine. I wonder if we might speak with you."

The woman hesitated, then she nodded and said, "Come in."

When the pair entered, she led them to a drawing room where there was a fire throwing out warmth. "What can I do for you?"

"I am an attorney from New Orleans, Mrs. Billaud. We need very much to find the woman who was Joanna Tubberville."

"That is my daughter-in-law."

Relief flooded Chantel, and she said quickly, "We need to find her very badly."

"Why would you want my daughter-in-law?"

Neville understood her apprehension and said, "There's no problem with Joanna or with your son, Mrs. Billaud. We simply need some information from her about her family."

Mrs. Billaud said, "I'm afraid I can't give out information to strangers."

"May I at least tell you why we need to find her?" Chantel asked.

Mrs. Billaud looked at the young woman, and something changed in her face. "I suppose it will do no harm for me to listen. Sit down." She took a chair herself, sitting stiffly upright.

Chantel at once plunged into the story of how she had lost her mother and her sister. She felt that this was the time for the truth, and she related everything that had happened. "So you see, Mrs. Billaud, I'm convinced that the girl who is living with Simon Tubberville is really my sister, and I need her back. She's all the family I have."

Something about Chantel's voice and features must have moved Mrs. Billaud, for she said, "I never heard of such a thing, but I would put nothing past Simon Tubberville!" Her face grew tense. "He's a vicious man. When Romain wanted to marry his daughter, I felt he was making a mistake. But we were wrong about Joanna." Her face eased, and she said, "She has been a good wife to my son."

"Could you tell us where they are? Do they live here in St. Charles?"

"No, Romain lives in Alexandria. He owns a general store there and has two fine children."

"We need to see your daughter-in-law and get the truth about how this girl came to her family."

"I think that is a good thing to do. That is no place for a child—especially a young girl."

"I think something may be done if Joanna could help us."

Mrs. Billaud went to a desk against the wall, where she wrote a note and put it into an envelope. "Give this to her," she said. "I think you'll find she'll be as helpful as she can."

"Thank you so much, Mrs. Billaud."

As the two left the house, Chantel said, "Can we leave today?"

"I'll have to change these horses. Perhaps there's a stable we can rent from while these two rest up. Yes, I think we need to press on as quickly as we can."

Alexandria was a much larger town than St. Charles, but finding the object of their quest was not difficult.

"I've been praying that this would be the end of our search," Chantel said as they pulled up in front of the store.

"So have I. Let's go in."

It was a rather large general store packed with merchandise of all sorts, from animal traps to bolts of cloth to groceries of many kinds. A woman stood behind the counter, and when they approached, she smiled and said, "May I help you?"

"We're looking for Mr. Billaud."

"That's my husband, but he's out of town on a business trip. Could I help you?"

"I have a letter here, Mrs. Billaud, from your mother-in-law."

"From my mother-in-law? Is she all right?"

"Oh, she's fine!" Chantel said. "She thought the note might introduce us to you."

Joanna Billaud opened the envelope, read the letter, and said, "We can speak privately in the room behind the store." She lifted her voice and said, "Claude, watch the store while I'm gone."

Chantel and Neville followed her down the aisle and then into a small room containing a desk, a safe, and several chairs.

"Would you care to sit down?"

"Thank you very much," Chantel said. "I'll tell you the same story I told your mother-in-law." She launched into her story, and Joanna Billaud listened. Her face changed when Chantel mentioned the little child who had disappeared, but she said nothing. Chantel left nothing out, telling how one of their number had been wounded in an attempt to get the child back.

"And so you see, Mrs. Billaud, I'm convinced that the child known as Jeanne Tubberville is really my sister, Veronique Fontaine. I want to take her out of that place and give her a home. I can provide for her very well and give her love and affection."

Chantel came to the end. For a moment she feared that the woman would not be willing to help, for Joanna's face had grown hard.

She sat there silently, but finally she said, "So you would take the child into your home and treat her as your own?"

"She's all the family I have. I just want to help her."

The woman looked directly at Chantel and examined her carefully, as though she were trying to memorize her features. Finally she said slowly, "I remember the day my father brought the girl home."

"Then she's not Simon's daughter! I knew it!"

"No, she is not his daughter. And you are right. Just one look tells you she's not like the rest of the family. Her hair and her eyes are different. Everything about her is different."

"What did your father say about her?" Neville asked.

"He said that a man had died and the mother was sick and had other children. He said she asked him to take the child as his own.

I never believed that, but no one ever questioned my father. Not in that house."

At once Neville expelled a sigh, and his eyes met those of Chantel. He turned again and said, "Would you testify to this, Mrs. Billaud?"

It was as if the woman did not hear him. She sat there staring blindly across the room, and finally she whispered, "My father, he is not—a good man." She seemed to struggle with painful memories that were coming back, then she turned to face them. "I had to run away because it was not safe for me to be there."

She turned to Chantel and said, "I love the girl Jeanne. Get her away from that place." Then she turned and nodded. "Yes, Mr. Harcourt, I will take an oath before God in court that Jeanne is not of Tubberville blood."

The sun had come out in full strength now, and heated the earth as Neville and Chantel drove along the rutted road. The rain had softened it, and the mud was splattered over the guard and had even gotten on their clothes. But it did not matter.

Neville had taken Mrs. Billaud to the local judge, and she had told her story. It had been set down, and she had signed it. Now he patted his pocket and said, "With this paper and Mrs. Billaud's testimony we're going to be all right."

"She was very worried about Veronique, and I am, too. Oh, we must get her out of there at once."

The buggy jolted along, and Neville turned to face her. "We will get her out," he said. "God is on our side."

Chapter twenty-eight

He looks more like a gambler on a riverboat than a sheriff, Chantel thought as she studied Sheriff Louis Prewitt. Neville had discovered that Sheriff Prewitt had jurisdiction over the area where the Tubbervilles lived, and the two of them came to his office and presented their case to him. Prewitt sat back in his chair, fondling the gold chain that hung across his colorful vest, and studied the pair. He was a short man, no more than five-foot-five, but he wore high-heeled boots to compensate. His white ruffled shirt was almost glaring, and a string tie decorated the area under his chin. From time to time, as Prewitt moved his hands, four diamond rings glittered. He had innocent-looking blue eyes, and overall Chantel was disappointed in his appearance. She had expected a strong looking man over six feet tall.

Prewitt brought his chair down and laid his delicate looking hand on the paper that Neville had brought to him. "And what you say these papers they mean?"

"That you have the authority to get Miss Fontaine's sister from the home of Simon Tubberville."

"And what I gonna do with her?"

"The papers explain that you may turn her over to us. There will be a trial to determine the parenthood of the girl."

Prewitt scratched his cheek gently. He had an olive complexion and a thin mustache that he touched from time to time as if to reassure himself that it was still there. He studied the pair before him, then turned to the tall, hulking man who stood with his back to the wall listening to all of this. "What you think, Odo? You think Tubberville give up this child if we say please?"

The deputy was at least six-foot-three and massively built. He appeared to have some Indian blood in him. He said stolidly, "I theenk we will maybe shoot him first. He will nevair give up nothing, him!"

Prewitt stroked his mustache fondly, then looked up at Chantel. "Why I should maybe get killed or get Odo here killed trying to get this girl?"

Neville said quickly, "Because you're a noble man, and I have a feeling that Tubberville isn't one of your favorites."

The words touched a nerve in the sheriff. "He is not, no!" Reaching down, he stood up, walked around the desk, and pulled up his right pant leg. "You see thees scar? Tubberville give him to me. He shoot me two years ago, and I promise I shoot him back someday." He said, "Odo, go get Jean Baptiste and Sonny. Tell them to bring plenty guns and bullets."

The big deputy moved out the door, making no noise whatsoever, and Sheriff Prewitt said, "You staying at the hotel. I'll send someone after you when we get back."

"I'm going with you," Chantel said.

"No, that is not good," the sheriff said at once. "He is a dangerous man."

"That's right," Neville said. "You mustn't come, Chantel, but I'll go."

The argument was rather long and lasted until Odo got back with the two other deputies.

"I'm going with you, and that's all there is to it! The girl will be very frightened, and she'll need a woman to comfort her. Who better than her own sister?"

The sheriff laughed. "I like your spunk. I say you go."

"Sheriff, you can't do that," Neville said.

"Yes, you come, too, lawyer mon. I geev you a shotgun. Don't worry if you kill this fellow. He's long overdue to die, him!"

As soon as the prow of the boat touched the land, Chantel stepped out and held it steady while Neville joined her. He moved awkwardly, for he had an enormous shotgun, and his pockets were stuffed with shells. He held the weapon gingerly and shook his head. "You don't need to be along for this, Chantel. You stay here at the boats."

"I don't want to seem stubborn, but—"

Prewitt interrupted her. "Come, we go quickly. You, Miss Fontaine, and you, lawyer mon, you stay with me." He turned to the three deputies and said, "Odo, you go and get on the other side. You go ahead of us. And you too, Sonny. You get on the east side of the house. And, Jean, you get on the other side. You surround him, no?"

The three deputies nodded, then trotted away like hound dogs on a scent. They disappeared almost miraculously into the tall trees and the undergrowth. Prewitt gave them a few minutes, waiting for a time and seeming to sniff the air. Finally he turned and said, "You two stay behind me a way. Thees ees one mean fellow."

He carried a rifle in his hand and looked completely out of place in his fancy boots and colorful vest. He was smiling and humming under his breath, and from time to time he broke out into a song just barely loud enough for them to hear.

The party moved silently—except for Prewitt's soft singing—and when they got within sight of the cabin, Prewitt held his hand up. "You stay here," he said.

He moved forward slowly, and they saw his head turn from side to side and point to point. When he was some forty yards away from the cabin, he called out, "Tubberville—Simon Tubberville, come out here—and let me see some empty hands or you be sorry!"

Silence followed his call. Chantel looked on both sides of the cabin but saw no signs of the deputies. She was sure, however, that they were there.

Slowly the door opened, and Mrs. Tubberville came out. She had no rifle in her hands this time. Immediately behind her came the girl she called Jeanne.

"Mrs. Tubberville, where's your husband?"

"He's not here."

"Just stay right there." Prewitt moved forward, studied the pair closely, then stepped into the cabin. The woman and the girl did not move but stood staring across the open space at Chantel and Neville. Prewitt came back out quickly and stood in front of the woman. "Where is Simon?"

"Hunting."

Prewitt laid his gun flat on the ground, reached into his pocket, and pulled out an envelope. He took out a paper and said, "You read this."

"I can't read."

"Well, I will read it to you." He started reading the paper, and suddenly Chantel moved forward. The sheriff stopped reading and looked at her. "What is it?" he said.

"Let me talk to the girl."

"All right. You stay where you are, Mrs. Tubberville. Girl, you go with this lady."

Jeanne looked like a frightened, stricken deer.

"Come along, Jeanne. I have something to tell you."

The girl hesitated, looking at her mother, but the woman simply shrugged. She was defeated looking, with lines of suffering on her face. Her eyes were dull, and this scene, it seemed to Chantel, was just one of a series of sorrows in her life.

Chantel motioned to the girl and said, "Don't be afraid, Jeanne."

"Why does the man have a gun? Is he going to hurt my mama?"

"No, but I have something to tell you." She hesitated and wondered if the speech she had rehearsed would work. "When I was about your age, Jeanne, I lived with my parents and my little sister on a plantation outside of New Orleans."

Jeanne kept her eyes fixed on Chantel as the story poured forth. Finally Chantel told her about the flood and said, "My mother's body was found in the river—but my sister was never found."

As gently as she could she said, "I do not believe the Tubbervilles are your real parents. I think you are my sister."

The girl's lips tightened, and she seemed to shrink. "Why do you think that?"

"Because you look exactly like our mother, and your hair and your eyes are not the same as your parents. When you were a little baby your hair was that color, and your eyes were violet as they are now."

"What do you want?" the girl whispered. She seemed unable to take her eyes from Chantel's face, and she shivered as if a cold blast had struck her.

"I want you to come and live with me. You're all the family I have. I want to tell you all about your mother and your father—our parents. I'll show you where you were born. You'll have your own room. I love you, dear sister, and I want you to come home with me."

A fit of trembling seized the girl, and tears began to gather in her eyes. Chantel put her arm around the girl. "Are you happy here, dear?"

A struggle seemed to take place within the girl. Fear was there, but also a longing. "No, I'm—I'm afraid."

Chantel said, "You must come with me, Veronique. That's your name. And I promise you that you will never be hurt. I know you're afraid, and I know you and I don't know each other, but I'll take you to our home, and you'll be safe. I'll take care of you always."

Veronique looked over her shoulder toward the yard, and she whispered, "My papa. He will not let me go. He will hurt anyone who tries to take anything that's his."

"Sheriff Prewitt will take us out of here. Your father won't know where you are. He can never hurt you. Will you come?"

Veronique nodded, and Chantel took a deep breath. "Come now, sister. It's time for you to leave. Get your things."

She led Veronique to the front and said, "Mrs. Tubberville, you've heard the sheriff. I'm taking my sister with me. Let her get her things, and we will go."

The girl did not do as Chantel said, but went to the woman and held out her hand tentatively. Mrs. Tubberville stared at it, then reached out and took it. They stood that way as if frozen for a time, and then the woman said, "It is better for you to go, Jeanne. This is no good place for you."

"You are not my mother?"

"No. Now go before your papa gets back."

Veronique pulled her hand away and went quickly into the house.

Chantel came over to the woman and said, "I'm sorry. I know you love her, but she shouldn't be here."

The woman did not answer for a time. Then she lifted her eyes, and Chantel saw the pure misery that was in them. "Take her quickly. Take care of her."

"I will. I promise you I will."

The door opened and closed, and Veronique stood there with a sack in her hands. She went over to the woman she had called mother all her life, and the woman suddenly reached out and embraced her. Chantel heard her whisper hoarsely, "Think of me sometimes." Then she released her and turned her back to them. She stood stiffly as if she could not bear to watch.

Prewitt said, "Your husband I will arrest. He will be charged with kidnapping." He put his fingers into his lips and blew a shrill blast. Almost at once the three deputies materialized, and the party moved away.

As they moved down the path, Veronique held tightly to Chantel's hand. She looked back once, and Chantel followed her glance. The woman was watching them. She did not move or lift a hand in farewell.

Tears were flowing down the child's face, and Chantel's heart went out to her. *I'll take this grief away from her. Before God, I will.*

The three deputies and Prewitt went first, and they were almost to the boat out in the clearing when a shot rang out. The deputy named Sonny fell to the ground and lay perfectly still. The other two deputies and Prewitt whirled and began a furious fire on the wood. Prewitt was shouting, "He's over there! Move around to your left! You people lie down!"

Bullets whistled around Chantel, and suddenly Neville was there, grabbing her and the child. He pulled them to the ground and shielded them with his body. Then, lying down, he leveled the shotgun, and a tremendous booming sound filled the space.

Chantel held her sister tightly, but she watched as Prewitt suddenly got up and ran directly at the spot from which the fire seemed to be coming. He seemed to have no fear whatsoever, and he was shouting and cursing as he ran. He emptied his rifle, pulled out a revolver, and fired three times. Chantel heard him yell, "I got heem that time!" He emptied the revolver, then suddenly turned and came back. He was limping badly, and Chantel saw him stop and pull up his pant leg. "Why, that devil got me in the other leg!"

"Is it bad?" Odo said.

"No, just a nick." Prewitt walked over to Sonny and bent over him. Prewitt did not move for a moment, and finally he stood up. "He is dead."

Jean Baptiste came to look down at the fallen man. He whispered, "He is my cousin. I will kill Simon for this!"

Chantel stared at the dead man, sick with the violence that had unfolded. She tried to speak, but found that speech was more than she could manage.

Prewitt was tying a handkerchief around his bloody leg. "I think maybe you will. Now, Odo, take these people back to town. You get Nick and his dogs out here—and send word to Sheriff Blevins to block off the bayou. Round up all the men you can. We throw a ring around this swamp. He will never get out. We catch him this time."

He turned to Neville and Chantel. "Get that child out of here. This is no place for her." The two deputies began to reload their weapons as Neville urged Chantel and Veronique into the boat. He shoved it off, and Chantel joined him as they paddled away.

Neville saw the girl trembling and said, "Don't worry, little one. You're safe now."

Chantel broke her rhythm long enough to turn and reach her hand out. "Don't worry. There's nothing to fear. You and I, we are sisters. I will take care of you always."

Chapter twenty-nine

As soon as they reached the landing at the Broussards' cabin, Odo mounted his horse and rode off at a furious pace. Neville said quickly, "Let's go back to the hotel."

The Broussards came out with curious looks at the girl but asked no questions. Chantel went to Michael Broussard and held her hand out. When he took it, she said, "I'll always be grateful to you, Michael, for the help you've given me in finding my sister."

"I'm glad it turned out happily for you," Broussard said simply.

Chantel turned and took Veronique's hand. The girl seemed to be stunned, unable to speak. "Come along and get in the buggy. You can ride between Neville and me."

Neville kept the horses at a fast pace. He and Chantel spoke quietly, mostly to break the silence. Chantel kept her arm around her sister. From time to time the girl would look at her, but she was silent all the way back. Chantel wanted to heap assurances on her, but she knew that things would be difficult for a time. When they reached the hotel, the three of them went inside. The room clerk remembered them. "Ah, Mr. Harcourt. You're staying with us again."

"Yes, I need three rooms."

Chantel spoke up quickly. "Oh, my sister and I can share a room, Neville. Will that be all right, Veronique?"

The trembling girl nodded.

"Come along," Chantel said as the clerk handed her a key. "I know we're all tired."

"You two get a good night's sleep, and we'll meet for breakfast," Neville said. He knelt down in front of Veronique, and she flinched slightly. "You sleep well tonight, Veronique. You and I will get better acquainted soon. There'll be lots of good things we can do when we get home. Good night."

Chantel was glad that Neville had taken the time to speak to her sister and to show her attention. She led Veronique up the stairs, and when they entered the room, she put the sack she had brought with her on the bed. "Why don't you put your bag over there by the wall? Then you and I can wash up. We may have to get some fresh water."

Without a word, Veronique put the bag down, and then Chantel said, "Are you hungry?"

"No." Veronique spoke in a whisper, and her frightened expression brought a quick sympathy to Chantel.

"I am. I think I'll get us something to eat if the restaurant's still open. I'll bring it up here, and we'll have a little picnic. Why don't you wash in the stand over there? Come, I'll show you."

Veronique seemed to warm up to the loving attention from her sister. She followed Chantel to the stand and watched her pour the basin full of water. "See, there's soap and a washcloth and a towel. Did you bring a nightgown?"

Veronique finally spoke. "Don't have one, me."

Chantel had noted that Veronique had the peculiar speech habit of the Cajun people, of adding "me" after a sentence instead of beginning with "I."

"I've got a spare. It'll be too big for you, of course, but when I was your age, I used to love to wear grown-up clothes. Here, let me get it." She opened her suitcase, pulled out a flannel gown, and said, "You wash and get into this, and then I'll be back with something to eat."

Going downstairs, she found that the kitchen was not yet closed, and she had the cook fix her two plates of hot food. She stopped by the desk and asked them to bring up some fresh water, then went back to her room, where she found Veronique wearing her nightgown and sitting stiffly in a chair.

"Well, you're all clean and have a nice, fresh gown on. Look, let's use this dresser as a table. This food smells good."

Veronique got up and pulled her chair closer. Without appearing to do so, Chantel noted that the child held her fork clutched in an awkward way. She bent over close to her plate and stuffed the food into her mouth as if she were afraid someone would take it from her. The juice ran down her chin and she wiped it with her sleeve. As she ate, she kept glancing fearfully at Chantel. She did not eat much, and she said nothing, but Chantel kept up a running conversation. She hardly knew what she said, and it mattered little, for all Veronique needed was the sound of a voice.

Halfway through the meal a servant brought water, and after they had finished their meal, Chantel undressed and washed herself as well as she could. She slipped into her other nightgown and said, "Now, we ought to sleep well tonight. "

She watched as Veronique moved to the bed and went to her side. She took the child in her arms and hugged her, saying, "I'm so glad I found you, little sister! I've always longed for you!" She felt the tension in Veronique's body at first, but gradually the child relaxed. Chantel kissed her on the cheek, saying, "You look so much like Mama!"

"Do I really?"

"Yes, indeed." Chantel ran her hand over Veronique's wealth of light hair, saying, "Her hair was exactly the color of yours—and your face is oval like hers. I'll show you her portrait when we get home and you'll see."

Chantel tucked the child into the bed, smiled, and said, "I'll see you in the morning, sister." She turned the lamp's wick down, and when she got into the other side of the bed she saw that the silvery moonlight was coming in through the window. She lay still for a while, hoping that Veronique would say something, but she did not. She could hear the girl's rapid breathing and knew she was not asleep, but decided to lie quietly without saying any more.

Soon she fell asleep herself, for she was exhausted. Sometime in the night she heard a cry that startled her. She sat up and saw that Veronique had buried her head in her pillow and was sobbing.

"What is it, dear?"

"I had a bad dream."

Chantel's heart went out to her sister. She had had her share of bad dreams, and now she reached out and pulled Veronique into her arms. She held her while the girl sobbed, soothing her, stroking her hair, and making meaningless sounds of comfort. Finally the sobbing ceased, and an idea came to Chantel.

"Now, that's better. But I want to show you something." She moved out of the bed, lit the lamp, and got something from her suitcase. She sat down on the bed and pulled Veronique into the circle of her arms. "Look. I want you to see this."

"What is it?"

"It's a locket. You see, it opens and there's a picture inside."

Veronique grew interested. She took the gold locket and with Chantel's guidance opened it up. She looked at the picture. "Who is this?"

"This is your mother. Isn't she beautiful?"

Veronique stared at the picture, hypnotized. She was still so long that Chantel said, "You look very much like her."

"Do I really?"

"Yes, you do. She had very nice teeth, so even and white, just like yours. I want you to have this locket. When you get lonely, you can open it up and see your mother."

Veronique turned suddenly. Her face was only inches away from Chantel's. She whispered, "It's mine? I can keep it?"

"For always and always. And someday when you have a little girl, you can give it to her."

Veronique suddenly threw her arms around Chantel and clung to her. She did not speak, but Chantel knew that a bond had been formed. Under her breath, she thanked God that she had brought the locket.

⌒

During the trip from Baton Rouge to New Orleans, Neville went out of his way to keep Veronique entertained. He had told Chantel that they must keep her mind off of the past and on the future.

On one long, level stretch he asked her, "Do you know how to drive?"

Veronique shook her head, but Neville handed her the lines and said, "There, you are now a driver." He winked over Veronique's head at Chantel and said, "We're in good hands now."

Veronique's eyes lit up, and when they stopped to water the horses, she got out of the wagon to stretch her legs along with the other two.

Chantel whispered to Neville, "That was a sweet thing to do."

"How do you think she's doing, Chantel?"

"She had nightmares last night, but I gave her my locket with our mother's picture in it. She's wearing it now."

"I've seen her take it out and look at it several times."

Chantel watched Veronique as she stood in front of the horses, reaching up to touch their noses. "She's a sweet girl, but she's had an awful life."

"She'll be all right now that she's with you."

Chantel suddenly reached out and touched Neville's arm. "What would I have done without you?"

Neville stood very still, and suddenly Chantel blushed and moved her hand. "How long do you think it will take us to get to New Orleans?"

"Not long," he said. He called to Veronique, lifted her up into the seat, then helped Chantel up. Climbing up into his own seat, he slapped the lines on the horses and got them to a sprightly trot. "Now, see if you can handle these, sweetheart."

The trip back to New Orleans had been trying, but Chantel didn't mind. She spent the hours getting acquainted with Veronique. The youngster was very quiet at first, but as Chantel told her stories about her own life then about things the two of them would do together, she became more talkative. Neville was a help with this, for he was gifted with young people, and kept Veronique entertained with humorous stories from his own life.

Finally they arrived at the town house, and as Neville helped Chantel down, he said, "I'm going to leave you here. I've got a lot of work to do. We're going to have to make sure that things go well legally."

"Will you come back and tell me as soon as you find out?"

"Yes, of course." Turning, he stooped down to say to Veronique, "Don't forget me now. When I come back, we can go downtown and see some of the sights. Would you like that?"

"Yes, please."

"Good. You take care of your sister now. She's a big girl, but she's apt to get into trouble." He was rewarded by a slight smile on Veronique's face.

When he had left, Chantel said, "Come inside. I want you to meet my stepmother and our brother."

"A real brother?"

"Well, he's what you call a half-brother. His father is our father, but his mother is different. Come along."

They entered the house, and as soon as the servant shut the door, Collette came to stand before them. "Chantel," she said, "where have you been?"

"I have a lot of things to tell you, Mama, but first I want you to meet Veronique. Veronique, this is Madame Fontaine." She had not known exactly how to introduce her. The idea of introducing a third mother would confuse the child even more. Now she saw the shock run across Collette's face and felt Veronique stiffen beside her.

"Come inside. Will you want a special room for the child?"

"Oh, no, we can share my room."

Collette said, "Well, you take her there, then come back and we'll talk."

"Yes, that would be best."

Collette watched as the two went up, and her lips grew together in a tight line. She shook her head and murmured, "What foolishness!" then turned and walked rapidly away.

"I don't think that lady likes me, Chantel," Veronique said when the two were inside the room.

Chantel had seen the same dislike, but she said, "Of course she does. Now, don't you worry about anything. I'll tell you what. I'll go down and see her for a few moments, and when I come back, you and I will go out and see some of New Orleans. Maybe we'll go by Neville's office and see him there, and we can all go out and eat somewhere. Would you like that?"

"Yes. But will you be gone long?"

Chantel sensed her fear. "You just look out the window there. And I have some books you might like to look through."

"Can't read, me."

"Well, you can look at the pictures then." She gave Veronique several books with pictures in them and went downstairs, where she found Collette in the study.

Collette was abrupt. "You should not have brought that child here. She's a stranger."

Chantel instinctively knew that the situation was hopeless, so she did not waste time arguing. She simply said, "She's my sister, Collette."

The use of her first name was not lost on her stepmother. Collette drew herself up but said nothing.

"We'll be leaving tomorrow to go to the plantation," Chantel said, "so she won't be in your way. Now, I must go. I don't like to leave her alone."

She turned and went back with a heavy heart. She had hoped for better things from Collette, but it didn't really matter. A fierce sense of possession came over her. *She's my sister. I don't care what Collette says. And I'll protect her.*

She did not want to leave the girl in the house, so they went out at once. They did go by Neville's office, but he was not there. They spent the afternoon shopping and stayed out late enough so that they would not have to encounter Collette.

They had just gotten home when Neville suddenly appeared, asking for her. Veronique was already in bed looking at picture books, so Chantel drew him into the library.

"How is Veronique?" he asked quickly.

"Oh, she's frightened at all the changes. But she's young and very quick." Chantel smiled warmly. "I can teach her, Neville. She's going to be fine."

Neville nodded, but then his face grew serious.

Neville was relieved to hear that Veronique was adjusting so well and felt it was the Lord's doing. He then paused and said, "I've got something to tell you. It may change things."

"Oh, Neville, don't tell me we're going to have trouble getting her."

"No, we won't have that trouble," he said grimly. He shook his head and said, "Simon Tubberville was killed resisting arrest."

"Oh, how awful!"

"He wouldn't have it any other way. I got a telegram from Sheriff Prewitt. He talked to the man's wife, and there'll be no challenge over Veronique."

"Whatever will I tell her?"

"I think eventually you should tell her the truth, but maybe not yet. She's had too many shocks."

"I'm not sure. She worries about her father coming after her."

"Well, then perhaps you had better tell her."

"Yes, but I will wait to do it when we are at the plantation."

Neville looked at her questioningly.

"I won't be staying in this house. Collette was not happy when I brought her home."

"She wouldn't be. Your father left his estate to be divided among his 'lawful lineal descendants,' so Veronique will get one-third of the amount. She doesn't like to see Perrin's assets reduced from a half to a third."

"I didn't think she would be that small." Chantel shook her head sadly. "He could have my share."

"No. Your father left it as he wanted. When will you be leaving?"

"Tomorrow."

"I'll stay here and get all the legal matters straight."

As he rose to leave, Chantel called his name. "Neville—"

When he turned, she came to him and put her hand out. "I seem to be thanking you a lot, but this would have been impossible without you."

"I'm glad we found her," Neville said simply. He held her hand in his, and for one moment something came into his eyes. Chantel was not experienced with men, but she knew that he wanted to kiss her. She did not move—then suddenly he nodded and left. A strange sense of disappointment came to her.

Chapter thirty

Marie Bientot set the heavy pot on the stove, took the lid off, and examined the contents critically. "I hope this gumbo will be as good as it was last time."

Clarice, who was chopping up vegetables, looked up and said, "Why would it not be good? I always make good gumbo."

"Yes, you do." Marie came over and sat down beside Clarice. "Where has the child gone today?"

"She is out riding with Miss Chantel." Clarice finished slicing the carrots into thin coins, wiped the knife on her apron, and smiled. "That child, she has brought a new life to this place."

"Yes. It is amazing how she has changed in a little less than a month. When she first came, I thought she was the saddest looking girl I ever saw."

Marie shook her head, but smiled. "She ate like a little savage, remember?"

"Yes, but she's learned very quickly."

"Yes, and she should have! Miss Chantel has spent almost every moment with her. The hours those two have spent shopping!" Marie smiled at the thought, then added, "The child has good taste in clothes."

"She's learning to read so quickly. Have you noticed how often she laughs now? She didn't smile for a long time when she first came."

"Well, who wouldn't be sad? Being yanked up from the only home she knew."

"It wasn't much of a home, from what I hear. Does she ever speak of it to you?"

"Never. And Miss Chantel says she only mentions the woman she called her mother. She had Miss Chantel write her a letter, but there is no answer yet."

Marie picked up a carrot slice and ate it. "It is amazing how much she looks like her own mother. She will be just like her when she is grown."

"It is a wonderful thing for the child that she was found."

"It's a wonderful thing for both of them. You know, Chantel never really believed that child was dead. I think the good God must have put it in her heart to have faith that she would be found."

Chantel was riding Bravo, and she had assigned Lady, her first horse, to Veronique. Lady was getting somewhat old and Chantel's weight was too much for her, but Chantel loved the horse still. When she gave the horse to Veronique, she said, "Papa gave the horse to me, and now he gives her to you because I give her to you."

The girl knew little about riding, but she fell in love with the horse, and the two sisters rode over the plantation daily. One afternoon they traveled down the road that led to New Orleans. They came to a river spanned by a bridge, and Chantel pulled up Bravo abruptly. He snorted and threw himself sideways, insulted at her rough treatment.

"What's wrong, Chantel?" Veronique said. "Don't we want to cross the bridge?"

"I—I don't really like to cross it."

Veronique touched Lady, and the mare moved forward obediently so that she was even with the big stallion.

For a moment Chantel hesitated, and then she said, "This is where our mother died, Veronique. I was on the other side, and she was crossing the bridge holding you in her arms. I saw the bridge break, and the carriage went into the river, and you were carried away in the flood. Ever since that day I've hated to cross this bridge."

Veronique stared at the river, which was now placid and slow moving. She reached out suddenly and took Chantel's arm. "But we're together now, aren't we?"

"Yes, we are, my sister." Chantel made herself smile. And truly, the river did not seem so ominous and formidable. She had dreamed about it many times, but now somehow she felt that time was over. "Come, we'd better go home."

They rode homeward in silence until Veronique asked, "Doesn't Mr. Neville ever come to see you?"

"Sometimes."

"But he hasn't been here since I came but one time, and then he didn't stay long. All he did was let you sign some papers, and then he went away."

"I think he's been very busy."

"I like him a lot. I wish he'd come back."

"I'm sure he will."

Veronique was not the only one who had noticed Neville's absence. It had been a month and, as her sister said, he had come only the one time. And even then he had behaved strangely. Chantel had been so happy to see him, but he had smiled only briefly and refused to stay the night.

"I wish he'd come back. We could go riding in the buggy, and he could let me drive again."

Chantel said abruptly, "There is a ball at the Taylors' next week. We're invited."

"Me too?"

"Yes, of course you, too! I'll write Neville and ask him to take us."

"But can't dance, me!"

"You will by the time the ball comes. I'll teach you. We'll get new dresses, and we'll be the prettiest girls at the whole ball."

"And Neville. Do you think he'll come?"

"I hope so. I'll write him today."

As they made their way homeward, Chantel thought, not for the first time, of how much she missed him. And with a start she realized she had thought only briefly of Yves. *He came into my life like a whirlwind, and I was carried away with him. He was not the man for me. I see that now.*

"Does Mr. Neville have a sweetheart?"

"Why—I don't know." The idea of Neville having a sweetheart was very disturbing. Chantel had taken him for granted, but now the question that Veronique had so innocently asked would not leave her. As soon as she got home, she wrote the note and had Brutus take it to be posted. Then she found Veronique and said, "Come along. We're going to teach you to dance."

Veronique had been staring out the window, waiting for Neville to arrive. She finally turned to Chantel and asked, "Are you sure he's going to come?"

"Yes, I've told you three times already. He said he'd be here."

"But it's late, and I thought he would come early for us."

Chantel had received only a brief note from Neville saying that he would be glad to take them to the ball, and he had signed it: *Sincerely, Neville.* The note was strangely unsatisfying, but there was nothing for it but to go on.

The sisters had bought new dresses, and Elise fussed over them and helped them fix their hair. The dresses were made from light green silk. Chantel's was sleeveless with a dropped neckline, tight bodice, and a long, flowing skirt with two rows of white lace at the bottom. Veronique's had a high neckline, a tight bodice decorated with tiny white bows down the front, three-quarter length sleeves ending with white lace at the elbows, and a long, full skirt with a large white bow trailing down the back.

"You look beautiful, Veronique," Chantel said.

"It's the prettiest dress I ever saw!" Veronique did indeed look pretty. She had gained some weight, and the dress had been carefully tailored for her. Now her violet eyes were beaming with excitement. "I wish Neville would come."

Five minutes later Marie opened the door. "Mr. Neville is here. Oh, you two look lovely!"

"Thank you, Marie. Let's go, Veronique."

Neville was wearing evening dress and looked very distinguished. He came forward at once and took Veronique's hands. "My word! I have never seen such a lovely young lady."

"Do you like my new dress?"

"Very much. As a matter of fact, I claim the first dance with you. And maybe all the rest of them."

Chantel waited for him to turn to her, and when he stood, he smiled briefly and said, "You look very nice, Chantel."

Chantel felt again a vague sense of disappointment. "Thank you," she said rather stiffly. "I'm glad you could come."

Neville hesitated, then gave a half bow. "I expect we'd better be going."

Chantel accompanied him to the carriage. He lifted Veronique in and then gave her his hand. Chantel gave it an extra pressure, but he simply released her and went to take his own seat. Chantel could not understand his attitude. He had been so excited when they had found Veronique, and now it was as if he were a stranger. She bit her lip and wished that she had not thought of asking him to come for the ball.

~

The Taylors' ballroom was not as large as some, but there were at least twenty couples there. There was also a group of young people somewhere close to Veronique's age, and she was overcome with shyness when she was introduced to them.

The room itself was beautifully decorated, and five musicians began at once to play the music for the first dance. Neville came and said, "I believe this is our dance, Miss Fontaine."

Veronique giggled and said, "I'm not very good."

"Well, I'm an excellent dancer. I'll teach you what you don't know."

Chantel watched as the two went around the floor. Veronique concentrated on her steps, but soon Neville said something that made her giggle. *He's so good with her,* Chantel thought. *He can make her smile so easily.*

At that moment she was asked to dance, and for the rest of the evening she had many partners. But to her anguish, Neville danced several times with Veronique but did not come to her.

At one point she managed to encounter him at the refreshment table.

"Veronique seems very happy, Chantel. Does she ever talk about her old life?"

"Not much anymore. Once, after she had been here about a week, she talked for a long time about it. It almost broke my heart."

"Well, she's a beautiful child. She's going to be a beautiful woman."

The conversation floundered. Neville was watching Veronique, and Chantel felt awkward and ill at ease. Finally she cleared her throat and said, "Neville, you haven't been to visit us lately."

Neville gave her a strange look. "I've—been rather busy."

At that instant a thought that had been dancing around Chantel's mind since Veronique suggested it found expression as clearly as if it were carved in bronze. *He's found a sweetheart!* She looked away blindly, not seeing the dancers. *He could at least tell me if he's found someone he likes.*

At that moment young Donald Mayfield came and pulled her out to the dance floor. She danced with him and others, but was dully aware that Neville was not even watching her.

The dance ended fairly early, and on the way home Veronique talked more than she ever had. "It was such fun! I hope there's another ball soon. You'll come back if there is, won't you, Neville?"

"I don't know. I hope so, Veronique. You're a fine dancer, but you don't want to be dancing with an old man like me."

Chantel had expected that Neville would stay all night with them, and when they returned home, the servants were waiting. She said, "We might have a little snack. You have something, don't you, Marie?"

"Oh, yes, there is plenty."

"I'm not really very hungry," Neville said. "And I'm a little tired. I think I'll turn in. Would you excuse me?"

"Certainly. Good night," Chantel said stiffly. "Are you hungry, Veronique?"

"Yes, I could eat anything."

"I'll go with you then."

She stayed until Veronique had eaten and then walked to her room, kissed her, and said, "You were beautiful tonight, and your dancing was wonderful."

"I like dancing with Neville, don't you?"

"I—" She broke off, because the hurt of his refusal to dance with her was more painful than she had dreamed it could be. "Good night," she said. She bent over and kissed the smooth cheek, then went to her room.

Chantel stood in the middle of the room for a moment, then sat down before the dresser and stared at her face in the mirror. She could think of nothing but Neville's strange attitude. *Have I done something to offend him? I don't know what it could be.*

She walked the floor for a time and then washed her face. After she had dried it off, she walked over to the window. A movement caught her eye, and she leaned forward and peered out into the darkness. By the faint light of the lantern, she caught sight of Neville walking along the brick walkway that led out to the gardens. His head was down, and he disappeared into the shadows.

At once she grabbed up her coat, slipped it on, and left her room. She ran quickly down the stairs and out the front door and ran down the walk. The moon was full overhead, a huge silver disk.

"Neville!" she called out, and then halted. She had come on a sudden impulse, and now that he turned and came to stand before her, she had not the vaguest idea what to say.

"I—I saw you walking. I was wondering if there's any trouble. Something you haven't told me."

"No, not really. I just wanted some fresh air."

His words sounded lame to her, and she said, "Let me walk with you."

"Fine. It's a little cold. People will think we're crazy walking in December in the middle of the night."

Chantel walked beside him and could not think of one thing to say. She finally asked how his work was going.

"All right."

"And the mission. Have you started it yet?"

"I've been spending a lot of time there. I rented an old building that needed a lot of repairs."

"So that's why you haven't been to see me."

There was enough of a pause that Chantel knew he was struggling for an answer. "Well, of course, it's been a little hard to get away."

The silence continued, and finally he said, "I saw Yves a few days ago."

"Is he all right?"

"Oh, completely recovered. I don't know how you'll take this," he said. "Dominique's husband died." He seemed to be fumbling for words, and finally he said, "I think they're seeing each other."

"Really? I'm not too surprised. I didn't think he ever got over her."

"I'm sorry. I know you had feelings for him. I hated to tell you."

"Why, Neville, I may have felt something for him once, but it could never have come to anything. I knew that."

Neville stared at her, and she saw consternation in his eyes. "Do you mean that, Chantel?"

"Why, yes. Did you think it was something else?"

"I thought you were in love with him. He is a romantic fellow. The kind of man I always wanted to be. Dashing and romantic."

"Neville! You don't need to be like Yves. You need to be exactly what you are."

Her words seemed to surprise Neville, and finally Chantel realized that she had to know the truth. "I want to ask you something, Neville."

"Why, go ahead."

"Have you found a sweetheart?"

"What?"

"You're seeing a woman, aren't you? Someone you care for."

Neville stared at her in shock. "What makes you think that?"

"Because you haven't been to see me. You were once in love with me, or said you were—but now you've found somebody else." Chantel found these words hard to say, and she turned her head away.

"Wait a minute!" She felt his hand on her arm, and when she turned around, he took a deep breath. "I don't want to be hurt again, Chantel. No man likes rejection. But I will tell you once more, I still love you. I always will. But I'm not the kind of man you want. Despite what you say, I know you want a big man who'll sweep you off your feet. If not Yves, somebody like him."

When she didn't speak, he added, "You do remember, Chantel, that you told me you could never think of me as a lover—that we were too much like brother and sister?"

"I—I did say that, but I've changed."

Neville's face lightened with hope, but he asked cautiously, "How have you changed?"

"I was swept away by Yves," Chantel replied, realizing even at that moment what had happened. "Perhaps because he looked like my father, but I was in love with love. I would have been miserable married to him."

She reached up and put her hand on Neville's chest. "I could never have been happy with him, Neville. When I think about the man I could spend my life with, I want someone who is steady and true and never changes." Even as she spoke these words, Chantel knew that she was, in effect, saying good-bye to the image that she had had of her father, for he did not have these qualities.

Her lips trembled, and she said, "I think of your patience and your kindness and how you put up with all my moods, and—" She could not finish, for he had put his arms around her and drawn her close.

As he kissed her, the heat of something rash and yet eternal touched them both. She knew at that moment that she had the power to stir him, and even more startling she knew he could stir her more than she had thought possible. She had always thought of love as something that came upon a woman like the striking of a bell, clear and complete, a roundness with no uncertainty to it. And she realized that he had been there for her all along, but she had been too foolish to recognize it.

Finally he lifted his head and said, "I love you, Chantel, but I'll be serving God in a mission and working in a law office. That's not a glamorous life."

"If it's your life, it will be mine." She put her hand on his cheek and said, "Neville, do you love me then?"

"Yes, of course."

"Then will you come courting me?"

"What!" Neville said with surprise.

"I—I think I love you, but I want you to take me places. I want other girls to see you with me and to know that you love me. And will you write me letters?"

"Letters? What kind of letters?"

"Love letters. And maybe a poem. I know you love poetry."

"I can't write poetry, Chantel!"

"Yes, you can," she said firmly. She smiled then and said, "It doesn't have to be a good poem, just a poem."

"All right. I'll write you a poem." He held her tightly and was stirred by her touch. "And I'll get a guitar. I'll learn to play, and I'll sing love songs under your window. My singing will be so bad that all the servants will laugh."

Chantel felt suddenly that she had come home. "I won't laugh," she said. She reached up, pulled his head down, and kissed him. Chantel put her head on his chest, then, while he held her tightly, she whispered in his ear, "We're going to have a beautiful courtship, Neville."

Neville held Chantel tightly, then laughed, saying, "You know, I feel like Job."

"Like Job? The man in the Bible who suffered so much?"

"Yes, he did suffer, but in the end, God made it up to him—for all of it." He had lost everything as the Lord tested him, even his children, but after all this tragedy, God gave Job seven sons and three daughters." Neville kissed her, and his face was glowing with joy. "And you are like the daughters of Job, sweetheart!"

"How am I like them?" she whispered.

"The Bible says, 'And in all the land were no women found so fair as the daughters of Job.'" He placed his hand on her cheek, and his voice was filled with emotion as he said, "That's how I have thought of you for a long time, Chantel—in all the world there is no woman so fair!"

The two clung together under the silvery moon, silhouetted in white light and filled with joy and hope.

About the authors

Dr. Gilbert Morris is a retired English professor. He is the author of more than 170 novels, many of them bestsellers and several of them award winners. He has been married for fifty-three years to Johnnie, and they have three children. His daughter, **Lynn Morris**, has coauthored many books with her father, including the *Cheney Duval, M.D.* series.

Look for the next book in

The Creole Series,

The Immortelles.